A Dragon Lives Forever

A Dragon Lives Forever

by John R. Riggs

Barricade Books Inc.
Fort Lee, New Jersey

Published by Barricade Books Inc.
1530 Palisade Avenue, Fort Lee, NJ 07024
Distributed by Publishers Group West
4065 Hollis, Emeryville, CA 94608

Library of Congress Cataloging-in-Publication Data

Riggs, John R., 1945–
    A dragon lives forever / John R. Riggs.
    (A Garth Ryland mystery)
    ISBN 0-942637-78-X: $17.95
    I. Title. II. Series: Riggs, John R., 1945–
Garth Ryland mystery.
PS3568.I372D7   1992   92-17748
813'.54—dc20   CIP

To the kid in all of us,
and to Carole,
the biggest kid of all.

"I had been permitted to correct time's arrow for the space of perhaps five minutes— and that is a boon not granted to all men. If I were to render a report on this episode, I would say that men must find a way to run the arrow backward. Doubtless it is impossible in the physical world, but in the memory and the will man might achieve the deed if he would try."

—Loren Eiseley,
from *The Star Thrower*

1

"It seems like something always has to come along and ruin Homecoming," Clarkie said.

I looked at him. A few minutes earlier Clarkie had picked me up at my office, and we had driven under a cloudless blue sky through the cool of that late-July morning to Hidden Quarry. Along checkered asphalt roads. Past brown yards and brown pastures and weeds thick with dust. Each alone with his thoughts, as we listened, on that last lonely stretch of road to the quarry, to the trees scrape the sides of the patrol car, and the locusts burst like quail from the tinder-dry thickets along the way.

1

Then we got out of the patrol car, walked to the edge of the quarry, and looked down. A body floated in the water about forty feet below us. White and still, it looked like a buoy floating there. And oddly in keeping with the steeped stillness of the day.

"You know what I mean, Garth," Clarkie continued. "Last year it rained. The year before that Mose Callaway's horse got diarrhea and left a four-block trail along Jackson Street." He stopped to think. "What was it the year before that?"

I also had to think about it. Homecoming ran a week, Sunday–Saturday, and usually included a carnival, a talent contest, another contest of some kind, a variety show, and then culminated with a parade on Saturday, followed by a fish fry that evening. After a few years, though, one Homecoming began to look a lot like another.

"The Jonker sisters," I said.

"That's right. They poisoned half the town with that rancid potato salad of theirs. It's a wonder some of us didn't die."

I nodded in agreement, even though I felt little sympathy for anyone who would eat the Jonkers' potato salad in the first place. Anyone who would willingly break bread with the Jonkers would probably also eat road kills. But I didn't tell Clarkie that. He had enough on his mind the way it was.

Clarkie was Sheriff Harold Clark of Adams County, Wisconsin. A round, bland, self-conscious man, who felt more at ease with calculators and computers than with the public he served, Clarkie had learned everything he knew about law-enforcement from my good friend and mentor, Rupert Roberts.

Rupert Roberts was Clarkie's predecessor and the only three-term sheriff in the history of Adams County. With patience, humor, and an unflappable presence that bordered on stoicism, Rupert had taught both Clarkie and me the ropes, the ins and outs of our town of Oakalla that we would have spent a lifetime learning otherwise. What Rupert hadn't taught us was how to get along without him on the job.

I was Garth Ryland, owner and editor of the *Oakalla Reporter*, a small weekly newspaper whose circulation continued to grow each year. I also wrote a syndicated column that also had grown in circulation over the years until it now reached nearly every town in Wisconsin, and even a few towns outside of Wisconsin.

For the past twelve years I had lived in Oakalla with my housekeeper, Ruth Krammes. Every day I walked six blocks to work at a job I loved. Occasionally I had the time to watch the sun rise and the sun set and every once in a

3

while the chance to put my nose to the screen and smell evening coming on. I had a place in the community and friends by the dozens. I had food in the freezer and money in the bank. I had a good life, a comfortable life, the life I'd always wanted. But for some reason, during that hottest and driest of summers, I wasn't feeling very satisfied.

I looked down into Hidden Quarry at the body floating on top of the water. "Somehow, I think this Homecoming's different, Clarkie."

Together we watched as Ray Fickle, a volunteer fireman, put one arm around the body and, swimming sidestroke, began to drag it to shore. "You're probably right, Garth," Clarkie said.

Hidden Quarry, a long-abandoned stone quarry, was so named because you could walk right up to it, without knowing it was there. Located two miles south of Oakalla back of a narrow gravel road, which was crowded by two picket rows of saplings that grew right to its edge, and overhung with grape vines as thick as my wrist, Hidden Quarry was a haven for anyone—hunters, fishermen, kids, lovers, and dreamers alike, who loved the out of doors and valued solitude above all.

As a kid on temporary loan to my grandmother Ryland for the summer, I had spent most of my days there, either swimming in the

4

quarry's cold green waters, or warming in the sun on its limestone shelves, or fishing for the giant bass, crappie, and bluegill that were supposed to be in there somewhere, if you could ever catch them. I never could.

And it was the Schiery kids on their way to swim who had found the body floating in Hidden Quarry earlier that morning. They had reported their find to their parents, who had called Clarkie, who in turn had called me. Clarkie was temporarily without a deputy, since his former deputy had quit only a week before, and the County Council had not yet met to hire another one. In Clarkie's mind, that vacancy left me with my tarnished special deputy's badge as his sole aid and comfort in a town that in the past had offered him precious little of either. Also, as of last Thanksgiving, when he had shot the person who intended to kill me, I had owed Clarkie my life.

We watched while Ray Fickle attached a rope and harness to the body and stepped aside as Danny Palmer, Oakalla's volunteer fire chief and owner of the Marathon service station, used his wrecker to hoist the body to the rim of the quarry where two attendants from Operation Lifeline bagged it and put it into their ambulance. From there it would go to Doc Airhart's house for examination, since

5

Ben Bryan, the county coroner, was on vacation until the end of the month.

"Looked like a man to me," Clarkie said. We neither one had gotten too close to the body—mainly because we neither one had the stomach for it.

"It was definitely a man," I said. The man was naked. I had been close enough to see that.

"Then these clothes could belong to him."

I glanced down at the pile of clothes at our feet. Included were a sleeveless black T-shirt, jeans, socks with brown sweat-stained toes, a fawn cowboy hat with a silver concha band around its crown, and a pair of soft fawn cowboy boots.

"That'd be my guess," I said.

We found a billfold in the left rear pocket of the jeans, and two crisp one hundred dollar bills inside it, but no driver's license, no credit cards, no photographs, no identification of any kind.

"Funny," Clarkie said, picking up the clothes and pocketing the wallet.

"Funny," I agreed.

A late-model Firebird was parked a few feet away from where we stood. Its silver paint shown brightly through the thin coat of dust it wore, and its chrome wheels and bumpers looked as if they had been spit-shined.

6

"Nice car," Clarkie said, running his hand along it.

The Firebird's driver-side window and passenger-side window were both rolled down; inside its red leather bucket seats and red floor carpet looked like new. But the Firebird wasn't new. Not by fifty thousand miles.

"It is a nice car," I agreed. "I wonder why he never bothered to tag it?" There was no license plate on either the front or the back of the Firebird.

Clarkie opened the passenger-side door, searched through the glove compartment, behind both visors, then through the rest of the interior. "Or register it," he said, leaning across the seat and popping the hood.

Clarkie raised the hood and stood dumbfounded for a moment before he said, "Would you look at that, Garth. Isn't that about the prettiest engine you've ever seen?"

He was talking to a mechanical dropout, who, in his father's words, couldn't figure out the mechanism of a potato masher. All I could see was steel and chrome, and lots of it.

"Beautiful," I said.

"Isn't it, though." Then Clarkie went on to rave about the engine, which he described as a TA, fuel injected, turbo-charged, big block V-8. "It'll flat outrun about anything on the road," Clarkie said.

"Even Jessie?" I said in reference to my car, which was the old-six banger Chevy sedan that Grandmother Ryland had willed to me along with the money to buy the *Oakalla Reporter*.

"You're kidding, aren't you, Garth?" Clarkie said in all seriousness.

"I'm kidding, Clarkie." I should have known better than to have wasted good sarcasm on him.

Humming to himself, Clarkie found the serial number on the engine block, wrote it down in the notebook that he always kept in his left front shirt pocket, then gingerly, and somewhat reluctantly it seemed, closed the lid on the Firebird.

"Ready?" he said, taking the keys from the ignition and locking the Firebird.

"Ready," I answered. "But what about his clothes?" Clarkie had laid them down on the ground when he searched the Firebird.

"Someone ought to look after them," he said.

"Yes," I said. "Someone should."

It seemed to take him the longest time to ask, "Would you?"

I sighed in resignation and picked them up. Owing someone your life wasn't all that it was cracked up to be.

"I didn't know you were so into cars," I said

to Clarkie on our way back to Oakalla. "At least you never mentioned it before."

We were riding in his patrol car, and we both had our windows all the way down. But it was still hot in there. Clarkie's uniform was soaked with sweat. I felt plastered to the seat.

"I used to be more into cars than I am now," he said. "As a kid, that's about all I could think about. Cars and . . ." His face reddened.

"Cars and what, Clarkie?"

Embarrassed, he shook his head. "Never mind. That's water over the dam. Long over the dam," he felt it necessary to add.

A few minutes later we stopped along Ferry Street beside the white concrete block building that housed the *Oakalla Reporter*. "I'll let you know when I learn something," he said.

"There's no hurry on my part."

I got out of Clarkie's patrol car, taking the dead man's clothes, boots, and hat with me, went inside my office where I dumped them in a corner, and sat down at my desk. Then I picked up the yellowed newspaper clipping that had come in the mail Monday, the morning before, and that had lain like a summons on my desk ever since.

2

The yellowed newspaper clipping told about thirteen-year-old Paul Samuel who had disappeared from Oakalla during Homecoming on his way to the carnival in Centennial Park. A search started early the next morning, and two days later included as many as two hundred searchers, but they didn't find Paul Samuel. A week later, searchers across the state were looking for Paul Samuel, but they didn't find him either.

No one had found Paul Samuel. Not then. Not in the twenty years since then. As Clarkie had said, something always seemed to come along to ruin Homecoming.

I turned the clipping over where someone

had written on the back in small neat script, *I know where he is.*

"Good for you," I said, as I put the clipping back in its envelope and laid the envelope back on my desk.

Then I rose and walked to my north window, which looked out across my corner lot to Gas Line Road. My grass was brown and crinkled, the air hot and still. Just the thought of doing anything at all wore me out.

If Paul Samuel had made it to Centennial Park twenty years ago, if something hadn't happened to him before then, he would have gone right past my office. It wasn't my office then. It wasn't even the *Oakalla Reporter* then but *Freedom's Voice*, the forerunner of the *Oakalla Reporter*. Still, if someone had been standing at his north window, as I was doing now, he might have seen Paul Samuel pass by.

He might have seen him and not known it because his thoughts were elsewhere. Or he might have seen him and not recognized him because he was near-sighted from reading newspaper print all of his life. Or he might have bent over to pick up a pencil at just the wrong moment and missed him. The possibilities were endless, as were the frustrations whenever we tried to unravel the past and reconcile it with the present.

I pushed away from the window, sat down

in my swivel chair, and put my feet up on my desk. *I know where he is*, someone had written. If that were true, then it would just have to remain the writer's secret.

I spent the next couple hours doing as little as possible, then walked uptown and ate lunch at the Corner Bar and Grill and returned to my office just as Clarkie pulled up in his patrol car. I got inside his patrol car. Unlike my office, it was air-conditioned.

"Fancy meeting you here," I said to lighten things up. Clarkie looked grim. Maybe it was the weather.

"I ran the serial number of that Firebird through my computer," he said. "It belongs to a Scott McBride of Ventura, California."

"What about his driver's license?" I said.

"He had it suspended four years ago in California for driving under the influence. As far as I know, it hasn't been reinstated."

I laid my head back against the seat and closed my eyes. It was cool and comfortable in there. I could have slept.

"Somehow the name Scott McBride is familiar to me," I said.

Clarkie didn't say anything.

"What about to you?" I continued.

"I've heard the name before," he said.

"Where? Do you remember?" I opened my eyes and sat up. My mind had started to drift; the rest of me felt dull and logged.

Clarkie shook his head. Either he didn't know or wouldn't tell me. "Doc Airhart says he wants to see you," he said.

"That's a first," I answered. "What about?"

"The body they found this morning. Something about it doesn't seem quite right to Doc."

"Shit," I said.

Clarkie's look said he couldn't have agreed more.

Doc Airhart lived in a big white house with stone pillars across the street from the United Methodist Church. Formerly the Cuyahoga County Coroner and at that time one of the ten top-ranked surgeons in the world, Doc and his wife, Constance, had moved from Cleveland to Oakalla during the 1930's, and he had lived there ever since. Constance had died several years ago, and Doc's ancient setter, Belle, had died last October, so Doc had been alone up until a few weeks ago when I bought him a setter pup that he'd named Daisy. When I asked him why he'd named her that, he said it was better than Buttercup. So I let it go at that.

"You going in?" I asked Clarkie.

"Nope," he said stubbornly. "If Doc had something he wanted to say to me, he would have said it by now." Clarkie was put out because Doc thought it necessary to tell me instead of Clarkie what he'd found.

13

"Whatever you think," I said and went inside.

Doc sat at his kitchen table, drinking a quart-sized glass of iced tea. A small spritely man with white hair and merry blue eyes, Doc drank coffee in winter, iced tea in summer, and Scotch straight up all year round.

I took a seat across the table from him. "Where's Daisy?" I asked, hearing her whine, but not seeing her.

"In the basement. I can't get a thing done when she's around." Doc had been writing his memoirs for the past several years. Or at least was pretending to write them. I hadn't yet read that first word.

"With the body?" I said, since Doc's morgue was in the basement.

"She won't eat it, if that's what you're worried about."

Doc took a drink of his iced tea. I took a look around his kitchen. The walls and ceiling were white, the cabinets white with black knobs, the linoleum a burnt red, the table and chairs yellow. The kitchen windows were open and a large ceiling fan turned lazily overhead. Like me, Doc didn't care much for airconditioning.

"Where's Sheriff Clark?" Doc asked. "I thought you two were an item these days."

"Outside in his car pouting. His exact words were, 'If Doc had something to say to me, he would have said it by now.'"

14

"It seems," Doc said, showing a flash of his famous temper, "that Sheriff Clark's skin is as thin as it ever was." As Clarkie was angry at Doc for not giving him more respect, Doc was angry at Clarkie for not demanding more.

"With good reason," I said, knowing too well how much grief the people of Oakalla had given Clarkie over the years.

"If you can't stand the heat, stay out of the kitchen" was Doc's answer.

"It appears that's exactly what Clarkie is doing."

Doc sighed, then rose and poured me a glass of iced tea nearly as large as his own. If I'd had all day and lots of help, I might have been able to drink it.

"What do you know about the man they brought here this morning?" Doc asked after returning to his seat at the table.

"Not much. What do you know about him?"

"I asked first."

So I told Doc what I knew, that the man's name was Scott McBride and that apparently he was a drunk from Ventura, California.

"You don't know any of his history?" Doc said.

"No. Not a bit. I don't even know if Scott McBride is his right name. For all I know, he could have stolen the car."

Doc assumed the thoughtful look he always used to wear right before he told you what was wrong with you. From looking at him, you never knew whether you just had a cold, or the worse case of double pneumonia in the history of mankind. But whatever you had, Doc knew what it was and what to prescribe to make you well again.

"It's like this, Garth," he said. "The man's somewhere in his thirties, mid-to-late thirties would be my guess, and considering what all he's been through, not in all that bad of shape . . . at least up until the time he died."

"What all has he been through?" I asked, because I knew Doc expected me to.

"A fire for one thing. A fire that left him terribly scarred and probably should have killed him." Doc spoke with rare compassion, as if the dead man had touched him in a way that most of life hadn't. "For another thing," Doc said, "I'd say he's been to war. If the tatoos on his arms hadn't told me that, the scar just under his left clavicle did."

"Bullet wound?"

"That's what it looks like to me. And several smaller scars where he likely caught some shrapnel, since there's some of it still in him."

"Not all bullet wounds come from war," I said, recalling a recent one of my own.

"No. But I'd be willing to bet that his did."

16

"What are his tatoos like?" I said when Doc didn't continue.

"An American eagle holding an American flag on his right forearm. A heart on his left forearm with the name Cheryl inside it." Doc shook his head. I couldn't tell if he was amazed at the man's condition or just moved by the man himself. "When you figure in his tatoos and his war wounds and his fire scars, except for his face, there wasn't much of him that wasn't marked in some way."

"Sign of the times," I said.

"I guess," Doc said. "That's about as good a way of putting it as any."

"Is it possible that those burn scars are from war?" I said.

Doc didn't think so. He told me why. "The burn scars are newer than the war scars," he said. "By several years, I figure. Also his left ankle's been broken at least twice and his right ankle at least once. I'd say that he broke one or both of them right about the time he got burned."

"Maybe in a car wreck?" I said, remembering Scott McBride's big-block-eight silver Firebird. Someone who drank and drove a fast car usually wrecked it at some time or another during his life.

"Yes. That'd be my guess."

Doc and I didn't speak for a while, as the

ceiling fan turned overhead and Daisy continued to whine and to scratch at the basement
door. Then it grew so quiet that I could almost
hear myself sweat.

"There's more, Garth," Doc said.

"Somehow I knew there was."

Doc nodded wisely and took a drink of his
tea. I took a drink of mine and wished that
Doc had put some sugar in it. No frills. But
that was Doc.

"The man had likely been in the water all
night, maybe longer," Doc said. "And in this
heat it doesn't take long for decay to set in and
ruin things. By that, I mean the telltale signs
that we look for to determine the cause and
the time of death. But, to make a long story
short, the man in my basement died of drown-
ing, brought about by a broken neck."

"Which figures," I said, "considering where
he was found." Scott McBride wasn't the first
to drown in Hidden Quarry, or the first to
break his neck there.

"It figures," Doc said, "if you don't take
into account the fact that there's no bump on
his head, which there would have been if he'd
dived into the quarry and hit something hard
enough to break his neck."

"Maybe he was wearing a helmet," I suggested.

Doc's eyes didn't even twinkle. "Not likely,
Garth."

18

"Is there any other way his neck could have gotten broken besides hitting his head on a rock?" I said.

"There are a lot of ways that could happen," he said. "But nearly all of them would have taken place before he went into the water."

"Oh," I said.

"There is one other possibility. The capillaries in his stomach, chest, and face are shattered, like he'd done a belly flop in the water from about forty feet. Water's like concrete, if you hit it flat like that. It doesn't compress. So he could have broken his neck that way, if it snapped back hard enough when he hit the water."

"Then why don't you think that's the way he died?" Because if I read Doc right, he had already dismissed that possibility.

"Something in my guts," he said. "If he hit the water hard enough to break his neck, he should have broken some ribs, or bruised his heart, or ruptured himself, none of which took place." Doc looked distraught. He hated uncertainty as much as I did. "I'm not saying it couldn't happen that way. I just don't think it did." Then he added, "Besides, what fool would dive forty feet into a stone quarry if he didn't know what he was doing?"

I listened to the fan overhead take a few more turns. "Maybe somebody trying to kill himself."

19

Doc dismissed that idea with a wave of his hand. "Not a man like that, Garth. Not after everything he'd been through. Because if he did decide to kill himself, he'd know how hard it was for him to die, and pick a surer way."

"What do you think did happen, then?" I said.

"I think somebody broke his neck and then threw him into the quarry. That's what I think happened."

I thanked him and left.

"Well?" Clarkie said after I had climbed into the patrol car.

I told him what Doc had told me.

He took his time digesting it, then said, "Figures."

"Do you want to translate that for me, Clarkie?"

He didn't answer.

"Then would you mind taking me back to my office?"

Again he didn't answer. He was off somewhere, where I couldn't reach him.

"Clarkie?"

He started the patrol car and put it in gear. "Sure, Garth. Anything you say."

3

But Clarkie didn't let me off at my office. He drove right on past it and into the park where the carnival had set up for Homecoming. A double row of game tents faced each other between the shelter house and the restrooms. Beyond the game tents to the south were the rides, and parked behind the tents, and scattered here and there about the park were the pickups, pop-up campers, and small house trailers that the carnies called home. Just one more gypsy camp in this age of flea markets, caravans, and life on the road.

"What's the deal?" I said. "Why are we stopping here?"

He avoided my question by saying, "I

talked to some of the kids around town, figuring that they would notice the Firebird if anyone would. They say it came in with the carnival on Sunday night. They say they saw it uptown early yesterday afternoon. They say they haven't seen it since."

"You've been busy," I said, impressed with Clarkie's legwork, which he usually bumbled if given half a chance.

He shrugged off my compliment. "Like Sheriff Roberts always used to say, it comes with the territory."

At the mention of Sheriff Roberts I grew silent. So did Clarkie. We both knew how much I missed him.

Once, not so long ago, I had pictured carnivals as a dizzy whirling ride, one right after the other, a cotton-candy smile on each and every face, and con men who'd take your last dime, if it wasn't sewn in your pocket; and knowing that I was still a sucker for a good pitch, I still stepped lightly around the gilded voices that rang up and down the midways and still kept one hand on my wallet at all times.

But that day I saw only tents and dust and weary carnies gathered in the shade, talking quietly among themselves while keeping a close eye on us. That was the trouble with growing up, I thought, and seeing the dross through the glitter. For every pearl of wisdom that you gained, you lost an ounce of pure gold.

We found the owner of the carnival between the Octopus and the Tilt-a-Whirl. He was a big, burly, nearly bald man with a barrel chest, thick tatooed forearms that looked like anchor cable, and ice-blue eyes that rolled like marbles with each turn of his head. At that moment he was angry, as his voice boomed across the park, "Let me tell you something, mister. The next time I find a loose bar on your ride, you're going to be out of here before you even have time to pack."

The thin swarthy man who stood before him didn't reply. He registered nothing, his eyes as blank as his smile. Then he just seemed to melt away. I looked for his puddle on the ground, but couldn't find it.

The owner of the carnival looked at us and frowned. "What do you want?" he said. "As you can see, I'm busy."

I glanced at Clarkie, who seemed to have swallowed his tongue and his confidence along with it. I doubted that I was going to get much help from him.

"I'm Garth Ryland, editor of the local paper," I said, stepping forward and offering my hand. "This is Sheriff Clark."

The carnival owner didn't shake my hand,

so I let it drop, as Clarkie just stood there, staring at him. I couldn't tell if Clarkie were thinking, or awe-struck.

"I'm Sean Ragan," the carnival owner said, returning Clarkie's stare. He seemed as intrigued with Clarkie as Clarkie was with him.

"We need to talk to you, Mr. Ragan," Clarkie said at last.

"What about?"

"Scott McBride. He's dead."

Ragan recoiled slightly, like a man who had walked too close to an open hearth. "Then let's get out of the sun."

We sat down in the shade of a sugar maple, I to Clarkie's right, Clarkie and Sean Ragan facing each other. A breeze stirred the leaves overhead. A dappled patch of sunlight lay at our feet.

"So talk," Ragan said. "The rides start at five."

Clarkie's look said that he was taking charge. He didn't want, nor need, my help. Fine with me. I lay back on the powder-dry ground and closed my eyes.

"Some kids found Scott McBride's body floating in Hidden Quarry early this morning," Clarkie said. "From the looks of things, he was there all night."

I opened my eyes. Sean Ragan seemed to be taking a long time to answer.

"What does that have to do with me?" he finally said.

"He rode into town with you and your carnival. That's what it has to do with you," Clarkie said with surprising verve and anger.

"Just because he rode into town with me doesn't make me his keeper," Ragan said, displaying some anger of his own.

"No," Clarkie answered. "But it should make you his friend."

I watched to see what would happen next. Clarkie's jaw was set as hard as I'd ever seen it. Ragan's jaw was set in the same way. But head to head, it would be no contest. Ragan would squash Clarkie like a water bug.

"What do you want from me?" Ragan said, looking away.

"Some answers, that's all. Like who is Scott McBride and what is he doing in Oakalla?"

Ragan's marble-blue eyes rolled our way. "You mean you don't know?" I couldn't tell if he was addressing Clarkie or me. Then he added, as if for my benefit, "Evidently neither of you follow stock-car racing."

Then I knew who Scott McBride was and why his name seemed familiar to me. In the late 1970's and the early 1980's Scott McBride was one of the leading drivers on the NASCAR circuit. Then he wrecked in one of those spectacular crashes that they show over

25

and over on network television, was burned to near death, spent several months in a hospital, and then dropped out of sight. The last I had heard of him, which seemed longer ago than it was, he'd started the comeback trail—the one that, particularly for old racers, almost never led back up to the mountain top.

"I remember him," I said. "Where was it he crashed? Daytona?"

"Talladega," Ragan said.

"Hell of a crash, if I remember right."

"Yeah," Ragan agreed. "It was a hell of a crash. And that was just the beginning."

"Of his rehabilitation, you mean?"

Ragan's eyes fixed on mine. I wouldn't have wanted those eyes looking down the barrel of a gun at me. "Of his nightmare. Catalepsy, drug addiction, alcoholism, every two-bit race in every dirt-bag town—you name it, he's been there. And now this." The irony seemed too much for Sean Ragan even. "Just when he was getting back on his feet again."

None of us spoke for several seconds. I didn't know what the others were thinking, but I couldn't help wondering how a man who had survived catalepsy, alcoholism, drug addiction, and who knew what else had come to die in a stone quarry. Sometimes life seemed unspeakably fickle and cruel. But Ruth said that was my biggest problem. I always expected life to be fair.

"I take it you've known Scott McBride for a long time," I said.

"A long time," Ragan answered.

"You were in the service together?" I took a guess.

"Yes."

"Vietnam?"

"Where else."

More irony. Add hell to the list of the things that Scott McBride had survived. "I'm sorry," I said.

"Sorry for me, or sorry for Scottie?" Ragan wanted to know.

"Sorry for all of us who were and who weren't there."

Ragan nodded as if he understood. Not all of Vietnam's casualties were casualties of war. Those of us who had stayed behind, for whatever our reasons, had paid the price in shame, guilt, and an incessant longing for our own red badge of courage to convince ourselves that we really weren't quite the cowards we seemed.

"You never went?" Ragan said.

I shook my head no.

"You mind telling me why?"

"My number never came up. I was one-ninety-nine. They stopped at one-ninety-five that year."

"You didn't miss anything," he said.

27

I nodded in agreement, though in my own mind I had missed a lot.

"You still haven't told us what Scott McBride was doing here." Clarkie was glaring at us. Apparently he didn't like the direction our conversation had taken. But then he was a decade younger than we were . . . or so I believed at the time.

"Scottie was on his way from Milwaukee to Terre Haute," Ragan said. "He'd raced at Milwaukee on Sunday and planned to race at Terre Haute next weekend. He sent his car and his crew on ahead and drove over here with me."

"So you're the reason he's here?" Clarkie seemed to want that to be the case.

"Part of the reason," Ragan said. "I hadn't seen him for over a year, and we had a lot of catching up to do." Ragan's brows furrowed and the sweat glistened on his broad forehead. He seemed to be heavily weighing his next statement. "The rest of the reason is that there was someone here who Scottie wanted to look up."

"Who?" Clarkie demanded to know.

"I assume it was probably a woman," Ragan said calmly.

Clarkie reddened, then rose and stalked off. The last I saw of him, he'd put the Octopus between us and was headed for the Kiddie Cars.

28

"Do you know her name?" I asked, Clarkie was obviously out of it for the being.

"No. I don't." Ragan's eyes never wavered. I couldn't tell if he was lying or not.

"Old love or new love?" I asked.

"More than likely an old love. Scottie didn't have many new ones."

"Since his accident, you mean?"

"Yes. Since his accident." Ragan's eyes were unmercifully hard. They neither gave quarter nor asked for any. "You'd understand if you'd ever seen him in the raw. Plastic man. That's what he called himself."

"Was he clean?" I said.

"In what respect?"

"Booze, drugs, the law, whatever."

"He was clean," Ragan said. "He had been for the past three years."

"Any reason why he had no registration, no driver's license, and there were no plates on his car?"

Ragan thought it over. "Not that I can think of. Scottie's license was suspended for one reason or another for most of his life, but that never stopped him from driving."

I rose and dusted myself off. Clarkie had returned to stand a few feet away. Sean Ragan stayed where he was on the ground. For a busy man, he seemed in no hurry to get going again.

"I've got a question for you," he said. "How did Scottie end up dead in that quarry?"

"That's what we're trying to find out."

"It was an accident, wasn't it?" His look said that it better have been.

"We're withholding judgment for now," I said.

"Until when?"

"Until we don't have any other choice."

Apparently Ragan bought my answer because he didn't say anything more.

"Coming?" I said to Clarkie, who was doing his best imitation of a wooden Indian.

"Coming," he said.

When we reached Clarkie's patrol car, Sean Ragan still sat where we'd left him in the shade of the sugar maple.

4

"My office is to the left," I said as we drove by it again, heading west on Gas Line Road.

"I know it is," Clarkie said. "I still need your help."

"Doing what?"

"Finding out the reason that Scott McBride came here."

"I thought you already knew that."

"Says who?" He gave me an angry look.

"Says your actions back at the park. For a while there, it seemed to me that you and Sean Ragan were old friends, up until you asked him who it was that Scott McBride came here to see."

Clarkie turned his attention to the road. "I've never met the man before in my life."

"What about Scott McBride? Have you ever met him before?"

Clarkie hesitated, then said, "Once. I met him once. At Atlanta. A bunch of us drove there to watch the race. He finished second that year."

"What year was that?"

"Seventy-six or Seventy-seven. I was just a wide-eyed kid in love with racing and race car drivers. I went down into the pits looking for autographs and ended up with his."

"Do you still have it?"

"Yes. It's in my dresser at home."

"You might have told me that sooner."

"Told you what?"

"Told me that you knew who Scott McBride was. Not only that you knew who he was, but that he was once your hero."

Clarkie looked at me in unalloyed astonishment, like the Clarkie of old. "How did you know that, Garth?"

"I didn't. But I also didn't know how else to explain your behavior."

Clarkie's face was a picture of sadness. "Wait until someone kills your hero, Garth. Then you'll know how I feel."

I didn't say anything more. I didn't know how to tell him that all of my heroes were already dead.

While Clarkie drove out to Hidden Quarry to dust the inside of Scott McBride's car for fingerprints, I went into the Corner Bar and Grill and asked if anyone there had seen Scott McBride the previous afternoon. No one had.

Then I crossed School Street and went into the Oakalla Savings and Loan where its owner, Wilmer Wiemer, greeted me with a big smile and good-old-boy handshake and assured me that no stranger with a tatoo on each arm had been anywhere near the Savings and Loan on Monday afternoon. I believed him, primarily because I knew that Wilmer watched his front door like a spider her web, waiting for the unsuspecting innocent to drop in.

From there I walked south along the west side of School Street to the Lutheran Church, found its front door locked, and continued on south to the Oakalla Mutual Insurance Company. The Oakalla Mutual Insurance Company, Oakalla's oldest continuously run business, had been in the same brick building since the turn of the century. Recently its limestone facade, added in the 1950's, had been torn down, its bricks cleaned and remortared, its carpeted floors taken down to the soft bare wood beneath, and its false tile ceilings removed in favor of the original high plaster ceilings. I liked the changes. Even

33

more, I liked the feeling that came with the changes.

Dorothy Sims had been the receptionist at the Oakalla Mutual Insurance Company for as long as I could remember. In May, she had received a lifetime achievement award from Oakalla Mutual's parent company, and she had been flown to Chicago where she and a dozen other lifetime achievers were feted with a banquet and gifts. On her return to Oakalla, she had described the experience to me as her "most memorable." I wondered then, as I interviewed her at the desk where she had sat for eight hours a day, five and six days a week, for the past thirty-five years, what my "most memorable" experience was. Probably not a trip to Chicago. Probably not a trip to any city.

"Good afternoon, Dorothy."

She looked up with a start. "Garth!" she said, grabbing her chest. "I didn't know anyone had come in."

Dorothy Sims was a short petite pretty woman with short dark-brown hair, large brown cocker-spaniel eyes, thin lips, and a nervous smile that never stayed very long before it turned to a worried frown. That day, as on nearly every other day, she wore small gold earrings, a plain cotton dress, red lipstick, and dark eye shadow that made her eyes look even larger and sadder than they were.

"Next time I'll knock," I said.

"I wish you would."

I didn't know if she was kidding or not. I never really knew how to take Dorothy Sims. She was one of those scrupulously good people, who, if you ever watched her walk down a sidewalk, as she deliberately stepped on every crack, deep in her heart, you knew was bad.

"Were you here yesterday afternoon?" I asked.

"When haven't I been here on a Monday afternoon?" she said with a hint of rancor.

I looked around the office. It had grown very quiet in there. All of the typewriters, printers, and word processors had seemed to stop at once. Apparently there was something heavy hanging over everyone's head. Either that or I was more captivating than I thought.

"I just wondered if this man came in here yesterday afternoon?" I described Scott McBride as best I could. I hadn't seen him in life, and only briefly and at a distance in death, so I was relying on Doc Airhart's description of him more than my own.

Dorothy Sims looked me right in the eye and said, "No. He wasn't in here."

I looked around the office, which suddenly was as busy as it had been still only moments before. But not everyone was busy. Maryanne

Markle, a large, ruddy, big-breasted woman with thin white curly hair, sat there in her print dress with her arms folded and a scowl on her face.

"That's a lie, Dorothy Sims," she said loud enough for the whole office to hear. "He was in here and you know it."

Dorothy Sims stiffened; even her hair went rigid. "Mind your own business, Maryanne," Dorothy warned.

"Which is it, Dorothy?" I said. "Was he here or not?"

"Not," she said, again looking me straight in the eye.

"Liar," Maryanne Markle answered. "He came in, took one look around, and went into there." She pointed to the manager's office which was separate from the main office. Then I began to understand what might be happening here.

Dorothy Sims stood up at her desk and turned to face her accuser. "Maryanne Markle, if you call me a liar one more time," she said with clenched fists through clenched teeth, "I'll tear what's left of your hair out. And don't think I won't either."

On hearing that threat, Maryanne Markle turned about the whitest shade of pale I'd ever seen. She sighed heavily and began to type.

Dorothy Sims turned back to me. "As I said, Garth, he wasn't here."

"Do you mind if I get a second opinion?"

"You had a second opinion. It turned out to be wrong."

"Nevertheless," I said, walking past her, through the office, and into the manager's office. But as luck would have it, the office was empty.

"Where is Cheryl today?" I asked Dorothy on my way out. Cheryl Loveless, the office manager, whose cool efficiency had kept Oakalla Mutual in the black the past ten years, was also Dorothy Sims' daughter.

"I don't know," she answered without looking up. I couldn't tell if she were still angry, or were embarrassed by what had taken place. I had never known Dorothy to raise her voice to anyone, let alone her fist.

"Are any of the other agents in today?"

"No. Neil Pate is on vacation, and Wilbur Snodgrass is out looking at somebody's car." She looked up at me. I couldn't quite read what was in her eyes. Fear perhaps. Perhaps a fear born of desperation. "I'm sorry, Garth," she said, then looked away.

My first step into the heat outside felt good after being in the air conditioning. But every step after that took its toll. When Clarkie met me on Gas Line Road, I was ready for a ride.

"You get your prints?" I asked.

"Yes. Did you find out anything?"

37

"I found out it's too hot to walk."

"I mean uptown."

I studied him. Clarkie seemed on edge, as if he couldn't decide what to do next, or couldn't wait to do whatever came next. "What do you think I found out?" I said, testing him.

"How should I know what you found out?" he asked testily. "I was out at the quarry taking prints."

I believed him, even though he hadn't come from the direction of the quarry, but from the direction of the park.

"I found out that Scott McBride was in Oakalla Mutual Insurance office yesterday," I said. Then I told him what had happened there.

Without saying a word, Clarkie turned his patrol car around in the middle of Gas Line Road and drove to the west end of Oakalla. I thought that I knew where we were going. When Clarkie stopped the patrol car in front of Cheryl and Butch Loveless' house, I knew for sure.

Cheryl Loveless and her husband, Duane (Butch) Loveless, lived in a small, neat, two-story brownstone house that had a red tile roof, two tall straight cedars growing on either side of its front steps, a grape arbor in its back yard, a rose of Sharon in its side yard, and a bay window that looked out over the rose of Sharon onto Madison Street.

Cheryl Loveless was a graduate of the University of Wisconsin at Whitewater and the office manager of the Oakalla Mutual Insurance Agency. She was also my insurance agent, and very good at what she did. Butch Loveless was a graduate of Northern Illinois University at DeKalb, a history and government teacher at Oakalla High School, and its track and wrestling coach. Cheryl drove a bright red Chevy Beretta. Butch drove a black Ford Bronco II. They had no children, pets, or servants.

If Clarkie had been out of character for most of that day, he had become his own worst self when we stopped in front of the brownstone. He was so wired that he forgot to put the patrol car in park and then to shut off the engine before he took his foot off the brake and opened the door to get out. As a result, we kissed the telephone pole in front of us. Then, without even looking at the damage, he slammed the patrol car into reverse and kissed the bumper on the Ford Bronco II that had pulled up behind us.

"Jesus Christ, Clarkie!" Butch Loveless said after jumping out of the Bronco. "Why don't you look where you're going?"

I thought Clarkie would be cowed by his blunder, and rightfully so. I was wrong, however. "Why in the hell don't you look where you're going!" Clarkie yelled. "You could see I was backing up."

They faced each other like two bucks in rut, neither one willing, or eager, to back off. Except that Clarkie was hopelessly over-matched. Butch Loveless had at least sixty pounds, all of it solid muscle, on him. Besides, Butch had the moves, the holds, and the guile that a lifetime of wrestling had taught him. It would be like a grizzly wrestling a panda.

"Let's all count to ten," I said, stepping between them. "Then if you still want to bash each other's head in, be my guest."

"There'd better not be so much as a scratch on it, that's all I can say," Butch said as he turned to examine the Bronco.

"And if there is?" Clarkie said, as belliger-ent as ever.

"For God's sake, Clarkie," I said under my breath. "Cool down before you get yourself hurt."

"The sonofabitch," Clarkie fumed, just as loudly as before. "One of these days he'll get what's coming to him."

"What was that, Clarkie?" Butch said, look-ing up from his bumper. His expression had turned from anger to one of cold rage. One more word from Clarkie, and I'd have a fight on my hands.

"Is Cheryl home, Butch?" I asked, hoping to distract him.

His eyes were still on Clarkie. He still smoldered, waiting for any excuse to tear Clarkie apart. "Who wants to know, and why?"

"It's police business," Clarkie said.

"That's funny," Butch said. "I don't see any policemen around."

Clarkie didn't even flinch. He'd heard it all before. It had almost become a standing joke in Oakalla, though not one that he found funny.

"What you see or don't see doesn't much matter," Clarkie said. "We still need to talk to Cheryl."

"Cheryl is not feeling well," Butch said. "I don't think she needs to be bothered."

I studied him. Butch Loveless was about six feet tall and weighed somewhere around two-hundred-twenty pounds. He had a broad face and mouth, dark heavy brows that almost grew together, a round thick torso, and enough hair on his arms and chest to stuff a mattress. But less hair on his legs, which he usually kept covered with jeans, and no hair at all in the growing bald spot in the middle of his scalp.

"In what way not feeling well?" Even though he should have been, Clarkie wasn't intimidated by Butch Loveless. Either that or the heat had made him a little crazy.

"She fell and hurt herself last night," Butch said. "Messed up her face some." He gave us

41

a little smile, or what I took for one. "You know how women are. If they can't look just so, they won't go out in public."

Clarkie didn't say anything. Maybe he didn't trust himself to speak.

"Did she break her jaw?" I said.

"No, no, it was nothing like that." Butch seemed almost genial now that he thought things were going his way. "Just a few bruises here and there, that's all."

"Then it won't hurt her to talk to us," I said.

"About what?"

"That's our business," Clarkie said, finding his voice again.

Clarkie started for the brownstone. I followed him. But Butch Loveless beat us to the door.

"Cheryl's business is my business," Butch said. "Nobody's talking to her unless I say so."

Clarkie's right hand rested on the butt of his .38 Police Special. I hoped he wouldn't pull it, but I didn't know that he wouldn't. The way he'd been acting, anything was possible.

"If you don't get out of the way, I'm going to arrest you for obstructing justice," Clarkie said.

"Or shoot me in the process? You'd like that, wouldn't you, you little turd?" Despite Clarkie's .38 Police Special, Butch still wasn't giving any ground. Maybe he didn't realize just how serious Clarkie was.

Then Cheryl Loveless opened the front door of the brownstone and stepped outside. "Shut up. Both of you," she said. "You're acting like children."

Cheryl Loveless was, to coin a phrase, a flaming redhead with creamy white skin, summer freckles, emerald green eyes, long arms and long legs, and a sharp smile that could alternately charm or infuriate you, depending on your mood and the thickness of your skin.

But today she had a big purple blotch on her left cheek, and her left eye and the left corner of her mouth were slightly swollen from what looked like a beating. She didn't seem to let it bother her though. Rather she gave me that sharp little smile of hers, as if to say, what of it?

"That must have been quite a fall you had," I said to her. "Butch was just telling us about it?"

"Was he now?" Her eyes fastened on Butch. I could feel the heat from them. "Where did he say I fell?"

"I didn't say," Butch was quick to answer. "And they didn't ask."

He pushed past her and went inside, closing the front door behind him. As he did, I felt the cool air from inside spill out.

"How did you get that bruise?" I asked. "If it's any of my business."

"It's not any of your business," Cheryl Loveless said calmly. Then she smiled.

"It is mine," Clarkie said. "If that sonofabitch has been beating on you again."

She gave Clarkie a look that said that this wasn't the time or the place to discuss it.

"Have it your way," Clarkie said, losing some of his steam. "But once, just once, I'd like to catch him at it. Then we'd see what Butch Loveless is really made of."

"He'd have you for lunch," Cheryl said gently. "You and I both know that."

"Maybe you know that," Clarkie said. "But I don't."

I watched while they exchanged looks. That wasn't the first time they had ever talked. They had the easy familiarity of old friends.

"Why is it you're really here, Clarkie?" Cheryl asked him, leaving me out of it. "It can't be because of what you're thinking because I haven't told anybody."

Clarkie looked to me for help. He didn't want to have to be the one to tell her.

"Where were you yesterday afternoon, say between two and four?" I said.

"I was in my office at work. Why?"

I might have believed her if she hadn't added the why, or if the concern hadn't entered her eyes when she did.

44

"Do you want to tell her, Clarkie?" I said, feeling that he ought to be the one.

He hung his head. He couldn't tell her. That left it up to me.

"Does the name Scott McBride mean anything to you?" I said.

"No. Why should it?" she answered.

"Because they found him dead in Hidden Quarry this morning."

Nothing happened for a moment. Cheryl Loveless just stood there in shock, like someone who had just taken a gut shot and didn't realize it yet. Then she wheeled and walked away from us. Clarkie went after her and tried to stop her, but she shook him off and continued walking. The last I saw of her was when she rounded the brownstone.

"Okay, Clarkie, what's the deal?" I said a couple of minutes later as we sat in his patrol car. "And don't give me some song and dance because I'm not in the mood for it."

"The deal is that I'm in love with Cheryl Loveless and have been since the seventh grade. But she can't see me for sour apples."

"That's not what I mean," I said.

"Then what do you mean?"

"Clarkie, don't play dumb with me. In the first place, you're not very good at it, and in the second place, I might take you seriously, and then where would you be?" I was out of patience with him. I didn't care if his feelings got hurt. "Where does Scott McBride fit into all of this? And don't try to tell me that he's Cheryl Loveless' childhood hero, too. Not with the name Cheryl tatooed in a heart on his arm."

Clarkie started the patrol car, waited for the air-conditioner to get going, then rolled up his window. I followed suit, because it seemed stupid to ride with one window up and one window down and the air conditioner on.

"Scott McBride was once Cheryl's lover," Clarkie said. "He was the first one to have her, the only one to have her that I know of, besides Butch." The thought of anyone having her, be it Scott McBride or Butch Loveless, hurt Clarkie more than he could stand.

"Did Cheryl tell you that?" I said.

"No. But I know it for a fact."

"How do you know it for a fact?" I persisted.

"Because," Clarkie said, fastening his seat belt and putting the patrol car in gear, "A couple years back Sheriff Roberts and I got called down here by the neighbors, who said that Butch and Cheryl were in the process of killing each other, if they hadn't already." He turned the patrol car around in the street, and we started back the way we'd come. "The long and short of it was that Cheryl got a letter

46

from Scott McBride, and Butch somehow found out about it. In the argument that followed, Cheryl lost her temper and threw it up in Butch's face that yes, Scott McBride had had her first, and yes, Scott McBride was twice the man Butch was."

"Who told you that?"

"Butch did. Later that night up at the Corner Bar and Grill, when I was off duty and he was crying in his beer." Clarkie stared straight ahead, as if he were afraid to look me in the eye. "It's the truth, Garth."

"So help me, God."

"What's that?"

"Nothing, Clarkie."

He stopped in the middle of the block. There was no reason to stop there that I could see, but he stopped anyway.

"Where do you fit into this?" I asked.

Clarkie still wouldn't look at me. "I told you. I'm in love with Cheryl Loveless and have been since the seventh grade."

"I mean with Scott McBride. Where do you and he come in?"

Clarkie turned to face me. He didn't like being questioned anymore than I liked doing it. "I told you, Garth. He was my hero."

"So you invited him here to Oakalla to screw the girl you'd loved since seventh grade. Come on, Clarkie, even you can do better than that."

"I didn't invite him here," Clarkie said. "He came with the carnival. And he wasn't my hero then, just somebody I got to know."

"Who in turn screwed the girl you loved?"

"That's the way it worked out," Clarkie said. "But that's not the way I planned it."

"What did you plan then?"

"Christ, Garth, how should I know? That was years ago."

Clarkie drove on. Two houses later I saw a familiar figure out watering his roses. "Stop here a minute, Clarkie," I said. "I need to talk to Hayden Sims."

Clarkie's look soured. "Be my guest," he said. "If it's all the same to you, I'll stay in the car."

"It's all the same to me."

Hayden Sims was somewhere in his mid-fifties, and was in many ways a smaller sleeker version of his son-in-law, Butch Loveless. He stood about five-ten, weighed somewhere around one-seventy, had sixteen-inch biceps, a thirty-two-inch waist, and slender, hairless, almost girlish legs. Like Butch Loveless, he had once been Oakalla's high school wrestling coach and now coached wrestling at the University of Wisconsin at Seaman's Point. Like Butch, he was a balding ex-jock, who, though he seemed to genuinely like his son-in-law, had confided more than once to me that Cheryl could have done better.

48

"It looks like you've got your work cut out for you," I said.

Hayden Sims wore a deep summer tan, yellow plaid bermuda shorts, a white golfing shirt, no socks, and sandals. He had just finished watering one rose bush and started on another. By my count, he had at least fifteen more to go.

"At twenty minutes a bush," he said, "I do have my work cut out for me."

"Does it do them any good to water them in the heat of the day?"

He glanced at his yard, which was nearly all in shadows, including the spot where we were standing. "It's after four," he said. "They'll be okay."

Sometimes Hayden Sims and I drank a late-night beer together at the Corner Bar and Grill and commiserated about the "good old days." His chief complaint was about the material, or lack thereof, that he'd had to work with lately—the "they don't make them like they used to" complaint common to old coaches and old newspaper editors.

My chief complaint was about the death of small town America—the loss of its schools, churches, families, neighborhoods, mores, and traditions that I sometimes had chafed under at the time, but missed now that they were all but gone. I wasn't a fanatic on the subject. But

49

after a couple of late-night beers, I felt like an authority.

"I just came from talking to Cheryl," I said, then let it rest there to see what would happen.

Hayden turned from the rose bush to me. "Why? Has something happened to her?"

"She's wearing a bruise that wasn't there yesterday," I said. "If that tells you anything."

"The bastard," he said. "I told him not to ever let it happen again."

"How often does it happen?"

"Not often," he said. "And sometimes I think it's as much her fault as his. But that still doesn't excuse Butch's behavior."

"No," I said. "That doesn't excuse Butch's behavior."

His concentration was back on the rose bush. He seemed intent on watering it into the ground. "As soon as I get done here, I'll go have a talk with him."

I nodded my thanks and started to leave.

"Garth, isn't that Clarkie there in the sheriff's car?" Clarkie had left his window up and the motor running. He was hard to see from where we stood.

"One and the same," I said.

"Why didn't he come with you?"

"You'll have to ask him," I said, not wanting to go into it.

50

"I will, the next time I see him."

I got back into the patrol car. It was as cold as a tomb in there. I wondered how Clarkie stood it.

"What did old 'Rosey' have to say?" he said in reference to Hayden Sims.

I rolled down my window to let in some warm air. "He wondered why you didn't come with me."

"He knows why," Clarkie said as he drove on. "Or after all these years, at least he should."

"Why? What do you have against Hayden? Besides the fact that he's Cheryl's father?"

"He drove me out of Boy Scouts," Clarkie said. "Or at least he made it so hard on me that I quit."

"Why would he do that?" I said.

"Because I was a fat little kid that he didn't think was good enough to be in his troop."

"Were you good enough?" I said, not wanting to take sides.

He shrugged. "Not in the things that mattered to him." Clarkie stopped at the stop sign for School Street. Even though there was no traffic coming, he didn't drive on. "You know, Garth, I think I actually hated him for a long time after that. He's probably the only person in my life that I've really actually hated."

"What about Butch Loveless?"

51

Clarkie turned onto School Street and headed north. "He comes in a close second."

"A lawman can't hold grudges, Clarkie. Not and do his job."

"How would you know, Garth? You've never been one."

"I wasn't the one who said it. Rupert Roberts did."

"God, in other words," Clarkie said bitterly.

"God, in other words."

"Garth, there are other lawmen around who are just as good as Rupert Roberts was."

"I know," I said, not liking his attitude. "But none of them live in Oakalla."

5

At home, I wiped the salt from my mouth and stood a moment in the shade before I found the energy to climb my front porch steps. I'd eat an early supper and wait for it to cool off some before I went back to my office.

Inside, Ruth was reclining on the couch, holding a large glass of iced tea in one hand, a stalk of celery in the other, and reading a women's magazine. She looked becalmed; she'd gone as far as she was going to that day, and if I wanted to keep peace in the family, I'd leave well enough alone.

"You don't have to worry," I said, sitting down in my favorite chair facing her. "I'll eat

53

up at the Corner." Short for Corner Bar and Grill, Oakalla's only restaurant.

She sat up, set the iced tea on the floor, and put the magazine aside. "I've been telling you for twelve years now that we need to air-condition this place, but, no, you know best."

Ruth was a large big-boned Swede somewhere in her early seventies. She had a mule's constitution and a will to match that usually kept her going in spite of hell or high water. Wisconsin born and bred, she couldn't take the freakish hot water that we'd had that summer. And since God wasn't handy, she blamed me.

"And how many days a year do we need air-conditioning?" I said.

"Thirty so far, and it's not even August."

"It's been a hot summer."

"I've never seen a cold one yet."

"Is there any tea left in the refrigerator?"

She picked up her magazine and lay back down. "Help yourself."

I went into the kitchen where I put some ice cubes in a glass and filled the glass with tea. Ruth liked her tea strong and sweet, the same way I liked mine. It really didn't quench my thirst, but it felt good going down.

I went back into the living room where I set my tea on the oak floor and sat back down in my chair. There were things I could be doing, should be doing, but I didn't have the energy. All I wanted to do was sit—maybe forever, if I could get away with it.

Ruth looked up from her magazine. "Something bothering you, Garth?"

I shrugged. How could I tell her when I didn't even know myself? Once, I went as the crow flies, from one adventure to another without worrying about what might lie in between. I spent part of my summers and many of my holidays there in Oakalla on Grandmother Ryland's farm. Home was the small town of Godfrey in west central Indiana where my dad owned a dairy and dairy bar, and my mother worked in the bank. Across the highway to the north of us was a small airport where Pop Stone, who owned the airport, used to take me joy-riding in his Piper Cub for fifty cents an hour. To the south and the west were neighbor kids who always could be counted on for a game of softball, croquet, or kick-the-can. To the east were farms and fields and beyond them a woods and stream I called my own. I was happy. I was free. I chased butterflies and baseballs until the cows came home and thought I would be a kid forever.

Then I went to college. Then I got out. Then I got a job with the *Milwaukee Journal*. Then I got married. Then I bought a house in the

55

suburbs. Then my son was born. Then my son died. Then I got divorced. Then Grandmother Ryland died and left me her car, farm, and some money. Then I bought the *Oakalla Reporter*, left Milwaukee and moved to Oakalla where I'd been ever since.

Somewhere along the line I'd lost sight of me. The old Garth could laugh easier at himself and the world around him, laugh heartier, too, from the toes on up. I missed that twinkle in his eye, that irrepressible boy in him who still clung to snips, snails, and puppy dog tails, and who still believed in happy ever after.

"I don't know, Ruth," I said, wanting to explain myself, but not sure that I could. "Earlier today, before all of this business with Clarkie started, I was sitting there in my office with my eyes closed and my feet propped up on my desk, thinking about nothing really, just enjoying the peace and quiet and the cool of the morning. When from out of the blue an old familiar scent blows in my window, and I'm sixteen-years-old, I'm up in the Superior National Forest, it's sunset, and my cousin, Dave, and I are on our way back from our first portage trip to Thompson Lake." I stopped. Here was where something always got lost in the translation. "Anyway, the river's behind us, there are northerns and walleye in the

56

bottom of the boat—not a boat load, but a respectable catch, the sun's dipped below the pines, and the lake's just lying there, cool, dark, and still, without a ripple showing, waiting to take us home." I smiled at her. "I can't describe the feeling. But I'd give almost anything to feel that way again."

Ruth returned to her magazine. I leaned back in my chair and closed my eyes. I knew she wouldn't understand.

"It's funny what we remember," she said. "Not more than an hour ago, I was thinking back to 1956 when Karl and I burned the mortgage on our farm. Here we'd survived a depression, a world war, another war, and buried both our children while on that farm, and Karl still broke out the French champagne he'd smuggled home from there after the war, and we toasted each other until we both were silly as geese. So when you talk about wanting to feel that way again, don't give up all hope. There's still a lot of life left to be lived."

For the next few minutes all I could hear was Grandmother's shelf clock ticking in my bedroom upstairs. Then Ruth rose and went into the kitchen where she began banging pots and pans around. I soon got up and followed her in there where I took a seat at the table.

"I thought you said it was too hot to cook," I said.

57

"I didn't say that. You did."

Ruth handed me a paring knife and some potatoes to peel, then took a package of hamburger from the refrigerator and began to make patties.

"This business with Clarkie you referred to," she said, "would it have anything to do with the body that was found in Hidden Quarry this morning?"

"Everything to do with it," I said.

She put half a stick of margarine into her favorite cast iron skillet, lit a fire under the skillet, and began slicing the potatoes into the pan as I got them peeled. She'd fry at least twice the potatoes we'd eat, but that was Ruth. She would rather throw food out to the neighbor's dog than have anyone leave her table hungry.

"Then it's not a simple case of some fool stranger diving into the quarry and hitting his head, like everyone is saying?" she said.

"I wish, Ruth. I think this thing has roots miles deep."

"Why do you think that?"

I told her what all had happened that day—from our arrival at Hidden Quarry to my conversation with Hayden Sims on our way back from Butch and Cheryl Loveless' house, as she finished slicing the potatoes, diced some onions to fry with them, and put the hamburgers on.

58

"On top of that . . ." I stopped. I had started to tell her about the twenty-year-old newspaper clipping, sitting on my desk at the *Oakalla Reporter.*

"On top of what?" she said. She washed and dried her hands, then began making a tossed salad.

"Never mind," I said. Ruth with a problem to solve was like a wolf with a T-bone steak. Once she sank her teeth into it, she'd never let go. And I was determined not to try to solve that particular problem.

She shrugged as if it were no concern to her. I knew better. "So what are you going to do about it?" she said.

"Do about what?"

"The body they found in the quarry this morning." She turned the potatoes and then the hamburgers. Both smelled equally good to me.

"I'm not going to do anything about it," I said. "Clarkie is the duly appointed sheriff of Adams County."

She sliced an onion and set a bottle of catsup on the table. "God help us then."

I left at seven for the *Oakalla Reporter.* The sun was low in the western sky, and the shadows were long and deep. But if it had cooled any since the afternoon, I couldn't feel it.

On my way east along Gas Line Road, I met Clarkie in his patrol car. He stopped the patrol car and rolled down his window. Reluctantly I walked around the patrol car to talk to him.

"Garth, I need a favor," he said, appearing as distraught as he'd been for most of that day. I wondered if he'd spent the last two hours driving around Oakalla in his patrol car, waiting for me to leave home, just so he could stop me on the street.

"What is it?" I said, feeling short on favors.

"I want you to take all of my calls tonight."

"And do what with them?"

"Answer them as best you can."

I flattened up against the patrol car as someone drove past on his way east. "Clarkie, I can't do that. I go to press in two days, and I just wasted the day on you the way it is. I can't afford to waste the night, too."

"It wasn't wasted," he said defensively.

I waited for a couple more cars to pass. I wondered what all the traffic was about, then remembered the Homecoming Fair in the park. What was it tonight, the beauty pageant or the pet judging contest?

"Maybe it wasn't a waste of time from your standpoint," I said. "But from mine it was. As you pointed out this afternoon, I'm not a cop. Furthermore, I have no desire to be."

"You're still a special deputy, Garth. Don't

forget that. And I can call on you any time I need you."

"Do you want me to turn in my badge?" I said, reaching for my billfold as if the badge were really in there. "If that's what it takes to get you off my back, then that's what I'll do." Another car came along and honked as it went by. I gave whoever was in it a half-hearted wave. Better than the alternative I had in mind.

"No. I just want your help," Clarkie said.

If he hadn't looked so earnest and forlorn, it would have been a lot easier to refuse him. "Not tonight, Clarkie," I said, pushing away from the patrol car. "Not tonight."

I crossed to the sidewalk to avoid all the traffic and continued east along Gas Line Road, as Clarkie waited there a moment, then drove on. I could tell just how hot it was when Mable Clendenning's old wooly shepherd looked up, curled his lip in a one-toothed snarl, and gave a weak woof. Any other day, he have been charging down the porch steps with Garth-chops on his mind.

Once at my office, I sat down in my chair, pushed some papers around, and tried to ignore the clipping that lay there on the desk in front of me. Either I ignored it completely, or I spent the next how many days, weeks, and years, looking for Paul Samuel? I couldn't

61

do anything half-heartedly. I blamed that character lapse on Grandmother Ryland, earth woman that she was, who had instilled in me a fierce loyalty to person, place, and community, and the continuity of things begun through things completed. Once you started something, you didn't quit until either you finished it, or it finished you. It was that simple.

I put the clipping inside my desk where I wouldn't have to look at it and began to lay out that week's edition of the *Oakalla Reporter.* As I worked, I could hear the sounds of the Homecoming Fair—the whir and grind of the carnival rides, the screams of young girls more thrilled than terrified, the occasional blare of a loud speaker announcing pet judging and lost car keys in the same metallic voice; and I could almost see the Ferris wheel tumbling in a fall of yellow light and smell the sweet corn baking within its husk.

Fairs were circular, it seemed, something you discovered as a kid, lost for a while in the confusion of adolescence, and rediscovered again with your own kids. Fairs were, like Christmas, never quite as good without kids.

Much later that night, when my conscience finally got the better of me, I called Ruth at home. For someone who owed Clarkie his life, I hadn't been very grateful.

Ruth answered on the first ring, which was unusual for her. That late at night she was usually asleep on the couch. "Whatever your problem is," she said, obviously out of sorts, "take it somewhere else. This isn't 911."

"Ruth, it's me, Garth. What's going on?"

"Sheriff Harold Clark, that's what's going on. The next time you see that little turnip, you can tell him personally for me that the next time I see him, I'm going to wring that chubby neck of his."

"Why? What has he done?"

"He's routed all of his phone calls here. That's what he's done. I haven't had a minute's peace all evening."

"Why would he do that?" I wondered aloud.

"I don't know. But I plan on asking him. Now, before I take the phone off the hook, what is it you wanted?"

"I just called to ask you if Clarkie had called. I was pretty sharp with him earlier this evening, and I'm afraid I might have hurt his feelings."

"It wouldn't be the first time his feelings got hurt."

"True. But this time he didn't deserve it."

She cleared her throat as if to say that was my opinion, then said, "No, he hasn't called. Nor has he stopped by here to see who did call."

"That doesn't sound like him," I said. "Usually he's a lot more conscientious than that."

"None of this business is like him," she said. "If you want my opinion, this job's gotten the best of him and he's gone off the deep end. Either that or the heat has gotten to him. God knows it's starting to get to me."

"To all of us, Ruth. But I don't think that's the problem."

"What is Clarkie's problem, then?"

"I don't know. I won't know until I ask him."

Outside, the stars were scattered and dim, more like ashes than diamonds, and the night unusually still, as if even the crickets and katydids found it too hot to chirp. I walked east along Gas Line Road to the park in the hope of finding Clarkie there. All of the rides had shut down and all the fair-goers had gone home. A dusty haze hung in strands between the tents and over the baseball diamond, giving the park the aura of a battlefield. Of those carnies still up, no one was moving very far or very fast—until fifteen-year-old Billy Hunter nearly ran over me in his hurry to leave the park.

Then I heard a woman scream somewhere ahead of me. I was between the merry-go-round and the haunted house just leaving the double row of game tents when it happened.

A moment later what looked like a white balloon came bobbing toward me, then abruptly turned to my right and disappeared. I started after it.

But others had also heard the scream and came running from all directions. I thought we were all in this together until one of them with an iron grip grabbed me and began to drag me in a direction that I didn't want to go. I twisted, broke away from him, and ran west in the direction that the white balloon had gone.

I got tackled for my trouble, and literally bit the dust as I went face down into the hard ground. By then I'd had enough. I got up ready to swing at someone.

But Sean Ragan was equally ready to take a swing at me. I lowered my fists. He did the same.

"Ryland, is that you?" he said.

I spat out a wad of blood and dirt. "It's me," I said.

"What the hell are you doing here?" he demanded to know.

"Looking for Sheriff Clark."

"You weren't just a minute ago."

"No," I said, spitting out another wad of dirt. "I was chasing someone. But thanks to you, he got away."

"Boss?" Someone came running up to Sean Ragan. "You'd better go check on Sally. She's pretty shook up."

Ragan pointed his finger at me. "I'll talk to you later," he said, then started off with the man.

"You can make book on it," I said, following him.

Ragan suddenly stopped. Preoccupied with my bloody lip, I nearly ran into him. "Where do you think you're going?" he said.

"With you."

"The hell you are."

I studied him. I could see the rage in his marble eyes. It was a living, breathing thing that might, at any moment, jump out at me. Not many people scared me. But Sean Ragan did.

"Yes, I'm going with you," I said, hoping my voice didn't crack. "You might not like it, but I'm a duly-sworn deputy sheriff of Adams County."

"Then show me your badge."

"If you like." I reached for my wallet.

"Forget it," he growled, taking off again. "I don't have time to play your Mickey Mouse games."

I followed him to a small trailer where a woman sat upon its steps crying. Her trailer door was open, and I could see broken glass on the floor inside.

"Are you okay, Sally?" Ragan gruffly asked, sounding more put out than concerned.

She stared at him in anger. She had long bleach-blond hair, a hard tired face, and the look of someone who'd seen it all in her day, and done most of it. I had seen her at the carnival on Monday, the first night it opened. Some kid behind me had said to his friend, "For six bits she'll guess your age and weight. For six bucks she'll do a lot more."

At the time I thought it was a lot of hot air, which adolescent boys had a lot of. But maybe he knew something I didn't.

"No. I'm not okay," Sally said to Sean Ragan. "I'm scared shitless, that's what I am. Some maniac just tried to break into my trailer."

The glass on the floor of the trailer had come from the small window in the door, which had been shattered by a blow from something. To me, Sally had reason to be upset.

But Sean Ragan seemed unconcerned. "It's happened before," he said.

"Not for a long time, Sean."

He shrugged. "Why don't you go on back inside. I'll get someone to fix your window tomorrow."

She balked at that idea. "And what if he comes back in the meantime? What am I supposed to do then?"

"Screw him, like you do everyone else," Ragan said, then walked away.

The rest of the carnies who had gathered in the shadows wasted no time in following Ragan's lead. Soon Sally and I were the only ones there.

"Do you have a last name, Sally?" I asked.

"What's it to you?" she said angrily, still feeling the sting of Ragan's last remark.

I studied her more closely. Perhaps she had been pretty once before her eyes and face had hardened into that permanent look of regret that the life-worn wear. She was still a handsome woman with sharp prominent features, a long lean body, and an innate something that kept her head up and her eyes in focus. But she looked better in shadow and from a distance. Up close, with her pale white skin and straw-yellow hair, in her faded jeans and blue denim work shirt, she looked like yesterday's queen of the rodeo.

"I'm just curious," I said. "Most people do have a last name."

"It's Sally Wampler," she said, scooting over so that I could sit down beside her. Apparently she needed a friend. Since no one else was around, I would have to do.

"Mine's Garth Ryland," I said, offering my hand. "I run the local newspaper."

She shook my hand. I liked her grip. It was dry, warm, and surprisingly soft. "At least you're not a cop," she said.

"I take it cops aren't welcome here."

She laughed at that. "Cops aren't welcome anywhere there's a carnival. Cops and carnies mix about like oil and water. That's because," she explained, "most of us are on the run from something. Either our past or ourselves."

"Just like the rest of us," I said.

We neither one spoke for a while. She watched the stars through weary eyes. I watched them with her.

"Speaking of cops," I said, remembering why I'd come to the park in the first place, "have you seen Sheriff Clark around here tonight?"

"Was he in uniform?"

I had to think about it before I said, "As far as I know."

"Then I haven't seen him." She smiled at me. "Believe me, I know when there's a uniform around. We all do."

Again we were silent for a while. My eyes had gradually grown accustomed to the dark, and I began to recognize the park again as a familiar place. With the carnival there, particularly at night, the park seemed anything but the quiet, collect-my-thoughts sanctuary that I had come to know and love. With the carnival there, it seemed strangely foreign, almost like alien ground.

"Do you have any idea who tried to break into your trailer tonight?" I said.

Sally Wampler didn't answer right away. That bothered me, since it might mean that she did know but wasn't going to tell me. "No. I don't know who it was. Like I told Sean, probably some sex maniac."

"You just called him a maniac the first time."

"Well, I meant sex maniac," she said. Then she added, "I mean, aren't all men?"

"I'm not."

"Then ninety-nine percent of them." She spoke with bitter authority. I didn't see the point in arguing with her.

"You and Sean Ragan seem to go a long way back," I observed.

"I taught him the ropes," she said simply, and with a hint of pride. "About a lot of things."

"You were lovers once?"

"God no!" she laughed. "Sean has never loved anything in his life. Except maybe this carnival." She paused as her eyes filled with tears. "And Scottie McBride." She sucked in hard as if she couldn't get her breath, then said, "Scottie's death has really gotten to him."

"I didn't realize they were that close." At least Sean Ragan's actions hadn't told me that.

"They went through Vietnam together. That should tell you something."

I nodded in agreement, then stood to spit out what I hoped was the last of the dirt in my mouth. My lip had stopped bleeding, but it felt as big as a basketball.

"Something wrong with your mouth," she said, as I touched my finger to it.

"Sean Ragan tackled me by mistake after you screamed. He busted my lip in the process."

"You're lucky that's all he busted."

Again I nodded. I felt the same way. "If not lovers, what were you and Sean Ragan to each other?"

She had to think about it. "Traders, I guess. I took what I needed from him. He took what he needed from me."

"Ayn Rand would say that's the purest kind of love."

"Who's Ayn Rand?"

"A writer. Dead now."

"Well, it was pure, but I wouldn't call it love."

"And Scott McBride, what was he to you?"

She shrugged as if she really didn't know. "Scottie was my friend. About the only real friend, male or female, I've ever had."

"He wasn't a sex maniac?"

She flipped me off, but without anger or malice. "No. Scottie was a very sexy guy. But we never made it together."

71

"Why not?"

"Because we were both afraid it would ruin our friendship."

"Reason enough," I said, preparing to leave.

"Heading out?" she asked.

"Yes. I'm heading out."

"You could stay here tonight. I'd make it worth your while." She spoke simply, bluntly, matter-of-factly, like an honest trader who knew the worth of her goods. Had it been another night, I might have considered it.

"I'm sure you would," I said. "But I have to get home."

"To the wife and kids, I suppose?"

"Yes," I lied. "To the wife and kids."

"Have a good one then."

"You too." I started to leave, then stopped. "Sally, are you going to be all right?"

"I'll be fine," she said. "Just fine."

If there was any irony in her voice, I didn't hear it.

6

"What happened to you?" Ruth sat up and asked on my return home. She had been lying on the couch reading. Or trying to read. Her eyes looked pretty blurry to me.

I sat down on the footstool in front of my chair. "Sean Ragan gave me a fat lip."

"Who's Sean Ragan?"

"The carnival owner that I told you about earlier." Then I went on to tell her what had happened in the park.

She thought for a moment, then said, "Does that make sense to you?"

"Does what make sense to me?"

"Any of it."

"Some," I said. "I think I know what Billy

Hunter was doing there. I'm not so sure about the person who tried to break into Sally Wampler's trailer."

"What was Billy Hunter doing there?"

"He was probably with Sally Wampler."

"Oh," she said, surprised at herself for not thinking of it. "Do you suppose Billy might know whoever it was that tried to break into the trailer?"

"It's a possibility."

"It wasn't Peg Hunter, Billy's mother," Ruth said with certainty. "Or she'd still be there with her hands around Sally Wampler's throat."

"What about Glen Hunter?" Who was Billy's dad.

Ruth was skeptical. "If I know Glen Hunter, he'd have been right there in line behind Billy. Maybe in line ahead of him."

"So who does that leave?" I said.

"The rest of Oakalla," she answered. "Not counting you and me."

"At least that narrows it down."

She gave me a quizzical look. "What is it you're not telling me, Garth?"

"It's what Sally Wampler didn't tell me. I have the feeling that she knew who it was, or at least why he was there."

"Someone from her past, you mean?"

Leave it to Ruth to speak my thoughts. "Yes. That's what I mean."

74

"Then whoever he is, he might not even be from Oakalla."

It was my turn for skepticism. "We should be so lucky."

The phone rang. Ruth and I exchanged looks. Neither one of us was expecting a call.

"I thought you said you were going to take the phone off the hook," I said as I rose to answer it.

"I did take it off the hook. But I couldn't stand the beep-beep-beep any better than I could the phone calls."

"Garth Ryland here," I said on answering the phone.

"Homer Hutchinson on this end. I called Sheriff Clark's house, but his answering machine said to call here."

Homer Hutchinson lived about a mile south of town at the top of Hutchinson's Hill. He had lived there all of his life, which was close to eighty years.

"What can I do for you, Homer?"

"Well, this might mean something, and it might not, but I think there's been a wreck at the bottom of my hill."

I felt something very close to panic, as my mouth went dry and my pulse began to race. Late-night wrecks weren't my specialty any more than late-night tavern brawls were. Rupert Roberts always took care of those things in the past.

"How sure of that are you, Homer?" I said.

"Pretty sure." Then he upped the ante. "Real sure."

"I'll be out there in a minute, Homer. In the meantime, you'd better put in a call to Operation Lifeline."

"For the good it'll do."

"Trouble?" Ruth said after I'd hung up.

"It looks like it."

Moments later I raised my garage door and looked skeptically inside. There sat Jezebel, alias Jessie, the brown Chevy sedan that I had inherited from Grandmother Ryland. I knew that Jessie didn't have a soul, that she didn't spend all her idle hours conspiring against me. It just seemed as if she did.

"Well, Jessie, what'll it be today," I said, patting her back fender, "cross fire or vapor lock?"

I climbed in and turned on the ignition. She started on the first try. She sometimes did that to confuse me.

I went via my back alley to Jackson Street, from Jackson Street to Perrin Street, and from Perrin to Colburn Road. Hutchinson's Hill, about a mile out on Colburn Road, was a long steep hill that used to put the fear of God in me every time I raced my bicycle down it on my way to Hidden Quarry. Invariably, at some point on the way down I would lose control to the hill, and from then on it was just a matter of holding on and riding it out in one awful exhilarating pause, suspended it seemed between air and earth, until the hill let go of me again.

And invariably, stiff-armed and rubber-legged from swimming in the quarry all afternoon, I could never pedal all the way back up the hill. Again I didn't have a choice in the matter. At some point my bicycle just stopped, and either I jumped off or I fell off. All of us did. Not a one of us could ride all the way to the top of Hutchinson's Hill without stopping. Not on a one-speed with balloon tires, which was all any of us had back then.

Homer Hutchinson stood out by his mailbox to flag me down. I opened Jessie's passenger side door and he got in.

"Tell me exactly what happened, Homer," I said. I switched on the bright lights, put Jessie in low gear, and began to creep down the hill.

"There's not time for all of it."

"The long and short of it then."

The long and short of it was that Homer had been sitting outside on his porch swing because it was too hot inside to sleep. He'd heard, rather than seen, a car drive past with its lights off and stop at the top of the hill, where it sat, in Homer's estimation, for a minute or two. Then he saw the car's lights go on and heard a door open and close, as the car started slowly down the hill, gathering speed as it went. Near the bottom of the hill the car veered to the left, jumped the ditch, and went into a pasture where it appeared to roll over a couple times.

As we approached the bottom of the hill, I glanced at Homer, who in his bare feet and bib overalls sat perched on the edge of Jessie's seat, like a bird about to take flight. "Is this about where the car went off the road?" I said.

"Right about here," he said. "We best get out and walk."

I parked Jessie as close to the edge of the ditch as I dared and left her parking lights on. Then Homer and I got out. He had thought to bring a flashlight. So had I, but his worked better than mine.

"Here it is, Garth," he said, shining his flashlight at the hole in the fence where the car had gone through. "Lucky for us it's as dry as it is."

"Why is that, Homer?"

"Because if this pasture wasn't burned up, there'd be cows in there now."

And if we were real lucky, maybe a Holstein bull.

We found the car lying upside down about fifty yards into the pasture. Its windshield and all of its windows were broken, and its roof had been smashed nearly flat. The only thing about Clarkie's patrol car that I positively recognized was the star on the door.

78

"I hope there's no one inside," Homer said.

"So do I, Homer."

He shined his light inside, slowly raking the interior of the car. I breathed a sigh of relief. No one was in there.

"That's Sheriff Clark's car, isn't it?" Homer said. "Or what's left of it."

I didn't answer right away. I was trying to get my heart to slow down enough for my mind to work.

"Do you figure he's still around here somewhere?" Homer asked.

I could hear what sounded like a siren in the distance. But it didn't seem to be coming any closer. Soon I couldn't hear it at all.

"He's around here somewhere, Homer," I said. "He can't be anywhere else."

Homer and I split up and began looking for Clarkie. He went back in the direction we'd come while I walked down to the small, nearly dry stream that ran through the pasture. The stream ran through a culvert under Colburn Road, then through another culvert under the old interurban before it emptied into Stony Creek about a quarter mile west of there. I was guessing that Clarkie had crawled out of his patrol car after it crashed and walked down to the creek, which would have been the easiest route to take if he were trying to hide from someone.

And why would he be hiding from someone? My guess was that someone had just tried to kill him by sending Clarkie and his patrol car on a free roll down Hutchinson's Hill.

I shined my flashlight into the culvert that ran under Colburn Road. "Clarkie, are you in there?"

He didn't answer.

Being careful not to step on the slippery green slime that had coated the bottom of the culvert, I wobbled my way through it and came out on the other side. Ahead was the culvert that ran under the old interurban, the one that, when I was a kid, held a dark fascination for me. Brown and crumbling, its entrance nearly blocked by debris and chunks of broken concrete, it was always the one place that I was afraid to enter. And at night, since I was more than mildly claustrophobic, it could still make my pulse quicken. I could almost hear the snakes sharpening their fangs on the rats inside.

"Clarkie, are you in there?"

No answer.

I dragged a snarl of brush out of the way and went deep into the culvert before being stopped by a huge slab of concrete that had broken loose from the top of the culvert and effectively sealed the other end to everything but small critters and water. Clarkie wasn't in the culvert, but wedged behind the concrete slab was something that intrigued me.

"Garth! I found him!" I heard Homer Hutchinson holler as I emerged from the culvert.

"Where is he?" I hollered back.

"In the ditch about twenty yards north of where we came in."

"Is he alive?" I was afraid to ask.

"He appears to be."

"Thank God. I'll be right there."

I climbed up onto Colburn Road and began running toward Homer. Again I could hear a siren in the distance. This time it appeared to be coming our way.

I reached Homer at the same time that the ambulance from Operation Lifeline crested Hutchinson's Hill. "You'd better flag them down," I said to Homer, "or they're liable to be in Illinois before they get stopped."

"No great loss," he answered.

Clarkie had a large bloody knot on his left temple, several small cuts on his face and arms, and a large welt just above his right eye that had already started to close the eye. But he had a strong steady pulse and seemed to be breathing normally.

"What do you think, Garth?" Homer asked.

I raised Clarkie's left eyelid, shined my

flashlight in his eye, and saw only pupil. "I think he probably has a concussion."

Homer and I watched the Operation Lifeline ambulance make a U-turn, rock from side to side as it narrowly escaped the ditch, and come back our way. The ambulance had whizzed right on past a frantically waving Homer and continued on for a couple hundred more yards before it got stopped. Now Homer stood right in the middle of Colburn road, waiting for it.

"I'm not sure that's wise, Homer," I said.

"Jesus Christ, Garth, surely they'll see me."

But they didn't see Homer until the last minute, and he had to jump out of the way to keep from getting run over. I had never seen Homer move quite so fast, and I had known him most of my life.

"Are you okay?" I asked him as the ambulance squealed to a stop and began to back up.

Homer sat rubbing his right ankle. "I think I sprained it, Garth. I heard something pop when I landed."

So a few minutes later, which, thanks to Homer, were probably the longest few minutes of the two young paramedics' lives, they in their Operation Lifeline ambulance took both Clarkie and Homer to the hospital.

7

Sometime between then and dawn it got cool enough for me to doze off, put a stranglehold on my pillow, and awaken with my right arm numb from sleeping on it. Sitting up in bed, I could hear a cow bawling somewhere to the east and the local freight chugging up the grade south of town. I rose and looked out my east window where a mist clung to the trees and the sun sat low in the sky, like a red rubber ball. It was going to be another hot one.

I went downstairs and called the hospital. I had followed the ambulance to the hospital where I learned that Clarkie did indeed have a concussion, which the doctor on duty rated a five out of a possible ten. Then I waited for them to X-ray and wrap Homer Hutchinson's sprained ankle before driving Homer home.

When I finally reached home, Ruth had already gone to bed, so I did likewise. But sleep hadn't come easily. I had a mind full of questions and very few answers.

My call to the hospital was routed to the nurses' station in the intensive care unit. "Judy Dellinger speaking."

"Judy, this is Garth Ryland. Is Clarkie awake yet?"

"Not yet, Garth. But we're hoping sometime soon."

"How's he doing?"

"As well as can be expected. He took quite a blow to his head."

"Do you have any way of knowing whether the blow came as a result of the accident or not?"

I waited while she spoke to someone nearby. "What was that, Garth? We're right in the middle of breakfast here."

"The knot on Clarkie's temple. Did it come with the accident?"

Again I waited while she answered someone's question about who got what breakfast. "That'd be my guess. We picked several small splinters of glass out of it, so I imagine his head went through the window when the car

84

rolled over. If the car rolled over," she added.

"It did."

I thanked her and hung up and went into the kitchen where a pot of coffee sat perking on the stove and Ruth sat at the kitchen table in her favorite flowered pink robe that was almost as old as she was. Ruth yawned, then asked, "What time did you get in last night?"

"I don't know. I never looked."

"How's Clarkie?"

I poured us each a mug of coffee and handed Ruth hers. "He's doing as well as can be expected. Whatever that is."

Ruth added some sugar and half-and-half to her coffee, then scooted them across the table for me. I had already set my coffee on the table and was about to sit down when someone knocked on the front door.

"Are you expecting anyone?" I asked.

"Not at this hour."

Captain Fillmore Cavanaugh of the Wisconsin State Police was, as Rupert Roberts had been, a good cop. He and Rupert had served as M.P.'s in Germany following World War II and then had joined the state police together shortly after their discharge from the Army. I'd first met Fillmore Cavanaugh several years ago at a euchre game at Rupert's house, where to Fillmore's everlasting regret, he and I were partners. Since then I'd seen him every now

85

and again whenever he was in town, and the last time I'd seen him, when I was in the hospital eight months ago, he had eleven months to go before retirement.

"Come in," I said, opening the screen door for him. "The coffee's on."

"I know. I smelled it from outside."

Fillmore Cavanaugh was a big man. Tall and thick with a flat belly and bull shoulders, short grey hair that he always wore in a flattop, a ruddy face, and a schoolboy grin, he looked like the all-American grandpa, or at least TV's version of him. But when you looked past the smile and the jolly-old-elf face into his cool grey eyes, you saw the cop there. And something else there that said you didn't want to cross him. Not ever.

"Congratulations on your promotion," I said, handing him a mug of coffee. He had only recently made captain, which was a promotion that was long overdue.

"Since I had only a few months to go, I guess they figured they'd throw me a bone," he said, setting his hat on the counter and taking a seat at the table.

"You know Ruth of course," I said.

He nodded at Ruth. "Of course," he said with respect.

I could have sworn that I saw Ruth blush, but later she denied it.

"So what's the deal with Clarkie?" he said, taking a sip of his coffee and smiling his approval. "When you called last night, I didn't have all my wits about me. I'm still not sure I do."

I filled him in on how yesterday had gone.

"I've got a couple people at Hidden Quarry now, dusting the Firebird for prints," he said.

"I think Clarkie's already done that," I said.

"Well, at least we won't miss any that way." Fillmore Cavanaugh had about as much faith in Clarkie as I did, which at that moment was very little.

He took another sip of his coffee and set his mug down. "You talk to Clarkie yet?" he asked.

"No. He's still out."

"For how long, do you think?"

"Not long, according to the nurse I just talked to."

"And Scott McBride, where does he fit into all of this?"

"That's what I'd like to know," I said.

"There'll probably be hell to pay when word of his death gets out."

I knew what he meant. Scott McBride was once a national figure, and even though he had long been out of the limelight, somebody short on news with a deadline to meet was bound to pick up the story on his death and run with it. Soon lights, camera, and action would arrive in Oakalla and we'd all be celebrities for a day. Then we, and Scott McBride, would be forgotten.

"Any chance that the word won't get out?" I said. "At least for now."

"I'll see what I can do," he said.

He rose without finishing his coffee, picked up his hat, and walked to the front door. I followed.

"The way I read it," he said, "is that whoever killed Scott McBride, if in fact someone did kill him, also tried to take Clarkie out because Clarkie was getting too close to the truth. Is that the way you read it?"

"Yes."

"Which means I'd better post someone outside of Clarkie's hospital door."

"That was my next suggestion."

"Any other suggestions," he said, looking a whole lot more like a cop than a grandfather, "like who we might call on today to explain things?"

"I'd start with Cheryl Loveless, who, unless I miss my guess, was with Scott McBride on Monday afternoon. While you're at it, you might ask Butch Loveless where he was Monday afternoon and then again late last night. I'll be covering the same ground, but at my own pace."

88

A breeze blew in my front door. My next door neighbor was watering his yard. For one intoxicating instant, it smelled like rain.

"Are Butch and Cheryl Loveless the only players in the game?" he asked.

"No. There are a couple others. But they're the main ones."

"Who are the couple of others?"

"Sean Ragan, the carnival owner, is one. Whoever tried to break into Sally Wampler's trailer last night might be another. Then there's Dorothy Sims, Cheryl's mother, who for some reason has been acting as far out of character as Clarkie has lately. And, since it seems to be a family affair, you might as well add Hayden Sims, Cheryl's father, to the mix as well."

He stepped outside and put his hat on. It made him look at least ten feet tall. "You seen Rupert lately?" he said.

"Not since he got back from El Paso."

"That was over three months ago."

I didn't say anything.

"What is it with you two, Garth? You won't go see him and he won't come see you. Have you had a falling out or something?"

"No," I said, remembering back to that cold lonely day last November when Rupert and his wife, Elvira, left for El Paso. "We parted on the best of terms."

"Then what's the problem?"

I had spent months of trying to answer that same question—why I felt so deserted, and betrayed. "I don't know, Fillmore. Whenever I think of him out there hoeing in his garden, or down in his basement making a clock for someone, it's almost like he doesn't exist anymore, that he's not the same man I knew and loved when he was wearing a badge."

"He's the same man, Garth. Believe me. We don't change for either the better or worse once we take off our badge and hang up our gun."

"I know that," I said. "Or at least part of me does. As a kid, I went through the same thing when my dad sold his dairy and went to work for someone else. I knew he was the same man as before. But it still took me a long time to forgive him."

"For not being there for you?" As a father himself, Fillmore Cavanaugh was trying to understand.

"For not being there with me. Not with me every minute of the day. I don't mean it that way. But around. In case I needed him, or wanted to show him something." Then I spoke the fear that had been growing in me ever since Rupert resigned. "I'm not ready for a changing of the guard, Fillmore. I'm not ready to go it alone. I'm not ready because I don't feel up to it."

"You still have . . ." He'd started to say that I still had Clarkie, then thought better of it. "Ruth," he said.

"It's not the same. Ruth's a great friend, as good a friend as I could ever hope for. But she's not a man. Sometimes I need another man to talk to. To help keep me on course, if nothing else."

"You mean a father?"

"Not exactly a father. But an older man like Rupert, wise in the ways of the world."

"You mean a father." Fillmore Cavanaugh's mouth tightened. He glanced away. "I know how you feel, Garth. I felt the same way when my dad died, like my shoes had just grown two sizes too big for me." His eyes found mine. They were eyes incapable of self pity. "But we all have to take our turn sometime. We may not want to, but life requires it."

"What a crock," I said.

"Isn't it, though."

After a shave, a shower, and a breakfast of orange juice and Cheerios, I walked to the Corner Bar and Grill. The regular morning crowd was there, drinking coffee and sharing gossip, and if like other mornings recently, complaining about the heat. Included were Butch Loveless and Hayden Sims, who sat in a booth facing each other, looking like (with their balding heads and bulging biceps) Tweedledum

91

and Tweedledee. If they were at odds with each other over Butch's beating of Cheryl Loveless, they didn't show it.

"Morning, Garth," Hayden said, scooting over to make room for me. "Buy you a cup of coffee?"

I glanced from him to Butch, who didn't appear quite as eager to share his booth with me. "Thanks, Hayden," I said. "But I can't stay. I just dropped by to see if anyone here could tell me Clarkie's whereabouts last night."

Hayden and Butch shared a knowing look. I wondered what it meant.

"I can't tell you Clarkie's whereabouts," Hayden said. "But I saw his patrol car parked in the alley behind our house when I finished watering my roses and went to put the hose away." Then he corrected himself. "Actually it was about halfway between the Samuel house and ours."

"What time was that?" I said.

"Along about dark, or maybe a little later."

"And Clarkie was nowhere around?"

"If he was, I didn't see him."

"What about you, Butch?" I said. "Did you happen to see Clarkie last night?"

"Didn't see him. Wasn't looking for him," he answered. "I spent the whole evening inside the house. You can ask Cheryl."

I planned to do that at my next stop. "How long was Clarkie's patrol car there in the alley, or do you know?" I said to Hayden.

Seeing that I wasn't going to sit down, Hayden scooted back to where he'd been sitting when I came in. "I don't really know," he said. "After I put the hose away, I came up here and drank a couple beers. The car was gone when I got back."

"What time was that?"

"Around midnight. But I can't say exactly."

"Thanks, Hayden," I said. "It's a start."

"How is the little turd anyway?" Butch asked.

It had grown quiet in there, as everyone had stopped talking to listen. "As well as can be expected," I said.

"He's not going to die or anything, is he?" Though I didn't expect it, I thought I heard real concern in Butch's voice.

"No. I don't think so," I said.

"I told you there was nothing to worry about," Hayden said to Butch, as if continuing an earlier conversation.

"Who was worried," Butch said.

Fifteen minutes later I stood on Butch and Cheryl Loveless' front door step. I had stopped at the insurance company after leaving the Corner Bar and Grill, but Cheryl Loveless wasn't there. For the second day in a row, she had called in sick. Or so Dorothy Sims told me through the locked front door.

I wiped my brow. Not yet nine A.M. and already I'd started to sweat.

When I got no answer at the front door, I went around to the back door of the brownstone, knocked, and got the same no answer. So I walked down the alley behind the brownstone to where Hayden Sims said that he had seen Clarkie's patrol car parked the night before. As I stood there in the alley, studying the lay of things, while trying to figure out where Clarkie might have gone, I felt my hackles rise. It was my built in warning that someone was watching me.

I slowly turned to see who it was and saw a door close. It was the back door to the Samuel house.

The first thing I noticed about the house was the high cedar privacy fence that ran between it and the Sims' house next door. The second thing I noticed about it was the yellow-and-blue stained glass window on the west side of the second story.

The rest of the house was plain by comparison. Grey wooden posts supported a grey porch. The house's two gables were joined by a black asphalt roof whose gutters had rusted through in several places, leaving rust stains on the once white clapboard siding that had greyed through the years to the color of slate. Except for the string of morning glories wrapped in a tight blue ribbon around the red brick chimney, it looked like a house in mourning.

I stepped up onto the back stoop and knocked on the door, waited a moment, then knocked again. When the door finally opened, I was glad I'd waited. Goldie Samuel was worth waiting for.

"Yes, what is it?" she said. Her look said that if I was a salesman, she wasn't buying.

"I'm Garth Ryland," I said. "I own the *Oakalla Reporter*. I just wondered if I might ask you a couple questions."

"About what?"

"About what you might have seen last night."

"Relating to what?"

"Sheriff Clark's nearly fatal automobile accident."

"What has that to do with me?" Her expression hadn't changed. Whatever I was selling, she still wasn't buying.

"His patrol car was last seen parked in the alley behind your house. Before someone cold-cocked him and sent him on a ride down Hutchinson's Hill," I said for effect.

She glanced away from the sun that had made its way through a break in the trees into her eyes. "Why don't you come inside."

95

I followed her through the screened-in porch into the kitchen. She was bare-footed and wearing crisp white cotton slacks and a light-blue halter top. Her hair, piled in a golden mound on top of her head, was threaded with silver. But her smooth tawny skin seemed untouched by age.

She pulled a chair away from the kitchen table and held it for me. "I hope you don't mind," she said. "It's the coolest room in the house."

I sat down as she sat across from me. "I don't mind."

"May I get you anything?"

"No thanks. I'm fine."

I'd been told Goldie Samuel wasn't beautiful. Her nose was too large, her face too angular, her mouth too wide. Yet, studying her, I threw out all that I'd been told. Somehow it all worked to her advantage, and when she looked up at me with those sleepy blue eyes of hers, I could feel myself respond.

"When you first knocked," she said, folding her arms and resting them on the table, "I was very sure that I wouldn't even allow you inside the door."

Goldie Samuel was a semi-recluse who had gone into hiding twenty years ago and was now rarely seen in public. Before then, she first had been a teacher's aid at Oakalla High

School, while at the same time taking night school and summer school at the University of Wisconsin in Madison. Once she earned her teaching degree, she had taught business and typing at the high school. Then her son disappeared. She hadn't taught a day since. All of this I had learned in bits and pieces over the years.

"What changed your mind about letting me in?" I asked.

"I was curious," she answered.

"About what?"

"You. We've taken the *Reporter* since it first came out. I always wondered what you were like in person."

"So what do you think now?" I said, not sure that I would like the answer.

"What do I think about what?" Her eyes were as blank as her smile. They reminded me of a puppet's eyes.

"About me."

"I haven't decided yet."

Stalemate. I looked at her. She looked at me. Neither one of us knew quite what to make of the other.

"Would you like some ice water?" she said.

Ice water to break the ice. I liked the irony. "Ice water will be fine."

While she poured us each a glass, I looked around the kitchen. Small and neat, with white cupboards and cabinets, a cuckoo clock on the wall above the refrigerator, and a grey-green linoleum floor, it reminded me a lot of Grandmother Ryland's kitchen. A one woman kitchen, and purposely designed that way.

"You still haven't said whether you saw Sheriff Clark or not last night," I said.

She set the ice water in front of me and returned to her seat at the table. "No. I haven't said," she answered. "Why are you asking again?"

I told her why, giving her a more detailed account of Clarkie's "accident."

"There's no chance that Sheriff Clark was alone in the car when it happened?" she said.

"There's always that chance," I said. "But I don't believe so."

I waited for her to give it some thought. Then she threw me a curve. "You know, of course, that our son, Paul, disappeared from Oakalla exactly twenty years ago today. During *Homecoming*," she emphasized.

"I heard that, yes."

She sat staring at me, waiting for me to continue. "Well?" she said.

"I'm sorry," I said, hoping that would be the end of it.

"Never mind. I can see you're not interested."

"It's not that I'm not interested . . ." I was interrupted by the cuckoo, which screeched nine times before it finally went back into the clock. By then, I'd lost my train of thought.

"What is it, then?" she said.

Stalling for time, I took a drink of ice water. "Twenty years is a long time ago," I said. "Sheriff Clark was attacked just last night."

"First things first, right?"

"It just makes sense, that's all."

She shrugged. "Then I have nothing more to say to you. Good day, Mr. Ryland. I'm sure you can find your way to the door."

I started to leave, but thought better of it. Whatever Goldie Samuel might tell me, about either Clarkie or her son, I doubted that I'd learn anywhere else.

"Okay," I said. "Tell me about Paul. He was thirteen right, when he disappeared?"

Already I'd said too much. I could see it in her eyes. "How did you know he was thirteen?"

"For some reason that number just stuck with me," I lied, not wanting to tell her about the yellowed newspaper clipping in my office desk.

"Yes," she said. "Paul was thirteen in March. We got him a new bicycle that year for his birthday."

I felt dread come over me. It was the feeling

99

of stepping into quicksand. "What kind of a bicycle?"

"I don't remember what brand. It was one of those with high seats and high handlebars that all of the kids were riding at the time."

"What color was it? Do you know?"

"Red, I think. That was Paul's favorite color."

"And Paul was on his way where when he disappeared?" I knew, but wanted her to tell me.

She didn't hesitate. It just seemed as if she did. "The park. He left sometime that morning."

"Do you remember what he was wearing?"

"Shorts and a Led Zepplin T-shirt." Her eyes were gentle, as she remembered her son. "Paul hated to wear shorts because he had skinny legs, and he said that shorts made him look like a duck. But that morning when he came downstairs in jeans, I told him that he'd roast in them and made him go back upstairs and change."

"Then I assume it was a warm day?"

"It was a *hot* day, about like it is now. I remember because later . . ." She stopped. Something in her voice said that she was treading on dangerous ground, coming too close to the edge of the pit. "Later I had all of the windows open, and I could hear the parade as it went through town."

100

"The Homecoming parade?"

"Yes. The Homecoming parade. They had it that morning."

"But you didn't go?"

"No. Without Dick here, I didn't feel up to it." Dick was Dick Samuel, Goldie's husband, Paul's father.

"Where was he?" If the clipping or any of the subsequent articles had told Dick Samuel's whereabouts, I didn't remember it.

"He was in Portage. He'd gone to Beaver Dam on business, and he'd stopped in Portage on his way home to tell me he'd be late. He wanted to speak to Paul. That's when I told him that Paul wasn't home yet."

"Did Dick normally ask to speak to Paul?"

"No. Not normally," she said, pondering that question herself.

"Do you have any idea why he did that day?"

"No. No idea at all." Her eyes were like two blue mirrors. They hid whatever thoughts were left unsaid. "Except that Dick is the worrier in the family."

"Did he have any reason to be worried about Paul?"

"No. Not that I know of."

An uneasy silence followed. It appeared that I had asked questions that Goldie Samuel had not tried to answer before.

"What was Dick doing in Beaver Dam? Can you tell me that?"

"He's a pharmaceutical salesman. He was trying to make a sale."

"On the Saturday of Homecoming?"

"You have to get it while you can," she said. Then she smiled. It was at her own expense.

"Did he make the sale?"

"Yes, he did, quite a large one as I remember. It hardly seems worth it in retrospect, does it? To make a sale and lose a son?"

She was asking the wrong person, if indeed she wanted an answer. "Don't ask me to judge," I said. "I haven't walked a mile in his moccasins."

"Neither have I. But I've never forgiven him."

"Or yourself?"

I caught her off guard. She didn't like that observation. "That's beside the point, Mr. Ryland."

"You're probably right. Sorry."

She nodded. Apology accepted.

"After Dick called you, was that when you called the sheriff?"

"Yes. Dick insisted on it. I wanted to give Paul at least a couple more hours to come home."

"Why was that?"

Again she only seemed to hesitate before

answering. "Paul kept his own hours, his own counsel. He wasn't very good about reporting in, either his thoughts or his whereabouts."

"He'd stayed away all day before?"

"Not all day and into the night. At least not as long as he did that day. But he had stayed away from home for hours at a time when I didn't know where he was. But . . ." She smiled as if she knew I'd understand. "He was usually home by supper."

"What time was it when you finally did call the sheriff to report him missing?"

"Around eight. It was already getting dark."

"That'd make it closer to nine."

She didn't like to be corrected. "Whatever," she said with an edge to her voice. "But," she added, "I didn't call the sheriff first. I called Eddie Vincent, who was Paul's best friend. He and Paul were supposed to go to the park together. That's why I wasn't as worried as I might have been."

"What did Eddie tell you?" I hadn't read about Eddie Vincent in the newspaper account either. It made me wonder who else had been left out.

"He told me that he was sick, so Paul went on to the park alone."

"And that's when you pushed the panic button?"

"Yes," she said, her eyes reliving that terrible moment. "That's when I pushed the panic button."

I hoped that was all. Already I'd spent more time there than I intended, and none of it on what I intended.

The ice tinkled against the side of her glass as she slowly swirled it. She was locked in a thought that had no windows. Then she looked up at me. On her face was a shy, almost awkward smile. "Would you like to see Paul's room?"

I stared dumbly at her for a moment, not knowing what to say. "I thought no one was allowed in there."

"They aren't. I'm making you the exception."

I didn't ask her why. I doubted that she'd tell me anyway. "Yes. I would like to see in there. If only to get to know your son better." The words were out of my mouth before I could stop them.

I followed her up the stairs to Paul Samuel's bedroom. "Go ahead," she said, opening the door for me. "I'll be waiting downstairs." I went inside the room with the stained-glass window as she closed the door behind me.

So far Goldie Samuel was wrong about one thing. With the door closed and the window shaded, *this* was the coolest room in the house.

Not unpleasantly cool, but comfortably cool, like a California wine cellar.

I stood for a moment not doing anything but surveying the room, as I might a museum, whose artifacts sat under several layers of dust, and which had had only one visitor in the past twenty years. I was almost afraid to touch anything for fear of destroying the sanctity of the place. But that would defeat my purpose in being there. So, slowly so as not to overlook anything, I took a tour of the room.

The model cars on the shelf above the bed—the red Corvette, the Robin-egg-blue Thunderbird, the black Indianapolis Five Hundred racer with the gold fourteen painted on it, and the silver Jaguar XKE had all been meticulously made and mounted as had the butterfly collection that hung on the wall between a photograph of Janis Joplin and a poster of the Rolling Stones. A Daredevil comic lay open on the bed. A pair of jeans with shiny knees lay on the floor beside the bed. At the foot of the bed was a large wooden box that contained an assortment of toys, games, and puzzles, including a yellow dump truck that looked like new, and boxes of Lincoln Logs and Leggos that also appeared like new. Either Paul Samuel took very good care of his things or he spent very little time at play. Judging by what I'd seen in the rest of his room and what I already knew in my heart, I guessed the former.

I dug through the toy box, stopping to examine each item in turn, until I reached the bottom. There, under a piece of cardboard cut to fit the box, I found a copy of the July 1971 issue of *Playboy*. I opened the *Playboy* and looked inside to my favorite page. But someone had taken out its centerfold. Perhaps not Paul, I decided, after searching the rest of his room and not finding it.

At Paul's dresser, I stood looking at the photographs I'd found inside its top drawer. One in particular caught my eye. It showed Paul at about age ten or eleven with an older man that I took to be Dick Samuel. Each with his hand on the stringer, and each with a smile as big as all outdoors, they held up a large northern pike between them. Another photograph, taken in May 1971, showed Paul in a white shirt and blue jeans, standing on the sidewalk in front of his house. The contrast between the two photographs was striking. One showed a grubby happy kid, at one with himself and the world; the other a gawky adolescent who wished he were anywhere and anyone but where and who he was. Or at least that's what I read into them.

On my way out, I had a second thought, and returned to the room. I picked up Paul Samuel's jeans and began to fold them when Paul's billfold fell out of the back pocket. Inside it were fifty dollars, which would have been more than my lifesavings at thirteen, some photographs of schoolkids, none of which I could identify, and a red-and-white foil wrapper that contained a Trojan condom.

I put the billfold back in the jeans, laid the jeans on the bed, and started down the stairs. Halfway down them, I stopped to look back. For a hair-raising second, I thought Paul Samuel was following me.

Goldie Samuel sat at the kitchen table. I handed her the photograph of Paul and Dick Samuel holding up the northern pike. "May I keep it?" I said.

She smiled in recognition. "Where was it?" she asked. "I've looked all over for it."

"In Paul's top dresser drawer."

"It's my favorite," she said simply.

"Is there another you'd rather give me?"

She gave the photograph back to me. "No, it's yours now. I don't think that Paul would mind."

I had a question that I needed to ask her, and I didn't know what else to do but to ask it point blank. "Was Paul sexually active?" I said.

She responded as I expected. I might as well have asked if he rolled first graders for their lunch money. "No," she said coldly. "Whatever made you think he was?"

"I found a condom in his billfold. Which may or may not mean anything, since a lot of boys carry condoms long before they use them." Then I said, "I also found fifty dollars there."

Goldie Samuel seemed genuinely puzzled. "Whatever would Paul be doing with a condom in his billfold? Or fifty dollars for that matter? He never carried that kind of money around. I didn't even know he had that much money."

"My question is, what was Paul's billfold doing in his room if he were on his way to the carnival? And why was he going to the carnival in the morning if the rides didn't start until the afternoon?"

"You're sure about that?" She looked even more puzzled, as if I had just thrown her two curves in a row. "That the rides didn't start until the afternoon?"

"They've always started in the afternoon as long as we've had Homecoming."

She looked down at her hands, then up at the ceiling. But whatever solace she was seeking, she didn't find it there. "I think I know why Paul's billfold was in his room." Her voice was strained, barely under control. "I think he probably left it in his jeans when I had him change into his shorts."

108

I'd come to the same conclusion, but that still didn't explain why he didn't come back after it once he discovered it missing. Unless, of course, he couldn't come back after it.

She followed me to the back door, holding it open while I stood a moment, looking at the privacy fence that ran between the Samuel's house and the Sims' house next door. "Is that new?" I asked.

She glanced harshly at the fence. She seemed to find it as offensive as I did. "No. Not new. Dick and Hayden Sims put it up about ten years ago," she said.

"Whose idea was it?"

"Mine," she said. "As you said earlier, I like my privacy."

For the first time that morning I didn't believe her. "That's the only reason you put it up?"

"That and the fact that Dorothy Sims kept accusing me of spying on her. So finally I hit on the perfect solution." Her smile was thin and mocking. "It is the perfect solution, don't you think?"

"I think it's a solution," I said. Then I changed the subject. "You say Paul was on his way to Eddie Vincent's house when he left here?"

"Yes."

"Where was Eddie's house then?"

"The same place it is now, a block east and a half block north of here. It's white with black shutters."

"Does it have a white fence around it?"

"Yes. That's the one." She pointed to show me. "If you stay in the alley behind us, you'll run right into it."

I crossed the back yard, opened a gate, and entered the alley as if I really was going to Eddie Vincent's. But once out of sight of Goldie Samuel, I turned south toward Billy Hunter's house. I was nearly there before I realized that I had been had. Goldie Samuel had failed to tell me whether or not she had seen Clarkie last night. Instead, she had steered me off in a new direction in search of her missing son. If that was her intention all along, why then did she open the door to me only after I had told her about Clarkie being attacked?

8

Billy Hunter and his friend, Tom Morrison, were in the process of making a mud hole out of Billy's back yard. They had spread a couple of large sheets of plastic end to end and watered these down with Billy's garden hose. Then they got themselves good running starts and dived headfirst along the plastic to see who could slide the farthest. Their hair plastered to their heads, their grinning faces spotted with mud, they were, as Grandmother would have said, as happy as two hogs in a wallow.

"Hi, Mr. Ryland. What's up?" Billy said.

Billy was a tall, thin, gangly kid, who had worked for me at the *Oakalla Reporter* for a

111

while that past winter, emptying waste baskets and pushing the dust mop around. But when he quit to run track in the spring, I wasn't sorry to see him go. He wasn't as industrious as I would have liked, and I wasn't as generous as he had hoped, so we were never quite comfortable around each other. But we parted as friends and had remained that way.

"Could I talk to you alone for a minute?" I said.

"Sure." He walked over to where I stood on the sidewalk, while Tom Morrison made a half-hearted slide down the plastic, then lay there on his stomach, looking the other way.

"It's been a while," I said, shaking Billy's hand. "How's everything going?"

"Not bad. Now that school's out." Billy wasn't the world's best student. I doubted that he would ever be the world's best anything.

"The reason that I stopped by is that I was wondering what you were doing at the park so late last night?"

Billy glanced at Tom as if for support. But Tom still had his head turned away from us. "Who said I was at the park last night?"

"No one. I thought I saw you there."

I'd just given Billy his out. He was quick to take it. "What time was that?"

"I don't know what time," I said. "Late. The rides had already shut down."

"Hey, Tom!" Billy yelled, more loudly than necessary. "What time did we leave the park last night?"

Tom turned his head our way. Like Billy, he was neither a great student nor a great thinker. But both proved to be accomplished liars. "Nine, ten, somewhere in there," Tom said. "Why?"

"Mr. Ryland here thinks that he saw me there way after that."

"Couldn't have been," Tom said with certainty. "You were with me."

"My mistake then," I said to Billy. "Sorry to have bothered you." Billy would keep for another day, until I had a better handle on what was going on.

"So I'm off the hook?"

I shrugged. "For now. But I might want to talk to you later."

"About what? I told you I wasn't there."

"So you did, Billy." I started to leave.

"While you're out asking questions," Billy said, as his face reddened in anger, "you might ask that fag up at the bank what he was doing at the park last night. Every time I turned around, there he was behind me."

Billy mistook my shock for ignorance. He quickly filled the silence.

"You know the one," he said. "That Eddie guy. The one with the blond hair."

113

Eddie Vincent, to be exact. Paul Samuel's best friend.

"You sure it was Eddie?"

"Sure, I'm sure. Ask Tom if you don't believe me."

"It was Eddie," Tom concurred. "I'd know that fag anywhere."

"Following you?" I wanted to make sure.

"Like Billy said, he had his nose up our rear the whole way."

The First Farmers Bank of Oakalla once had frosted windows, fluted marble columns, and a black-and-white tile floor, but during a recent remodeling it had been modernized to look more in step with the times. The operation had succeeded, but that was about all I could say for it.

Inside the bank, Eddie Vincent, vice-president in charge of loans, sat with a customer within his air-conditioned office, like the heir apparent to the throne. Eddie's eyes were large and slightly protruding, his jowls round and slightly puffed, his shirt white, his suit, tie, and vest a dark green. His hair was white-gold, nearly platinum, and lay in dense shining waves. It was, without a doubt, the most beautiful hair I'd ever seen on a man.

While I waited for the customer to leave, I sat down in a chair and tried to remember what I knew about Eddie. I knew that he had never married and lived with his widowed mother in the near west end of town. I knew that he was a big sports booster, perhaps Oakalla's biggest, and that at one time, before he put on twenty extra pounds of jelly, he was a strikingly handsome man. I knew that he was a member of the Oakalla Playhouse, that he had starred in several local productions, including musicals, and that if Eddie had one fault, either as a player or a man, it was a tendency to overact, and over react.

"Garth! How are you!" Eddie stood to shake my hand, as I entered his office. Then when he realized that he couldn't raise his right hand because of the sling that he wore on his right arm, he offered his left hand instead. We shook hands, but it was awkward for both of us.

"What happened to your arm?" I asked.

"Tennis elbow," he whispered confidentially, as if his reputation as a sportsman was at stake. "Doc Combs says I have to wear the darn thing for another week or two."

Eddie sat back down at his desk. I sat in a large comfortable blue-upholstered chair facing him. If I'd closed my eyes, I probably could have slept.

"So what brings you here, Garth?" Eddie appeared ill at ease with me there, though he had seemed fine a moment ago.

"A lot of things, Eddie," I said. "But primarily I'd like to know what you were doing following Billy Hunter around the park last night?" Perhaps Billy was telling the truth, or perhaps he was lying to cover his own tail.

"Billy Hunter? I don't believe I know the boy." Eddie was a good actor, but a poor liar. He couldn't do it and look me in the eye.

"Tall, skinny kid," I said. "Runs around with Tom Morrison."

Eddie gave me his most sincere frown. "I'm afraid I don't know him either. Sorry, Garth. I wish I could help."

I sat there in silence, deciding what I should do. Billy Hunter had lied to me about when he had been at the park. Maybe he was lying about Eddie Vincent, too, though judging by Eddie's reaction, I didn't believe so.

"Thanks, Eddie," I said, starting to rise.

"You'll never guess who just called me," he said.

I sat back down in the chair. "Who?"

"Goldie Samuel," he said. "Twenty years, and I haven't heard word one from that woman. Then bam! Right out of the blue, she calls me."

"What did she want?"

"She wanted to know if you had been by yet. When I said no, she was silent for the longest time; then she started asking me all of these questions about Paul."

It was time I left. But I couldn't make myself. "What kind of questions, Eddie?"

"Where we were really going that day that Paul disappeared. And why didn't I go along with Paul since I was supposed to be his best friend. Questions like that."

Eddie's eyes were red and watery. He appeared to have been genuinely shaken by Goldie Samuel's phone call, but when you wore your heart on your sleeve as Eddie did, a broken cuff link could turn into a Greek tragedy.

"And you told her?"

"I told her the truth, that Paul and I were going to the carnival together, but that I got sick and couldn't go with him."

I could have left it at that and should have. "Do you remember if Paul was walking or riding his bicycle?" I said.

"Why?"

"I just wondered."

He thought a moment. "Riding his bicycle. I remember standing on my porch, watching him ride away. It was the saddest day of my life." He looked sad, as if it had happened only yesterday.

"Do you remember what kind of bicycle it was?"

"A Schwinn, I believe. It was red. I know that much."

"Did anyone ever find it?"

"No. Not that I know of. But then I'm not sure if anyone was looking for it."

"Thanks, Eddie. I appreciate it." I rose and walked to the door of his office. "One more question, If you don't mind?"

He seemed offended that I would have to ask his permission. "Why should I mind? Paul was my best friend. I'd give anything to know what happened to him."

"Okay, my question is, why did Paul have a condom and fifty dollars in his billfold, and why were you going to the carnival in the morning, rather than in the afternoon when the rides would have been going?"

His eyes clouded momentarily, then found their focus again. "I really don't know, Garth. The carnival was Paul's idea. I was just going along for the ride."

"Paul was thirteen, right?"

"Right."

"And how old were you?"

"Fourteen, going on fifteen."

"Thanks again, Eddie."

He sighed a deep sigh as I left. It sounded like a sigh of relief.

Eddie Vincent's mother, Cora Vincent, worked in Fleenor's Rexall Drugstore, which was right next door to the bank. I went into the drugstore, sat down at the counter, and ordered a vanilla Coke from her.

A dinosaur, like some of the rest of us in Oakalla, Fleenor's drugstore still had a soda fountain, and a six-seat counter and two wooden booths where on a hot summer day or a cold winter afternoon people could come in, drink a soda or a cup of coffee, and do absolutely nothing for a while. Fleenor's drug store also sold popsicles and penny candy, comics and crackerjacks, and a lot of other things that you couldn't get anywhere else in town. The only thing wrong with it was that I always stayed in there longer than I intended to. And never regretted it.

Cora Vincent set my vanilla Coke down on the counter in front of me. "Will there be anything else, Garth?"

A short, stout, rosy-cheeked Irishwoman with small mischievous eyes and red-and-white hair, Cora had worked in Fleenor's drugstore for as long as I had been going in there. Widowed early in life, she had almost single-handedly raised Eddie and then put him through a two-year business school. Justifiably proud of her accomplishment, she liked to refer to Eddie, loudly and often, as "my vice president." Eddie, on the other hand, seldom spoke of her, if he spoke of her at all.

"You might tell me when Eddie got home last night?" I said.

"From his meeting?"

"From wherever he was."

She eyed me suspiciously. "Why is it that you want to know?"

Unlike Eddie Vincent, I was a good liar. But then I'd been practicing since I was old enough to talk. "I was working late at my office when I saw someone out on a tractor dragging the Little League diamond. I figured only Eddie would be dedicated enough to be out there doing that at midnight." As long as I was at it, I might as well make it a whopper.

"So that's where he was," she said, obviously relieved. "Why didn't he just tell me that?"

I took a drink of my vanilla Coke. "You know Eddie," I said. "He's not one to toot his own horn."

I thought I had things in hand. But I was wrong.

The next thing I knew, Cora Vincent started crying. She wiped her eyes with the back of her hand, then took a napkin from its holder and used it to blow her nose.

"No, Garth, I'm afraid I don't know my son at all. It used to be I could trust him, believe every word he said. It used to be he thought his mom was the best thing since sliced bread. Now, he acts like he doesn't ever want to be in the same room with me, like he's ashamed of

120

me." Cora Vincent stopped crying, as she balled her fists in anger. "And all because of that Samuel boy. All because I wouldn't let Eddie go with him to the parade that day."

"Eddie told you that? When, twenty years ago?"

"Just last night," she said, using another napkin to blow her nose. "Just because I was sitting up, waiting for him when he got home. He had to find some way to hurt me."

"When *did* Eddie get home last night?" I asked.

"You said you saw him there at the park at midnight," she said. "It had to be after that."

Now I wished that I hadn't lied to her. But I didn't see how I could take it back. "You don't remember looking at the clock?" I said.

"I remember looking, but I don't remember what time it was."

What would Eddie Vincent have been doing out at that hour, whatever the hour was? Then another thought occurred to me, one that also had to do with Eddie Vincent.

"You said that Eddie and Paul were on their way to watch the parade when Paul disappeared," I said. "It was my understanding that they were on their way to the carnival."

"No. They were . . ." She started to correct me, then stopped. "So that's where they were going!" she said with a vengeance. "Eddie told me they were going bike riding and then to watch the parade. He knew how I felt about the carnival."

"Then Eddie wasn't sick after all?"

She wore a look of betrayal, the one my mother made famous. "Oh, he was sick all right. He was sick as a dog when I got home from the parade, and stayed that way for two days. He could hardly keep anything down, my homemade vegetable soup included. I thought that I was going to have to take him to the hospital."

I didn't say anything. She appeared to have more to say on the subject, and I didn't want to sidetrack her. Soon my patience was rewarded.

"But the reason he was sick," she continued, "was that filthy pinup I'd found in his room just that morning. I told him we'd talk about it when I got home. Until then he was grounded."

"By any chance, was that pinup from *Playboy* magazine?"

She had a dish towel over her shoulder. She used it to rub a coffee spot from the counter. "I don't know where it was from, Garth. It didn't survive long enough for me to find out." Patrolling the counter, she found another spot to rub out. "Thank God, Mr. Fleenor has never carried those filthy things in here. Or I don't know what I would have done."

122

"So Eddie was grounded? That's why he didn't go with Paul?"

"Yes. That's what he was." And might be again when she got home.

I drank the rest of my vanilla Coke and left.

9

At home Ruth had a load of clothes in the washer and another one on the clothesline in the back yard. A farm wife for most of her life, she regularly hung clothes outside to dry until the first real snow, or Thanksgiving, whichever came first.

"Where have you been?" she said, pouring herself a glass of iced tea and taking a seat at the kitchen table. "This came for you this morning."

I noticed the letter addressed to me on the table. I also noticed that it was opened. "Since when did you start reading my mail?"

"It was marked urgent," she said with no

124

show of remorse. "How was I to know when I'd see you next?"

I searched the refrigerator for something to eat and found nothing that suited me, so I made myself a peanut butter-and-honey sandwich on oatmeal bread. "Do you want one?" I asked Ruth.

Her look said I knew better. "What do you think?" In ascending order, Ruth hated peanut butter, cold meat, and leftovers, which, during the depression, was about all she had to eat.

After pouring myself a glass of milk, I sat down at the table across from her.

"Are you going to read it or not?" she said impatiently.

"You read it. Why don't you tell me what's in it?"

She snatched the letter from in front of me and began to read aloud the yellowed newspaper clipping inside. By now, I almost knew it by heart. It was the account of Paul Samuel's disappearance.

She turned the clipping over and laid it on the table in front of me. "Now read the back of it."

I know where he is, someone had written in the same precise handwriting as before. My reaction was the same. Bully for you.

"Interesting," I said between bites of my sandwich. "But I've got one just like it in my desk at work."

125

Her brows rose. "Since when?"

"Since Monday. Early Monday morning to be exact."

"And what are you doing about it?"

"I'm not doing anything about it," I said, knowing where we were headed, and not wanting to go there. "I've got enough things to do without trying to find a boy who's been missing for twenty years."

"Like what? It can't be putting out a newspaper because you haven't been in your office all morning. I know. I've called there three times already. And I don't know how many calls have come here for you."

"Well, if you wouldn't read my mail, you wouldn't have to call my office," I said, as I rose from the table in search of something more to eat. "As for what I've been doing, I've been all over town trying to find out who tried to kill Clarkie and why, which might also tell me who killed Scott McBride and why." I searched the cupboards, but didn't find anything else that looked good to me. "But it seems that all anybody wants to talk about is Paul Samuel. Including you."

"He's been on our minds for twenty years now, Garth," she said. "Something like that just doesn't go away."

How well I knew. One morning with Paul Samuel, and already I was having a hard time thinking about anything else. "Then why don't you find him," I suggested. "You're as good at this as I am. Maybe even better. And it's your town, not mine. At its heart, anyway."

She took her time in answering, which was intended to make me think about what I'd just said. And to take it back, if I was inclined. But I was too stubborn to give her that satisfaction.

"I never thought I'd hear you say that about Oakalla," she said, obviously disappointed in me. "If there ever was a town that belonged to a man, or a man that belonged to a town, it's you and Oakalla. You love this town, Garth. You and I both know that."

"Blame it on the heat," I said. "It's making me a little crazy."

"All of us, for that matter."

"But it would help if you would tell me what Eddie Vincent was doing at the park, following Billy Hunter around. And why he didn't get home until way late last night."

"Who told you that?"

"His mother. The last part of it anyway." I rose, took an apple from the refrigerator, and rubbed it on my jeans to clean it. "I'll be at the park if anybody calls."

"Why the park?"

"I need to talk to Sean Ragan, the carnival owner. I'm still not convinced that he and

Clarkie don't know each other from some-where."

"Do you think he's the one who sent Clarkie on his ride down Hutchinson's Hill?"

I took a bite of the apple. It was so cold it hurt my teeth. "I'm not ruling out anybody at this point."

"But how could he have, if he was at the park when you were?"

"Across country it's a fifteen minute walk from the park to Hutchinson's Hill. Or a ten minute run."

"But how would Sean Ragan know to go across country?"

"He wouldn't," I said. "Not unless he's been here before, which would also explain how he and Clarkie know each other."

"How do you plan to find that out?"

"Ask him."

I took another bite of the apple. Already it was losing its zing.

"You said Eddie Vincent was following Billy Hunter last night at the park. What does that have to do with anything?"

"Nothing. Except that if Eddie was follow-ing Billy, he might have followed him right to Sally Wampler's trailer."

"For what purpose."

"None that I can think of. Though Billy and Tom Morrison both called Eddie a fag. Do you put any stock in that?"

"As much as I do in Elvis' resurrection. Eddie might be a mama's boy, but that's as far as it goes."

"Some mama's boys have turned out to be serial killers."

She tried to stare me down, but I knew I had my facts straight. "None that I've known," she said.

I was almost to the back door when she asked, "Garth, are you serious about not looking for Paul Samuel?"

"Yes. I'm serious, Ruth. I've neither the time nor the heart for it."

"Why? If it's any of my business. Are you afraid that after twenty years you won't be able to find him?"

"No," I said, admitting the truth that I had been avoiding. "I'm afraid I might."

"Would you care to explain that?"

"If I could."

I drove to the park, instead of walking, as I normally would have. The heat and the frustration of getting nowhere had gotten to me. I simply didn't have the energy to walk.

Sean Ragan wasn't in sight, so I went looking for him. After passing through the double row of game tents, I circled the rides, but with no success. Those few carnies who were about answered me with a shrug when I asked if they'd seen him. I couldn't have felt more alone if I had been in a foreign country.

Then I saw Sally Wampler sitting on the steps of her trailer. She seemed to be wearing the same clothes as when I left her. I wondered if she had been sitting there ever since.

"Hi, Sally," I said. "Have you seen Sean Ragan around?"

She nodded in the direction of the outfield. "The last time I saw him he was headed out of here."

"On foot?"

"Yes."

I wondered where Sean Ragan might be going in that direction, which was southwest. Two places came to mind. One of them was Hutchinson's Hill, the other Hidden Quarry.

"You mind if I sit down?" I said.

She shrugged. "It's a free country."

She scooted over. I sat down beside her on the step. We shared the same space easily, like two old trail hands after a long hard day.

"Last night I got the impression that you might know the man who tried to break into your trailer," I said. "Am I right or am I wrong?"

She stared out across the park. She looked weary, and sad. "You're wrong," she said. "I don't know him, but I know his type."

"Which is what?"

"Frustrated, and angry. He blames me, and all women, for what he isn't, which is a man."

"Why blame you, if he doesn't even know you?"

She gave me an indulgent smile. "Come on now, Mr. Newspaperman. You're smarter than that. When haven't whores gotten more than their share of the blame for whatever's wrong with men. What they can't find at home or in themselves, they try to find in us. Or through us. We're just a tool to be used and discarded. And sometimes, if we don't work right, to be broken."

"Billy Hunter is hardly a man," I said.

"Who is Billy Hunter?"

"The fifteen-year-old boy you screwed last night."

Her smile hardened. Sally Wampler was not, with all apologies to Bret Harte, a whore with a heart of gold. "If you're looking for an apology, you've come to the wrong place."

"I'm just trying to understand."

"Don't try to understand. It's a losing proposition." Then she smiled. "No pun intended."

"Answer me this, then. Did you see whoever it was that tried to break into your trailer?"

"Not to identify him, no. A man. That's all I know."

"Could he have anything to do with Scott McBride's death?"

She frowned. "I don't see how."

131

"Could Sean Ragan have anything to do with Scott McBride's death?"

Her eyes showed her anger. "You don't know either one of them, or you wouldn't ask that question."

"Then enlighten me."

"Like I said before. They've been friends forever. They went through Vietnam together. Sure, they've had their disagreements. What friends haven't over the long haul. But they've always stayed in touch, even through the tough times. And believe me, Scottie's had his share of those lately."

Including death, which seemed to me the toughest of times.

"And it was Sean," she continued, "that saw Scottie through them. He's the one who, when Scottie hit the skids, checked Scottie into the hospital and paid for all his bills. Then when Scottie got back on his feet again, bought him a car and started him back racing."

"The carnival business must be more profitable than I thought," I said.

"Oh, there's money in it," she said. "But most of the money came out of Sean's own pocket. He wouldn't risk the carnival. He'd do about anything before he'd do that."

"Even kill his best friend?"

Her silence said that it was a possibility that she hadn't considered before.

132

Several backfires and a stall later Jessie and I were on the gravel road that led along Stony Creek to the back side of Hidden Quarry. We passed corn fields and bean fields, woodlots and wheat stubble, where thistles stood in purple islands and monarchs soared lazily, like the bright orange leaves of fall. Spring with its tulips, jonquils, and snowdrops, its redbud, dogwood, and magnolia, seemed a very long time ago.

The woods behind the quarry hadn't changed much in thirty years. It was still dark and cool, and rich with the smell of age and humus; and its trees, some of which stretched fifty feet to the first limb, seemed the columns on which heaven sat. I remembered the days that I had spent there as a boy when time was something that I always forgot to bring along. I couldn't stand a schedule, even then. I wondered why I tried to keep one now.

A splash came from the quarry. I walked in the direction of the quarry until I could see its limestone walls and its turquoise water. Someone was swimming just under the surface toward me, his body yellow through the blue-green water. Then he surfaced and I saw his face. It was Sean Ragan.

Ragan swam to shore and easily climbed the thirty foot wall to where I stood. Then he picked up a stone and threw it into the water.

Together we watched its rings outgrow themselves and disappear.

"How deep would you say it is?" he asked.

"I've heard it's over two hundred feet in some places."

"Any fish in it?"

"They say there are. I've never caught any."

Ragan wore no shirt, cut-off jeans, and the look of a man who'd rather be left alone. He lay down on the hot rock and closed his eyes. It was my cue to go elsewhere.

"You taking the day off?" I said.

He opened his eyes. He wasn't pleased to see me still standing there. "Something like that. I came after Scottie's car."

"Who gave you the keys?" Implied also in that question was, who gave you permission?

He stared at me. He had tiny orange specks in those cold blue eyes of his, like fire on ice. "Where I come from, you don't need keys."

"Where do you come from?"

He sat up. For a moment he seemed ready to go back into the water again, and just as ready to take me with him. But then the moment passed.

"Ryland, for somebody with no stake in this, you sure ask a lot of questions."

"No stake in what?"

He shrugged and stared off into the distance.

"Then answer me this question. How did you find this place? It's not exactly on the beaten path."

He lay back down, lying on the hot limestone as comfortably as he would his own bed. "I asked some kids at the park where it was."

"And they told you?"

"Why wouldn't they? I like kids, Ryland. I just don't like what they become."

I sat down on the rock facing him. "Have you always been with the carnival?"

He glanced at me, then away. "Ryland, what does it take to get rid of you?"

"The truth."

"Truth, like beauty, is in the eye of the beholder. Don't flatter yourself by pretending to be its champion."

"Okay, just answer my questions then, and I'll get out of your hair."

It seemed Sean Ragan almost smiled. "I have no hair to get out of. Or haven't you noticed?"

We neither one spoke, as the wind went slack and the sun beat down on us. Then he said, "Ask your questions. It's getting hot on this rock."

"Have you always been with the carnival?" I said.

"Since when?"

"Since Vietnam."

135

"No. After I got home, I knocked around for a while, taking whatever I could find. Then I went to college on the G.I. Bill."

"To do what?"

"Teach."

I liked that answer better than if he'd said, "To be a teacher."

"Did you teach?"

He sat up and used the heel of his hand to wipe the sweat from his eyes. "A couple of years, long enough to realize I wasn't going to change anyone's life for the better." Then he qualified his answer. "Or to change those that mattered the most to me, who were the ones that everyone else had given up on." He smiled at me. It was a harsh bitter smile. "The thinkers, in other words. The square pegs in the round holes. It didn't make a damn bit of difference what I said. They were going to learn the same way I did, and that's the hard way."

"Is what you're doing any better?"

"What? Running a carnival? At least they come to me now with a smile on their face, and I don't have to stand around and watch them grow old."

"How do you not grow old before your time?" I said. "How do any of us? That's what I'd like to know." Without intending to, I'd spoken my own worst fear.

136

Sean Ragan shook his head. Either he didn't have the answer or didn't want to bother giving me one.

"Tell me about Scottie," I said, finally getting around to what I'd come for. "Tell me why anyone in Oakalla might want to kill an over-the-hill race car driver."

"Who said he was over-the-hill?" Ragan took exception.

"I do. And anyone else who knows his history."

"You never saw him drive, did you? Scottie was a screw-up, that's true. He broke every heart he touched, including his own. But when he got behind the wheel of a car, he was pure poetry, if that can be said about a man who races cars." Ragan's voice spoke his envy. "I would kill, Ryland, I think, to be that good at anything. I don't know whether it was Scottie's absolute fearlessness, or a gift, or what, but when Scottie was in his prime, and if his car held together, everybody else was racing for second place."

"We're not talking about his prime. We're talking about now."

"Now he was merely great," Ragan said. "Not quite as fast through the turns, but faster than most, including the best. But once he was *God*, faster even than his own shadow. Think about it, Ryland. We should be so lucky." He

137

rose and walked to the edge of the rock. "How deep did you say it was?"

"You still didn't answer my question," I said. "Why would anybody want to kill him?"

"Maybe it was a case of mistaken identity. Maybe they thought he was someone else."

"And who might that be?"

"Don't ask me. It's your town, not mine."

He dived the thirty feet into the quarry, barely rippling its waters. I waited for him to surface, then began the long walk back to Jessie.

An hour later I parked Jessie at the bottom of Hutchinson's Hill, rolled up my jeans, took off my shoes and socks, and chasing tadpoles and water striders ahead of me, followed the small stream two hundred yards upstream to its source. Its source was an old cedar standpipe that had never run dry, and from it flowed the coldest sweetest spring water in Adams County. After drinking my fill, I felt better.

The culvert under the old interurban didn't look any more inviting in daylight than it had in the dark. Its opening was narrower than I remembered it, its walls weak and spongy, and likely to crumble with the first good shake of the earth.

I went inside, and without wasting any time, retrieved the bicycle that I'd found wedged behind the slab of concrete the night before. The bicycle's tires were flat, its frame rusted, its front sprocket sprung, and several of its spokes broken. It looked to me as if it had been in a wreck, but that wasn't what intrigued me. What gave me pause was its name, Schwinn, and the red chip of paint on its frame that hadn't yet rusted away.

After carrying the bicycle back up to the road, I put it in Jessie's trunk and started back to town. At the city limits sign I first smelled the antifreeze and saw the temperature gauge slowly creeping toward red. I kept on going. Jessie's last trick had nearly gotten me killed. I planned to return the favor.

When I reached Edgar Shoemaker's welding shop, steam was rolling out from under the hood and water was pouring from the block. I was all smiles.

Edgar sat in the shade outside his welding shop, eating a late lunch. He momentarily glanced at Jessie, then started to unwrap a sandwich. "Looks like you've finally killed her this time," he said. "God knows you've tired hard enough in the past."

"Likewise, I'm sure," I said.

Sandwich in hand, he got up and walked slowly to where Jessie sat. After raising the hood, he fanned away a cloud of steam and examined the block. "Nope. Not this time, Garth. You only blew a freeze plug."

"One can only hope," I said, not feeling as bad as I should have.

We went to sit in the shade of Edgar's shop. Everywhere I looked was a broken something. But if anyone could fix it, Edgar Shoemaker could. He had only one lung and sight in only one eye, but he got the most out of what he had.

"What can I do for you, Garth?" he said.

"It can wait until you're done eating."

He finished unwrapping his egg salad sandwich and handed half of it to me. "There's beer in that cooler over there," he said. "You might bring one to me and help yourself while you're at it."

I did as he asked, handed Edgar's beer to him, then popped the tab on mine. It wasn't spring water, but it'd do.

"Isn't that your Model A block lying over there?" I said. It looked like the same block that I'd seen the last time I was here, the same cigar lying on top of it.

"Yep, it's the same one," Edgar said. "I haven't gotten around to it yet."

"Shouldn't you take it inside?"

"I plan to the first time it rains." Edgar glanced at the milky blue sky above, then took a bite of his sandwich. "Whenever the hell that is."

A few minutes later I opened Jessie's trunk

and took out the bicycle. It was once a red Schwinn with a high seat and high U-shaped handlebars, just like Paul Samuel's bicycle.

"So what do you want to know?" Edgar said, bending down to examine it.

"I want to know if it's been in a wreck."

"That's obvious, Garth," he said, running his hand over its frame. "I've only got one eye, but I can see that."

"Do you suppose you could keep it here out of sight for a while?" I didn't yet know what I was going to do with it, if anything.

"I can keep it here as long as you like."

"Thanks, Edgar. I'll stop by the Marathon and have Danny come pick up Jessie."

Edgar rose and walked over to where his cigar lay on the Model A block. He sucked on it a couple times, but couldn't get it to go. "You mind telling me where this bicycle came from, Garth?"

"It came from the old interurban culvert below Hutchinson's Hill."

"Any idea who it belongs to?"

"Some," I said. But that's all I would say.

10

I stopped by the Marathon on the way to my office and then spent the rest of the afternoon calling my sources and learning what had been happening in and around Oakalla since I last talked to them. This gathering of and then the sorting, arranging, and printing of all the little details about people's lives was my least favorite part of newspaper work. But it was those very details that paid the rent, for nothing stirred a reader's interest more than seeing his own name in print.

At six P.M. I left my office to walk home. In the east a huge white-topped thunderhead had flattened out and filled the sky. It was so large that I wondered how it could have missed us on its way through, but somehow it had.

At home Ruth sat at the kitchen table with one of her scrapbooks open on the table in front of her. For someone who had no love affair with the past, she surely had a lot of pictures of it.

"Don't sit down," she said to me just as I was about to. "I want you to look at something."

I stood behind her to see if I could see what she saw. But I couldn't. "Enlighten me," I said.

"Dick Samuel was supposedly out of town the day that his son disappeared. But if I'm not mistaken, that's a picture of him right there," she pointed to show me, "watching the parade."

I studied the photograph that included Dick Samuel and several others standing along Jackson Street. I was amazed at how full and green the trees and yards looked.

"That could be Dick Samuel," I said. He looked to be short, maybe five-eight, and stocky, with brown hair and an honest face, just like the man whose photograph I carried in my shirt pocket.

"It *is* Dick Samuel," she insisted, closing the scrapbook to further argument.

"Goldie Samuel said he was in Beaver Dam that day."

143

"Well, she's wrong." She picked up the scrapbook and began to fan herself with it.

"Or she's lying," I said, not finding that too hard to believe.

"Whichever. But you won't know until you talk to Dick Samuel."

I studied her. Ruth had something up her sleeve. But I wasn't about to go along with her.

"Ruth, I'm not going to do that," I said. "He's not even in town that I know of."

"He's not in town," she said with certainty. "He's staying at the Hilltop Motel in Balboa, number 103."

"And how did you find that out?"

"Simple. I called Goldie Samuel and asked her."

"Well, you won't have any trouble finding him then," I said, looking in the refrigerator for something cold to drink. A beer would have done nicely. But since I planned to return to my office shortly, I settled for a Dr. Pepper.

"What's wrong with you?" she said, not liking my suggestion.

"I told you, Ruth. I'm not trying to find Paul Samuel. I'm trying to find out who killed Scott McBride, and who then tried to kill Clarkie."

"And how much luck have you had so far?"

"A little," I lied.

"For instance?"

I found the bottle opener and popped the

144

top on my Dr. Pepper. Ruth was still waiting on my answer when I finished my first swallow. "Okay," I said, "I didn't get anywhere today. I needed to talk to Cheryl Loveless, but she was neither at home nor her office. Either that or she wasn't answering her door. And everybody else who might be involved didn't know anything or weren't telling me what they did know. I'm just hoping Fillmore had more luck than I did."

"He didn't," Ruth said. "He stopped by here on his way out of town. He said he'd call you in the morning."

I sat down at the kitchen table. The Dr. Pepper had started to sweat the moment I had taken it out of the refrigerator and already felt warm in my hand.

"So what am I doing wrong?" I said, knowing that she was going to tell me anyway.

Ruth opened the refrigerator and began setting food on the table. "You might be looking for the wrong person."

"I'm looking for whoever killed Scott McBride. How can he be the wrong person?"

"Try looking for Paul Samuel."

"Why? He didn't kill Scott McBride."

She set plates, then forks and napkins on the table. "I made a suggestion. You don't have to take it."

"Just tell me this," I said. "How is finding Paul Samuel going to help matters?"

145

"Think about it, Garth," she said. "Clarkie told you himself that Scott McBride had been in Oakalla before. With a carnival, he said. By my calculations, since Scott McBride was a Vietnam veteran, and the war in Vietnam ended in 1973, that would have to have been just about twenty years ago. And don't forget Paul Samuel disappeared while on his way to the carnival."

"But you don't know for certain that Scott McBride was here when Paul Samuel disappeared?"

"No. But I'm working on it."

"It's still a long shot, Ruth."

"True. But better than no shot at all."

I took my time deciding. For my own reasons, I still didn't want to go in search of Paul Samuel. But maybe I wouldn't have to go all the way down that road to find Scott McBride's killer.

"I'll need to borrow your Volkswagen," I said. "Jessie's out of commission."

She gave me a look of disgust. "What else is new."

The Hilltop Motel was a misnomer. The only hill around was a small man-made one built for geriatric skiers about five miles to the west of the motel, just off of I-94.

After a quick supper of potato salad and cold fried chicken, I had started out for Balboa

146

in Ruth's Volkswagen Beetle. Like Jessie, the Volkswagen wasn't known for its speed. On the way I passed a Model T Ford, a self-propelled combine, and a kid on a mo-ped, but nothing else. Even the dogs along the way got tired of chasing me after a couple miles or so.

I arrived at the Hilltop Motel to find a crowd of people sitting around the pool, drinking tall drinks and looking very glad to be there. Maybe next time I'd phone ahead and have a Tom Collins and a rubber raft waiting for me.

A shiny black Chrysler New Yorker was parked in front of Dick Samuel's motel room. He answered the door with a smile on his face and what looked and smelled like a Scotch in his hand. He didn't seem surprised to see me. If anything, he had been expecting me.

"I'm Garth Ryland," I said, offering my hand.

"I know," he said, shaking my hand.

He had a soft powerful grip that belied his small stature. He couldn't have spent all of his life behind the wheel of a car. Some of it must have been spent at hard labor.

"Would you like to join me?" he asked, offering me a drink.

"Sure," I said. "Why not."

I followed him into his room where he filled

a plastic cup with ice and then Johnnie Walker Red. His movements were sure and unhurried, those of a man at ease with himself.

"Goldie said when I called that you stopped by today," he said, handing me my drink.

His eyes were smoky blue and calm, about the color of a dog-day sky. They reminded me a lot of his wife's eyes, except that hers were self-centered while his were centered on me.

"Tell me, Garth, what do you honestly think of Goldie Lenore?" he asked. Dick Samuel was a good salesman. By asking your opinion, he knew how to make you feel important.

"I honestly don't know what to think of her," I said. "If I even like her or not."

He took my answer in stride. "That's understandable. I'm not sure I know what to think of her myself, and I've been married to her for the past thirty-three years." Then he shook his head in self-reproach. "No. That's not true," he said. "I fell in love with Goldie when I was fourteen and I'm still in love with her." He glanced around the motel room—at its all-weather, heater-air-conditioner, its cable-color television, simulated oak dresser, and single bed. "After thirty-three years of these, that's a tribute to her."

"You've been a salesman all of your life?"

"All of my adult life."

"You seem awfully fit for a salesman," I observed.

148

"I work out every chance I get."

"Weights?"

He smiled as if that were the last thing he'd do. "No. Mostly racquetball and tennis. Maybe some wallyball whenever I'm in Madison."

"I've never played the game," I said, referring to wallyball, which, as I understood it, was a combination of handball and volleyball, played over a net in a handball court.

"You should try it," he said. "It's a lot of fun."

"Maybe the next time I'm in Madison." I said with half a mind to really do it.

He took a drink of his Scotch. I took a drink of mine, then watched as the *No* in the No Vacancy sign flashed on in the twilight outside. Already, it seemed, we had run out of things to talk about.

"So," he said, "Goldie tells me that you were asking some questions about Paul."

"I was," I said, not yet sure how much she had told him.

"What have you learned so far?"

I studied him, wanting to, but not knowing if I should trust him. My last words to Ruth were. "For the record, Ruth, what kind of man is Dick Samuel?"

Her answer was "A good man." From Ruth, that bordered on sainthood.

"Not much," I said. "Though I did wonder

149

why, on the day Paul disappeared, that you said you were in Beaver Dam when in truth you were in Oakalla?"

Dick Samuel stood there a moment in total surprise. Then he put down his plastic cup and walked to the window to stare outside. "Did Goldie tell you that?" he said.

I listened as someone bounced three times, then went off the diving board into the pool. "No. There's a picture of you standing along East Jackson Street watching the parade."

He walked to the dresser, shook a cigarette from its pack, and offered the pack to me. When I shook my head no, he said, "Do you mind?"

"It's your room."

He lighted a cigarette and sat down on the edge of the bed to smoke it. He looked young for his fifty-some years. His face had no wrinkles, his hair only a dusting of grey around the edges, and his eyes, which for the moment had turned inward, still had the sparkle of youth in them. Dick Samuel seemed an earnest, honest, forthright man, uncomplicated and uncompromised by self-doubt. In no small way, I envied him.

"The reason I was there," he said, "is my business."

"But you were in Beaver Dam at the start of the day?"

150

"At the start of the day, yes. But not for long."

"What did you do once the parade was over?"

"I went to Portage where I knocked on doors until I called Goldie later that evening."

"Did you make any sales?"

He smiled at me. It wasn't a happy smile. "Surprisingly, yes. But I told Goldie that I made the sale in Beaver Dam."

He had a cigarette to smoke. I had some thinking to do. Finally I said, "What was it that made you think Goldie was having an affair?"

He put the cigarette to his lips, then put it down again without taking a drag on it. "Who said Goldie was having an affair?"

"It's the only reason that I can think of for you to be spying on her."

He had forgotten about his cigarette. A long roll of ashes fell on the bed. He seemed not to notice.

"What was it that tipped you off?" I said. "Or did someone tell you?"

He took a long drag on his cigarette, letting the smoke leak slowly from his nose. "Nothing really tipped me off. Nothing I could ever prove. Just a lot of little things that over time began to add up. Phone calls that went unanswered. Absences that went unexplained. Ex-

151

planations that for no apparent reason became excuses. And then at home a lot of screwing, but not much love-making." He smiled at me. "Really not all that much screwing."

"Better than none, I suppose."

"Not much," he said. "Not when I knew what it used to be."

"So you decided that something had to be going on?"

"Yes," he said, leaning over and putting out his cigarette in the motel ashtray. "I decided that something had to be going on. I'm not very proud of what I did, but I was desperate at the time. I was afraid that I was losing Goldie to someone else."

"Did you have anyone particular in mind?"

"No. That was the worst part of it. I couldn't think of any of our friends or acquaintances who would do that to me. I still can't."

"So you still think she was having an affair?"

He got off the bed and made himself another Scotch. He didn't offer me a second one, but that was just as well because I still had to drive home.

"I don't know what to think, Garth. If Goldie was having an affair, it ended shortly after that. At least the absences and the unanswered phone calls did. Of course, with Paul missing, a lot of things ended after that."

"Do you have any idea what might have happened to Paul?"

"None whatsoever." He seemed sincere.

"Were you and Paul close?"

He shrugged. "At one time we were. But the older Paul got, the less we seemed to have in common."

"Yet when you called Goldie the night he disappeared, you specifically asked to talk to Paul. Why was that?"

Dick Samuel didn't like that question, or its implications. But he was polite enough not to say so. "Because on my way into town, I was sure I'd seen Paul walking along Colburn Road."

"In which direction?" I interrupted.

"South, out of town."

"Go ahead."

"At least at first glance I thought it was Paul," he said. "But he had his head down and was kicking a rock, or something, along the edge of the road. That didn't seem like Paul, I thought. Not wearing shorts, and certainly not on foot."

"As opposed to what?" I said.

"His bicycle. Paul never went anywhere without it."

I wished I'd passed on the first Scotch. Then I would better know what to ask next. "But if you couldn't be sure it was Paul, why did you ask to talk to Paul when you called home?"

Dick Samuel was trying hard not to let his anger and frustration show. "Because I was almost certain that it was Paul. And if it was Paul and he had seen me, I wanted to make sure that he didn't tell his mother that I was in town."

"Would Paul do something like that? What I mean is, would he say something to her about it before he said something to you?"

"Yes," he said without hesitation.

"So he and Goldie were close?"

"Very close." He sounded jealous, but I didn't know of whom. "Paul was a lot more his mother's child than he was mine."

"But he was your child?" I felt I had to ask.

"Without a doubt. He was the reason why Goldie and I got married in the first place. Not that we weren't going to anyway. She'd just planned on going to college first."

I supposed that explained a lot of things, but I didn't know what. "Thanks for your honesty." I rose and took one last drink of what was by then mostly ice water, then set my plastic cup on the dresser.

"Does Goldie have to know about this conversation?" he said.

"I don't know," I said. "A lot depends on where I go from here."

I avoided I-94 and took the back roads home. But even on them there was traffic, and

154

though not heavy, more like a slow drip that came just often enough to be annoying, it took some of the romance out of the barns, the hay fields, and the Holsteins on the hill.

It wouldn't have mattered anyway. My mind was on my recent conversation with Dick Samuel and the fact that he had seen Paul Samuel walking out Colburn Road. If that was true, where was Paul's bicycle and how did it end up in the culvert under the old interurban? And where was Paul going, and what, if anything, did that have to do with Scott McBride's death?

I didn't see the car fast approaching from the rear. Not until it was nearly upon me. I watched it close to within a few feet of me before I realized that it wasn't going to pass.

My next moves were instinctive, as my reflexes took over. I hit the brakes, geared down, and swung hard to the right, jumping a ditch in a burst of sparks that I soon learned was a single strand of electric fence, and bouncing across a pasture that had to be the hardest ground in Adams County. I had my seat belt on and a death grip on the steering wheel, but that didn't seem to ease my ride any. After the Volkswagen finally came to a stop in the middle of a nearly dry creek bed, I spent the next few moments counting teeth, while waiting for my heart to slow down and my brain to unscramble.

I climbed slowly from the Volkswagen, stood a moment to clear my head, then tested my legs on the rocky creek bed, which was the east fork of Stony Creek. I walked downstream and found a cattle crossing that I could use to get the Volkswagen back up into the pasture again. Then I waited there in the dark for the other car to return. When it didn't return, when after a few minutes I was certain that it wasn't going to return, I got back in the Volkswagen, found a gate that led onto the road, and went home.

11

At home I parked the Volkswagen in the garage and got out to take a look at it. The wire of the fence had scratched its hood and front bumper, but otherwise, it looked okay—and a whole lot better than it would have looked if I hadn't gone through the wire. Still, I doubted that Ruth would find much consolation in that.

Then I took a walk to the near west end of town. "Garth, is that you?"

Goldie Samuel sat outside on her porch swing. She wore a sleeveless white cotton dress, and she had let her hair down, to spill in a golden fall across her bare shoulders.

I climbed the porch steps and sat beside her

157

in the swing. "It's me," I said, belaboring the obvious.

A hush had fallen over Oakalla, setting in like a sea fog for the night. I liked the peace and quiet, which gave me time to sort my thoughts. Right then I wasn't too sure of anything, least of all me.

"What are you thinking?" she asked.

"I'm thinking how many roads a man must walk down before they call him a man."

"How many is that?"

"More than I care to count."

Then I leaned over and kissed her. Her mouth was moist, yielding, the softest mouth I'd ever kissed. Her eyes half opened at the same time as mine, and they were glazed with a look that made me feel all man. I pulled away, sat staring out into the street, and wondered what in the hell I was doing.

"Do you have someone?" she asked.

"No. I don't have anyone."

"I do. Though I can't really call us lovers anymore. We're more like old friends who know each other too well to be comfortable with anyone else."

"I'd say that's quite a bit."

"Is it?" A sliver of ice crept into her voice. "I wouldn't know."

"I'd think you would by now."

"Do you mind if we change the subject?"

"No, I don't mind. What would you like to talk about?" I said.

"Why you came by here tonight."

"I'm not sure why I came by here tonight," I said. "Is that answer okay with you?"

"Okay with me . . . I guess."

We swung in silence as the lights in the nearby houses went out, and the damp night air wavered between warm and cool. With both her hair and her guard down, Goldie Samuel looked younger that night than she had that morning, much as I imagined she looked twenty years ago, before she lost her son and went into hiding. I wondered how she had survived as well as she had—and if she enjoyed her solitude more than she knew.

"You knew Dick was in Oakalla the day Paul disappeared?" I said.

She stopped the swing by dragging her bare feet across the concrete. "No. I didn't know," she said. "Who told you that he was?"

"He did."

"Did Dick happen to say why he was in Oakalla that day?" she asked when I didn't continue.

I started the swing again. I felt safer when we were swinging. "He said that he thought you might be having an affair, so he came back here to see if it were true."

"I see." There was anger in her voice. "And you just had to tell me that, right?"

I stopped the swing and kept it stopped. "Yes. I had to tell you," I said.

"Why?" She tried to kick start the swing again, but I wouldn't let her.

"Because I need to know whether it was true or not." I raised my feet and away we went.

"Why should it matter after twenty years?" she said.

"I'm not sure it does," I said. "I'd just like to know."

"I'm not going to tell you," she said. "It's none of your business."

"Not even if it might help me find Paul?"

I thought that she would at least consider that angle. But she didn't. "No. Not even if it will help you find Paul."

I studied her as we swung back and forth, back and forth across the porch, and tried to imagine how she had looked as a girl. She would have been, like that soft elusive summer night, the stuff of which my dreams were made—the one I told Dick Davis about when we sat behind his barn smoking grapevine; the one waiting for me in the endzone when I scored the winning touchdown; the one, when I ran the three minute mile to finally win her, I would have put up on my mantle and dusted every two weeks.

And she was more. Hers was the face in the wilderness, the one who celebrated me, made

160

me ache with desire for fire and home. The one who said no matter where you go and what you do, here I am, I'll be waiting. The one, if I could unlearn everything that I had learned in the past thirty years, I still embraced in my heart—until I realized that I wasn't a kid anymore, and neither was she.

"Do you really want me to find your son?" I finally asked.

"What do you think?" she said.

"I don't know. That's why I'm asking you."

She gave me a look that promised everything, revealed nothing. "When you do know, then I'll tell you."

"When I know, then I won't be asking."

She brought the swing to a stop. "Would you like to go inside?"

I felt my heart go thud, the way it had when she had asked if I would like to see her son's room. Once you reached a certain point, in life or in love, there was no turning back.

"For a nightcap?" I said.

Her smile was noncommittal. "Whatever you want to call it."

I followed her inside. We got as far as her bedroom when she said, "If you'll excuse me a minute."

She left for what I assumed was the bathroom. I sat down on the edge of the bed. As I glanced around the room—at the plaster walls and the oak woodwork, the polished hard-

161

wood floor and the white throw rugs, the purple-and-white Japanese fan hanging on the wall beside a print of a purple Iris, the old Singer sewing machine used as a night stand, the Jenny Lind bed on which I sat—I was doing okay until I saw the 5 x 7 of Dick Samuel on Goldie's dresser. An early Sixties photo by the look of it, with him wearing a flat top, white bucks, a ten-dollar suit, and a million-dollar smile.

When I had left him earlier that evening, he was getting ready to bed down in a motel room several miles from home. With a worn green carpet and a simulated oak dresser. To the sound of passing traffic and the laughter of someone else's kids playing in the pool. While here was I, in his own home, ready to bed down with his wife.

Somehow I couldn't see the fairness of it. So I left.

At home Ruth was sprawled in her favorite chair with her eyes closed and her mouth open. On my way upstairs I stopped to turn off the television.

"Where have you been?" she asked. She didn't miss much, even with her eyes closed.

"I went to Balboa, remember."

"After that. You've been back from there for over an hour."

"I went to see Goldie Samuel," I made the mistake of saying.

"About what?" I now had all of her attention.

"Not what you think. I had a few questions I needed to ask her. That's all."

"I'll bet," she said.

I let that pass. It was too late to start an argument.

She yawned. "You going up to bed?"

"I thought I might."

"Then good night."

But thanks to a guilty conscience, I still stood there. "Ruth, something happened earlier tonight."

She got up and shut off the window fan in the south window of the living room. "What was that?"

"Some drunk ran me off the road on my way home from Balboa." I assumed that it was a drunk. I couldn't think it would be anyone else.

"And?" She was suddenly all ears.

"And I went through an electric fence, ended up in Stony Creek, and put a few scratches on the Volkswagen." I felt like a kid again, telling my mother I'd just wrecked her car after I'd begged her to let me borrow it.

"A *few* scratches?" she said in disbelief.

"Several scratches then. But nothing that a good paint job won't cover." When she didn't say anything, I said, "It was better than the alternative. Which was to let him run over me."

163

"The alternative is for you to get a car that runs. So you don't have to borrow mine."

It wasn't the first time she'd told me that. "You're probably right. I'm sorry."

Looking weary, she sat down in her chair and stared straight ahead at the wall. "Well, it couldn't be helped, I suppose."

"Honestly, Ruth, I did everything I could to avoid it. And it's really not all that bad. You'll see in the morning when you look at it."

"Karl bought that car for me. Did I ever tell you that? Just before we found out he had cancer." She looked at me. Her eyes were fixed, resolute. "We'll keep the scratches, Garth. I don't want a new paint job."

"Whatever you say. I'm going to bed."

I went upstairs and took a long hot shower, thinking that it would help me sleep. But it didn't help me sleep. So I got up, and without turning on any lights, went to my east window, letting what breeze there was cool me through the dusty screen. Scott McBride was out there somewhere—in someone's memory or someone's conscience. So was Paul Samuel. You just didn't walk away from your childhood without a reason. Either it was taken from you or you were driven away. Either way, you, or your shadow, kept searching until you confronted it again. And made peace with it once and for all.

164

12

The phone rang on my way down the stairs the next morning. It was Fillmore Cavanaugh. "Did I get you up?" he said.

"No. The birds did. What's on your mind?"

"Clarkie, for one thing. I talked to him late yesterday morning, and he says he can't remember a thing."

I glanced outside where the sky had gone from red to blue. Already it felt hot. "Not a single detail?"

"No. He says it's all one big blank."

My neighbor dragged out his garden hose and started to water his lawn. There were days when I wished that was all I had to do. But I didn't begrudge him. He'd spent forty years in a factory earning the right.

"Maybe I'd better give Clarkie a call," I said.

"Maybe you had."

"What about the others you talked to? Did you learn anything from them?"

Since dawn a robin had been singing in my apple tree out back. Apparently he liked the weather better than I did.

"I tried to talk to Cheryl Loveless," he said. "But I didn't have any luck finding her. How about you?"

A fox squirrel in the top of my walnut tree started barking at something, probably the robin. "No. I didn't have any luck with her either. My guess is that she's lying low."

"Why?" he asked.

"It's probably because of Scott McBride," I said. "Clarkie said they were lovers at one time."

Ruth came down the stairs, gave me a grumpy look, and put the coffee water on. "Damn squirrel," she muttered to herself.

"I heard that," I said.

"What's that?" Fillmore Cavanaugh asked.

"Nothing. I was talking to Ruth. What about Butch Loveless? Any luck with him?"

"No. He swears he was in the high school lifting weights from two to four on Monday afternoon. After that he went home."

166

"Do you believe him?"

"I believe he was at the school lifting weights. I'm not sure he went directly home from there."

Ruth sat down heavily at the kitchen table while waiting for the coffee to start perking. She didn't appear to be listening, but I knew that she was hearing every word.

"I have a woman named Edna Pyle who swears she saw Butch Loveless drive by her house late Monday afternoon," he continued. "He was headed east at the time, which, as you know, is in the opposite direction of his house."

"Have you told Butch Loveless that?"

"No," Fillmore said. "I thought I might wait for a more appropriate time."

The coffee water boiled over, spilling onto the stove. Grumbling to herself, Ruth got up and turned the fire down under the coffee, then wiped off the stove before sitting down again.

"So where do you go from here?" I asked Fillmore.

"I'm not sure. We got at least four sets of prints from the inside of the Firebird. That's more than we bargained for."

"Two sets of them probably belong to Clarkie and me," I said. Then I remembered something that I didn't like telling him. "Speaking of the

167

Firebird, it's probably still not out at the quarry."

"Then where in the hell is it?"

"At the park, if I'm not mistaken. Sean Ragan came for it yesterday."

"On whose authority?"

"His own, I presume."

"Why didn't you stop him?" He was outraged.

"I and whose army. Besides, you were done with it. I didn't see the harm."

Captain Fillmore Cavanaugh, however, did see the harm. "Christ, Garth, you'd make a piss-poor cop."

"That's why I'm not a cop," I said.

"It's more than a matter of semantics, Garth. We've got an eye witness who swears he saw Clarkie's patrol car sitting in the park late Tuesday night."

"How late Tuesday night?"

"Right about the time that Clarkie took his ride down Hutchinson's Hill."

I didn't believe it and told Fillmore so. "I was there in the park late Tuesday night, looking for Clarkie. I didn't see his car anywhere."

"Our witness claims it was hidden behind some bushes at the south end of the park. Then, after all that business with the trailer died down, he saw someone drive it out across the ball field."

168

I was looking at Ruth who was looking hard at me. "Just who is this witness anyway?" I asked.

"One of Ragan's own. He works there at the carnival."

"Local or import?"

"Import. He came in with the carnival. But he says he's leaving it once Homecoming is over."

"What did Ragan have to say when you told him?"

"I didn't tell him." Fillmore made a point of saying. "I could never track the man down, like you did. Why is it," he pondered, "those dogs with the best noses usually have the smallest brains?"

"Murphy's Law," I said, hanging up on him.

I called Clarkie at the hospital. "Clarkie, this is Garth. How are you feeling?"

"Garth, did you say?" He sounded half-asleep. Or half-drunk.

"Yes. Garth Ryland."

"Oh? That Garth." His voice sounded as if it were coming from the moon. "How are you, Garth?"

"I'm fine. How are you?"

"As well as can be expected."

"That's a comfort."

Ruth got up, turned off the stove, and poured us each a mug of coffee.

"What's that, Garth?"

"Nothing, Clarkie. Maybe I'd better talk to you later." If he was faking it, he was doing a good job of it.

"Sure. Anything you say, Garth."

"There is one thing, Clarkie," I said before he could hang up. "Two things actually. I need to know what happened the night you got hurt."

"What night was that?"

"Tuesday," I said, running out of patience with him. "You know that as well as I do."

He didn't answer. I hoped he hadn't hung up.

"Clarkie, are you still there?"

"Tuesday, you say?" The longer we went, the more feeble he sounded.

"Never mind. And never mind the second question. You probably won't remember it either."

"Remember what?" The change in him was miraculous.

"Those prints you took out of the Firebird. I wondered how many sets besides ours you got?"

He hesitated, conveniently I thought. "Three," he said, his voice again feeble.

"*Three*? You're sure, Clarkie?"

"I'm sure. And I'm betting that two of them are women's." He hung up.

170

"Clarkie's faking it," I said to Ruth. "I don't know why, but he's faking it."

"Faking what?" she said, taking a drink of her coffee. "It can't be incompetence. He's already cornered the market on that."

"Amnesia," I said. "He says he can't remember what happened to him Tuesday night."

"Maybe nothing happened to him Tuesday night," she suggested. "Maybe he tried to end it all on Hutchinson's Hill."

"You don't believe that anymore than I do."

"No." she said. "But maybe Clarkie does."

I didn't agree. "No. He's covering up for somebody. Maybe even himself."

"Why would he be covering up for himself?"

"He wouldn't be, unless he was up to something that he shouldn't have been Tuesday night."

"Impersonating a law officer. That's what he was up to," Ruth said.

A half hour later I'd shaved, showered, and was ready to leave for work. "One thing you might do," I said, hating to broach the subject, "is to get the Volkswagen tuned up sometime."

Ruth was up to her elbows in dishwater. She didn't even bother to turn around. "When you sell that wreck of yours."

171

"Another thing you might do is have your steering checked. I think it pulls a little to the right." Or at least it did after I drove out of the pasture.

She eyed me angrily. "It was fine the last time I drove it."

"Just a suggestion," I said. "You don't have to take it to heart."

The first thing I did when I got to my office was to call around to find out the name of the farmer whose electric fence I had run through. When I reached him, however, his wife said he wasn't there. He was out in the road chasing cows, she said. I said I'd call him back. About Christmas, I figured.

The rest of the day I spent in my office, working on Friday's edition of the *Oakalla Reporter*. By six P.M. I had nearly everything ready to go but my weekly column, which I'd yet to write. I had tried to write it several times, and even had made a couple drafts, but I couldn't get it right. I wanted to say something significant about childhood—I didn't care what—but the subject was either too vast or too personal because I choked every time I tried. Or I preached, which was worse, much worse.

I walked to the Corner Bar and Grill for supper. Oakalla's shops and businesses were closed for the night, and the cars that were left uptown were all parked around the Corner Bar and Grill. The smell of dust was everywhere—overhead and underfoot and in the cracks of the buildings themselves. Glancing at the western sky where a dark cumulus ridge lined the horizon like a far mountain range, I wished to hell it would rain.

Inside, the Corner Bar and Grill was packed with customers and seats were at a premium. Hayden Sims sat on my usual seat at the counter, so I had to take the seat beside him. Normally I wouldn't have minded, but that night I didn't want to be elbow-to-elbow with anyone. I needed room to think.

"Evening, Hayden," I said, noticing the strong scent of his lime aftershave. "Got your roses all watered?"

"I plan to do that later," he said, "after it cools down a little."

"Amen to that."

Paula Wiggins, the night waitress, came to take my order. I ordered a fish sandwich, a tossed salad, and a large 7-Up. A tall frosty draft of Leinenkugels would have gone well with the fish, but I still had my column to write and needed a clear head for that.

"How's Cheryl doing?" I asked Hayden, seeing what I could learn about her whereabouts.

"Not bad. But she's still pretty shook up."

"You've talked to her, then?"

Hayden wore shorts and sandals, was drinking a beer and eating a steak and french fries. It was strange to see a man with slender nearly hairless legs, and a wrestler's arms and torso. It was like seeing bicycle wheels on a Cadillac.

"I saw her just a few minutes ago," he said. "We thought it best that she stay at our house until all of this blows over."

"We?"

"Her mother and I."

"What does Butch have to say about that?"

As if on cue, Butch Loveless came into the Corner Bar and Grill. He didn't seem pleased to see either Hayden Sims or me. He didn't seem pleased about much of anything.

"Hayden, I need to see you outside," Butch said.

Butch wore jeans, tennis shoes, white socks, and a white tank-top, which showed every muscle in his upper body, and accentuated every rise and fall of his massive chest. He looked like a highly tuned thoroughbred, ready to explode out of the starting gate.

"When I finish my supper," Hayden said calmly.

"Now!" Butch growled.

Hayden cocked his head and looked up at Butch. I didn't like the look in Hayden's eyes. It made me fear for Butch.

"What did you say, Butch?" Hayden said. His voice was low, flat, calm. "I don't think I heard you right."

"You heard me okay," Butch said, backing off a little. "You got no right to lock Cheryl up like that."

Hayden turned back to the counter to cut a bite of steak. As he did, blood shot out of the steak onto his plate. "Call it protective custody," Hayden said, eating the bite of steak. "But if you don't like it, take it up with Garth here. It was his idea."

Immediately it became obvious that Butch would rather take it up with Garth than he would with Hayden. Perhaps because Garth's arms and chest were inches smaller than Hayden's.

"Is that right, Ryland?" Butch took a step toward me. Another step and he'd be right in my face, which wouldn't work for either of us.

I glanced around the Corner Bar and Grill, which had grown very quiet and self conscious. No help there, I decided. Where was Rupert Roberts when I needed him?

"That's right, Butch," I said, as Paula Wiggins brought me my tossed salad and fish sandwich. "It was my idea." Originally anyway, two long days ago.

Butch put his hand on my right shoulder. His was a hard heavy hand, and it hurt where he squeezed. "Then maybe you and I better step outside."

"To do what?" I said, picking up the fish sandwich with both hands, while trying to ignore the screaming pain in my right shoulder.

"Butch, that's enough," Hayden said. "I think you're hurting Garth."

But Butch wanted his pound of flesh, namely mine. He squeezed even harder. I could feel my right arm going numb. "He ain't seen nothing yet," Butch said.

"I said that's enough," Hayden repeated, with conviction this time.

I reached over with my left hand and took the steak knife off of Hayden's plate. "Butch," I said. "If you don't let go, I'm going to plant this in your family plot."

He increased the pressure even more. It felt as if my shoulder was about to pop. "I'd like to see you try."

Hayden Sims' right hand closed over my left wrist. Apparently he knew me well enough to know that I wasn't bluffing. I felt staked to my seat. Of the two of them, I didn't know which was the stronger.

Then Butch let go of my shoulder and left the way he'd come. An instant later Hayden let go of my wrist. I could feel neither my right arm nor my left hand. And I had two full columns left to type.

"Thanks," I said to Hayden, while working my right arm up and down, trying to get the feeling back. "I think."

He took the steak knife from me and used it to cut himself another piece of porterhouse. "I just didn't want you to do something that you'd be sorry for later," he said.

When the feeling began to return to my right hand, I used it to massage my left wrist. "It was something I might regret," I said. "But I can't guarantee you that I would've felt sorry about it."

Hayden Sims looked at me with admiration. "You're tougher than I thought," he said.

"Ditto."

My last comment seemed to please him as he returned to eating his steak and french fries. When I could work both hands again, I ate my now cold fish sandwich, drank my now watery 7-Up, left my salad on the counter, and went back to work.

13

I finished typing my column shortly after midnight and called in my printer, Cecil Edwards. The idea had come to me on the way home to my office, as I walked along the alley beside the cheese plant, flexing my fingers and thinking about nothing in particular.

I wrote that alleys, like barns, were once a vital part of a kid's education. In them you could find stones for your slingshot, stones for your rock collection, and stones to hit with a board when you wanted to kill some time and no one else was around. You could hide in them, race your bicycle down them, steal apples and cherries from the trees that grew alongside them, and come Halloween, find enough tomatoes in the nearby gardens to get you in enough trouble to last until the next Halloween.

Alleys—real alleys, those with rocks, dirt, weeds, and broken bits of glass in them, and grass, trees, and gardens surrounding them— were a part of small town America that was disappearing along with everything else. Their loss seemed one more nail in the coffin of imagination, that for every alley you paved, a poet was lost, a book was buried, an old man's life went unheard by the boy next door.

I thought that I said it well, but the real test came when Cecil Edwards walked into my office carrying the first paper off the press. He sat down on my desk and ate an apple while he read my column.

"What do you think?" I said when he finished.

He threw the apple core into my waste basket and wiped his hand on his pants. "Pretty good." From Cecil that was shameless flattery.

A couple hours later, Cecil, his wife Millie, and I had all the mailing stickers on and that week's edition of the *Oakalla Reporter* ready to go to the post office. Cecil and Millie would drop the papers off there on their way home. I would then, as I always did, turn off lights, empty waste baskets, and generally unwind until I felt ready to go home.

179

After helping Cecil and Millie load the papers into their Pontiac station wagon, I watched them drive off, then stood a moment, watching lightning light up the sky all around me. To the south was a storm that I could both hear and see, as thunder bumped and rumbled and fiery red veins appeared in the clouds; to the far north a storm that silently flickered, then paused, then flickered some more; and to the east a storm whose wind I could feel, whose rain I could smell, and whose wake left me hungry for a storm of our own.

I felt something else in the air that night. Fear. A nameless faceless fear that rose up in me without warning and sucked all of the courage out of me. I shivered and went back inside.

There I turned on a light I didn't need and sat down at my desk. I should go home. I was dead tired. Fatigued. As Vince Lombardi said, it makes cowards of us all.

But I didn't want to go home. I didn't want to go home because I didn't want to go out into the night.

I went to my north window and stood there watching—for what I didn't know. Clouds raced by overhead, stars came in, then passed out of sight, and the sound of insects rose and fell with the wind. It was a restive fickle night, one that couldn't quite make up its mind what it was or what it wanted to do.

Outside, I waited for a cloud to pass, then left under a clear dome of sky. Once I reached Gas Line Road, I began to feel a little better. I was out in the open there and could fairly well see what was ahead. Whatever goblins were waiting there in ambush, they would have to be quick to get me.

I neither saw nor heard the speeding car behind me. A whisper in the wind said to jump out of the way. I heeded it. It likely saved my life.

Landing on my left shoulder, I rolled over, got to my feet, and tried to identify the car that had passed within inches of me, so close I could feel its heat. But by then it was too far away to identify. I saw it brake for Perrin Street and turn left. Only then did it turn its lights on. I could see them spray the trees as it sped south.

I had two choices. I could either go on home or return to my office. Since I couldn't make myself go home, I returned to my office.

About five A.M. I awakened with my head hanging down and my face resting on the top of my desk. From then on I slept in fits and snatches until at six A.M. the phone rang. It was Ruth, checking up on me. I told her I'd be home in a few minutes.

I spent the next five minutes staring bleary-eyed at my green office wall, trying to find a reason to move. My right shoulder hurt where Butch Loveless had grabbed me, my left shoulder hurt from my landing on it, my left wrists felt sprained where Hayden Sims had grabbed it, and my head hurt for reasons of its own.

Normally I at least would stay the morning and take what praise or lumps I had coming from my subscribers. But on that morning I wasn't up to it. So I pulled down the blinds, put a note on the door that told whoever read it where I wouldn't be found, and went home.

Ruth was waiting for me in the kitchen. She had coffee on, bacon frying, and a stack of bread ready to go into the toaster. Sometimes even I thought I didn't pay her enough.

I sat down in my chair. I didn't care if I ever moved agian.

"Rough night?" Ruth asked.

"Yes. It was a rough night."

"Care to tell me about it?"

"After I've had something to eat."

Two eggs, two pieces of toast, four strips of bacon, and two cups of coffee later, I told her about it. The telling didn't make me feel any better, but at least I wasn't hungry anymore.

"Why didn't you come on home after he tried to run you down?" she asked.

"Because I was afraid to," I said, hating to admit it. "Plain old wide-eyed, knock-kneed, chicken-shit scared. I thought that he might try again and this time succeed."

"Even if you'd stayed on the sidewalk?"

"To be honest, Ruth, I didn't even consider it."

She picked up her mug of coffee and leaned back in her chair. "You said *he* tried to run you down. Are you sure it was a man driving the car?"

I got up and poured myself a third cup of coffee. I'd regret it later when the caffeine kicked in and put me in overdrive, but what the hell. Staying within my limits hadn't done me any favors lately either.

"No," I said, sitting back down. "I'm not sure it was a man. I just assumed it was from everything else that's happened."

"Such as?"

"Scott McBride's death. Clarkie's accident. I don't see how a woman could be physically strong enough to have carried those off. At least not any of the women I know."

"How strong would you have to be to knock Clarkie over the head and then drive his car to the top of Hutchinson's Hill?" she said.

I thought about the three sets of fingerprints that Clarkie said that he had taken from the

183

inside of Scott McBride's Firebird. Two of them, he thought, might be women's. Ruth had a point. But so did I.

"Okay, that's possible for a woman to do," I said. "But not break Scott McBride's neck with her bare hands and then throw him into the quarry. That's not possible."

Ruth's brow furrowed, which meant that she was thinking. "Maybe the same person who killed Scott McBride and then arranged Clarkie's accident, if that's what happened, isn't the same one who tried to kill you. It doesn't have to be, you know."

"I know," I said.

"So it is possible that there are at least two different people involved," she said.

"It's possible," I agreed. "But I don't see how. Not unless he has an accomplice."

"Why couldn't that be?"

I shrugged. "No reason, I guess. Except let's say that two people are involved in Paul Samuel's disappearance, which happened twenty years ago. That means that for the past twenty years two people have had to keep the same secret. In a town the size of Oakalla, that seems unlikely."

"But not impossible."

"No," I said. "Not impossible." Then I noticed a glimmer of a smile on her face, which meant that she knew more than she was telling. "What are you getting at, Ruth?"

She took a drink of coffee, prolonging my agony. "I thought it might interest you to know that this is the same carnival that was in town the day Paul Samuel disappeared. It was B and R Entertainment then. It's Sean Ragan Amusements now."

"And?" I said, hoping for more.

"And Sally Wampler, the woman at the carnival who was attacked on Tuesday night, was also here then."

"With the carnival?"

"Yes. With the carnival."

"Who told you that?"

"Billy Hunter's grandmother. It seems that Billy overheard his dad telling someone about Sally Wampler." Ruth grimaced at what she had to say next. "About what a hot number she was, according to Glen Hunter. Billy, it seems, took it from there."

It was my turn to lean back in my chair and think. But nothing came of it. "I'm sorry, Ruth," I said. "I wish it all fit together. But it doesn't. Except I think you're right about one thing. Scott Mcbride's death is somehow tied to Paul Samuel's disappearance."

"It would seem like it," she said.

"But I won't know until I talk to Cheryl Loveless alone, without her husband or either one of her parents around."

"And what are the chances of that?"

"I'll never know until I try."

At nine A.M. I stood outside the Oakalla Mutual Insurance Company, waiting for it to open. I had been there for the past half hour and hadn't seen Cheryl Loveless go into the building. Neither did I see her red Beretta anywhere. But that didn't mean that she hadn't walked to work early and wasn't somewhere inside.

When Dorothy Sims unlocked the front door, my hand was already on the handle. Before she could reach the security and authority of her desk, I cornered her.

"Is Cheryl in today?" I asked.

Dorothy Sims seemed on the verge of panic. She clearly didn't want to talk to me, and she clearly didn't want to be seen talking to me.

"No," she said, "Cheryl is not in today. She went with her father to a wrestling clinic in Eau Claire. I don't expect them back until late this evening."

"What are you afraid of, Dorothy?" I asked, mainly because that was the way she was acting.

She glanced at me, then at her fellow workers, then shook her head as if to say that she couldn't say anything with them there.

"If I come back later, when you're on lunch break?"

"No, Garth," she said, finding her voice

again. "I think it's best that you leave me and mind alone."

"By mine, do you mean Cheryl?"

"Yes. I mean Cheryl," she said. "She's had about all she can take right now."

"Which is why she is with Hayden in Eau Claire?"

"Yes. Which is why she is with her father in Eau Claire."

"What about Butch? Does he know where she is?"

Her answer was to look the other way.

"What about it, Dorothy?"

"No," she snapped. "He doesn't know where she is. And don't you tell him either. The farther he stays away from her, the better."

"I won't argue with that," I said. "But after all, he is her husband."

Anger showed in her brown eyes, as she pulled her small frame erect, ready to do battle with the world. She reminded me of Grandmother Ryland's bantam hen, who was content to cluck and scratch in the dirt all day, until you messed with her one and only chick. Then she became a wild-eyed demon, Flogging everything in sight.

"Men," she said, marching past me to her desk. "You're all alike."

I stood for a moment, staring at her. When it

became obvious that she'd said all that she was going to say, I left.

A few minutes later I stood on her front porch. The Sims' house was a two-story brick house, with two concrete steps leading up to its front door, a black wrought iron railing on either side of the steps, a deep-green carpet-like front yard that Hayden Sims watered daily along with his roses. A blue spruce, an ornamental fir, and a corkscrew willow grew in the front yard. A red maple and a couple pin oaks grew in the back.

I knocked on the front door, but received no answer. When I knocked a second time without an answer, I tried the latch, heard it trip, and went on inside.

"Cheryl, are you in here?" I stood in a brick anteroom with a brick floor. It felt close to freezing in there.

When Cheryl didn't answer, I went into a small formal living room that had a powder-blue carpet, a modern dark blue couch and two modern dark-blue chairs to match. Two walnut-veneer end tables with brass lamps and matching crystal shades sat at either end of the couch. A brick fireplace with a bare brick mantle faced the couch. The fireplace looked as if it had never been used. Probably because there was a brick Santa Claus stuck somewhere in its brick chimney.

"Cheryl, it's Garth Ryland. I need to talk to you."

From there I went into the kitchen, briefly onto the stairs that led down to the basement, then off the stairs and out of the kitchen and down a short hall into the master bedroom. The master bedroom had a king-sized bed, a large walk-in closet, two narrow ceiling-to-floor windows, blue drapes, and a blue shag carpet. Its adjoining bathroom had a gold tub, a gold stool, a gold-and-white vanity, and a brown shag carpet. Cheryl Loveless wasn't in either the master bedroom or the bathroom.

Returning to the anteroom, I climbed the stairs to the second floor and found myself in a long hallway with white plaster walls, a walnut baseboard along each wall, and no carpet on its hardwood floor. Three walnut doors in turn led into a clothes closet, a bathroom, and a spare bedroom that, like the fireplace, looked as if it had never been used. The fourth walnut door led into Cheryl Loveless' bedroom—or what had once been Cheryl Sims' bedroom.

Her carpet was dark-green, almost black, her walls and ceiling light green, about the color of spring's first leaves. She had a white canopy bed, a white wicker dresser and chair, and a white wicker chest of drawers. Piled on the unmade bed were a monkey, a panda, a

189

couple teddy bears—one black, one brown, and a white flop-eared rabbit with a pink ribbon around its neck. Lying on top of the pile was a green nightshirt that appeared to have been worn recently.

"Cheryl?" I said, feeling her presence, even though she wasn't there.

I walked over to her closet and looked inside. Hanger after hanger held a dress or a skirt from her past. Sack dresses, tent dresses, tie-dyed dresses, formals, senior cords and mini-skirts were stuffed so tightly into the closet that they bowed the steel clothes rod on which they hung. Puzzles, games, and magazines filled the shelves above them, and shoes of every kind and color covered the floor below. Like my closet at home, the closet smelled of mothballs.

Unlike the closet, which was jam-packed with mementoes, only one memento hung on the wall above her bed—a poster of a race car driver. The rest of her walls were bare, though chips showed in the paint where things had hung, and then had been taken down.

The race car driver wore a white racing suit with red lettering and cradled a red racing helmet in his right arm. He had dark brown eyes, long sandy-brown hair that hung down over his collar in back, an easy smile, and the carefree slouch of a man who feared nothing but anonymity. He had addressed the poster: To Cheryl. He had signed it: Love always, Scottie.

The poster itself looked several years old, and the man on it was several years younger than the one found floating in Hidden Quarry. But the masking tape on the back of the poster looked new. I guessed that it had been hung up only recently; or hung back up again, since there were old tape marks that suggested it had been hung at least once before.

Then I searched the rest of the room for something that might speak for Cheryl Loveless, since she herself wasn't there to tell me what she knew. I found it in her wicker dresser drawer, in an old photograph of her, Clarkie, what appeared to be a young Scott McBride, and someone else that I thought I recognized. They all had their arms around each other and were sitting on the bumper of a black 1952 Chevy pickup.

I turned the photograph over. On the back someone had printed:

EVERYDAY OF THE WEEK
I AM YOURS
YOU ARE MINE
WE ARE TODAY
WHAT WE SHALL BE TOMORROW

Knowing the principals involved, I agreed in part. But only in part. Scott McBride was not today what he would be tomorrow. Unless you counted dead.

I'd put the photograph in my shirt pocket and started down the stairs when I thought I heard someone enter the house by the back door. I retreated to the top of the stairs and stood there listening while someone moved quietly about the house, opening and closing drawers. Afraid that whoever it was would eventually come up the stairs and see me, I went back to Cheryl's bedroom and stood in the doorway.

I heard footsteps on the stairs. I wanted to see who it was, but if I stayed there to find out, I might be the first one seen. So I hid deep in Cheryl's closet where it would take a bloodhound to find me.

Soon the bedroom door opened, and I could hear someone going through Cheryl's chest of drawers, as I had done only a few minutes earlier. Whoever it was was being very quiet about it, as if he or she had no more right to be there than I did.

Then the closet door suddenly opened, and I felt myself flinch even though I knew I was well hidden. Looking through the hangers down the row of clothes, I saw Goldie Samuel standing at the closet door.

She spread some dresses apart and looked behind them. Apparently finding nothing there, she leaned into the closet and spread another section of dresses apart. She leaned even further the third time and barely missed my nose with her hand. I was sure that she had seen me, but when she straightened the clothes that she had moved and closed the closet door, I knew that she hadn't.

A moment later she left the room. A couple minutes after that, when I felt safe to move again, I went to the head of the stairs, listened momentarily, heard the back door open and close, and took off down the stairs, hoping to catch up to Goldie Samuel before she reached home. On my way through the living room I almost ran headlong into Butch Loveless. I didn't know which of us was the more surprised. Until Butch saw who it was. Then he was angry.

"What are you doing here?" he said.

"I might ask you the same thing."

"I'm looking for my wife," he said. Then I saw his anger deepen and knew right away what he was thinking. "For your sake, she'd better not be here."

"She's not," I said, hoping not to give too much away. "At least she didn't answer when I called."

"If you don't mind, I'm going to see for myself."

I stepped aside to let him pass, then took a seat on the couch. I needed to talk to Butch Loveless, whether I wanted to or not.

"She's not here," he growled, after returning from upstairs.

"I told you she wasn't."

"Lucky for you."

I patted the couch. "Have a seat, Butch. Take a load off your mind."

He glared at me as if I'd just propositioned him. "If you don't mind, I'll stand."

He went over to stand by the hearth. Neither one of us found it comfortable to be there together.

"Where did Cheryl go? Do you know?" he asked.

Butch wore jeans, tennis shoes, and a black T-shirt. As always, he looked like Mr. All-America. But at that particular point in time, he was an unhappy Mr. All-America. He missed his wife. He couldn't hide that fact.

"No. I don't know where Cheryl went," I said. I thought about telling him the truth, since he looked as if he needed it, but that might be telling him too much. "Hayden's not here either, so maybe she's with him."

"Probably," he said, angry with them both. "She always was a daddy's girl."

"Better than a mommy's girl, I suppose."

"I wouldn't bet on it."

Then I noticed the large wad of paper in Butch's right hand. It looked like the poster of Scott McBride.

"Do you think you should have done that, Butch?" I said.

"Done what?"

"Taken that poster off of Cheryl's bedroom wall," I said without thinking.

His eyes narrowed. He was about to get surly. "What were you doing in her bedroom?"

"The same thing you were. I was looking for her, thinking that she might be hiding up there."

"Why would she be hiding from you? You don't scare me any," he seemed to feel it necessary to add.

"Because I want to talk to her about Scott McBride."

"She didn't kill him, if that's what you're thinking," he said. Then he began to pace around the living room. I liked him better where I could keep my eye on him.

"I never thought she did kill him," I said. "I'm not so sure about you."

That got his attention. He stopped his pacing. "Says who?"

"Says that poster you're holding in your hand."

He threw the wadded poster at the fireplace, but missed, as it hit the mantle and bounced back my way. I reached down and picked it up.

"What do you think you're doing?" he said. "That belongs to Cheryl."

"Then I'll see that she gets it."

"Like hell you will."

He came after me, fully intending to take the poster away from me. Since I didn't see how I could stop him, I tossed it at him, and much to my surprise, he caught it.

I nodded at the hearth. "Now sit down and act like you've got some sense."

"I could take you right here," he said. "I could tie you up into a knot and drop you on your head."

"You probably could, Butch," I said. "But what's the point? I'm not the one who screwed your wife. For that matter, neither is Clarkie."

"No. But that little butterball would sure like to."

"That's beside the point."

He stood opening and closing his hands, as if he couldn't quite decide what to do. He needed to take his anger out on someone, and since Cheryl or Hayden wasn't handy, and Scott McBride was dead, I was his next best choice. But there was also a chance, granted a remote one, that I might hurt him in the process. And Butch Loveless didn't seem to be a man who liked pain—unless, of course, he was the one inflicting it.

He walked to the fireplace and stood with the poster in his right hand and his right arm on the mantle. I liked his pose. All he needed were a moose head and a 30.06 hanging over the fireplace to make it complete.

"You've got nothing on me either, Ryland," he said. "I was pumping iron when Scott McBride got himself killed. Or when he drowned, I should say, since no one knows for sure what really happened to him."

"Edna Pyle says differently. She says she saw your Bronco go by on its way to Hidden Quarry late Monday afternoon." Actually, Edna hadn't said where he was going, but he didn't know that.

"That's a lie!"

"Is it, Butch? Do you want to tell Edna that, face to face?"

He turned to the fireplace, resting both hands on its mantle and staring down into it. "Edna Pyle has been on my case for the past three years, ever since some of my wrestlers cut through her yard during conditioning. You can't believe a word she says about me."

"So you deny that you were out at Hidden Quarry Monday afternoon?"

"Yes. I deny it." He turned to face me. "And like I said, anyone who says differently is a damned liar, including Edna Pyle."

197

I didn't believe him, but I didn't see anything to gain by telling him that. "What about Cheryl?" I said. "Was she at Hidden Quarry on Monday?"

"I don't know," he said, his eyes avoiding mine. "You'll have to ask her."

"Then why did you beat her up?"

That was the wrong thing to say. Butch was again ready to fight. "Who said I beat her up? Not Cheryl, I can tell you that."

"No," I said, rising. "She wouldn't. She's probably too afraid of you to say anything."

"She's not afraid of me, damn it. I'll hurt the man who says so."

"I just did," I said. "Say so."

I stared at him. He stared at me. Both of us wanted to take a measure of the other, but neither one of us wanted to throw the first punch. "One of these days, Ryland, you'll get yours."

"As we all will."

He went out the front door. I went out the back.

14

Goldie Samuel lay on a lounge chair in her back yard sunning herself. She wore large round sunglasses and a black one-piece swimming suit that went well with her gold hair and brown skin. But I wondered how she stood it there in the sun, since I was hot in the shade.

She lowered her sunglasses to look at me. "Back so soon?" she said.

"I can't seem to stay away."

She laughed and put her sunglasses back on. "Tell me another one."

I sat down on the grass and took off my shoes and socks. Then I lay back on the ground. The leaves of the sugar maple above

199

me hung stock still, as if painted on the limbs. Between the maple and its fellow maple to the west, I could see a light blue patch of sky.

"Mind if I take a nap?" I said. Already the day seemed long. I could have stopped right then and there and been satisfied.

"Be my guest," she said.

I lay there for a while, occasionally glancing at Goldie Samuel, who seemed oblivious to me. Sweat had beaded on her forehead and pooled in the hollow of her breasts and navel. She couldn't be comfortable lying there. No one could.

"So what brings you to my door today?" she said without looking at me. "More questions?" Her casual tone almost hid the hard edge to her voice. Goldie Samuel sounded angry to me.

"More questions," I said, sitting up.

She took off her sunglasses and looked me straight in the eye. "Would you like to ask them *inside*?"

Then I realized what she was angry about. I had left her the other night without an explanation. "I think I'd better ask my questions out here. It's safer."

"Safer for whom?"

"Both of us."

The heat in her eyes intensified. I felt myself melting into the ground like a chocolate bunny. "I'm not afraid of you," she said.

200

"Safer for me, then," I said, lying back down and counting to ten.

When I looked at her again, she had her sunglasses back on. "So ask your questions," she said. "Then get out of here." She sounded more hurt than angry. It made me feel that much worse.

So I started to explain myself, then stopped. What good would it do her to tell her my views on love and marriage? What good would it do me?

"Okay," I said, "my first question is what were you doing in the Sims' house?"

"When?"

"A few minutes ago." Though by then it was more like an hour.

"Who said I was in the Sims' house?" If she was worried about it, she did a good job of hiding it.

"I saw you there myself."

"Sure you did," she said, unconvinced.

"I was on my way to talk to Cheryl Loveless and saw you come out the back door," I said. Then I described the yellow jumpsuit she had been wearing.

"I didn't see you," she said. "Why didn't you say something?"

"I intended to. But Butch Loveless got in the way."

She stared at me for several seconds before

she said, "And where was he hiding? You sure you're not making this up?"

She had me where she wanted me. I couldn't tell her the truth without giving myself away. She knew that. Instinctively, or otherwise, she knew she had the upper hand.

"I'm not making it up," I said, deciding that I had nothing to lose by going on the offensive. "You were there and we both know it. If you want to continue to play games with me, then that's your business."

"Go to hell," she said, turning away.

"Gladly. If you'll tell me the truth. Do you want me to find Paul or not? If you do, then you'll level with me."

She took off her sunglasses and sat up in her chair. The anger that had been smoldering in her finally erupted. "What do you know about it?" she said. "It's not your son who's been lost, your life that's been ruined. You've got nothing in this but a few hours of your time, and maybe, if I give you more credit than I think you deserve, a vicarious interest in Paul. Your life's not at stake here, as mine is."

"That's where you're wrong," I said, feeling a little angry myself. "Last night someone tried to run over me and damn near got the job done. And the night before last on my way home from Balboa, I think he did the same thing with about the same results. So don't lecture me on lives that might be lost."

202

"It's still not the same," she insisted.

"Maybe not. But it's close enough not to split hairs."

I put my socks and shoes back on. She lay back in her chair and stared at the sky.

"I can't tell you, okay," she said, "what I was doing in there. Not until I'm sure."

"Sure of what?"

"Myself."

"That's no answer and you know it."

She shrugged. "Maybe so. But that's the best I can do for now."

I rose and walked to the gate that led into the alley behind her house. I could feel her eyes on me the whole way. At the gate I stopped and turned back to her. "Just out of curiosity, what kind of car does Dick drive?"

"A black Chrysler New Yorker," she said, which was the same car that I thought that I remembered seeing parked outside his motel room door.

"He wasn't by any chance in town last night, was he?"

"Not that I know of. Why do you ask?"

"I just wondered."

"It wasn't Dick who tried to run you down," she said on my way out the gate.

"Then who was it?"

She closed her eyes and lay there, soaking up the sun. "No one. I just know it wasn't Dick."

203

A long hot walk later I found Sean Ragan at the shelter house in the park, eating his lunch. Watching him down his Italian sausage-with-peppers-and-onions sandwich, I wished I had stopped at the Corner Bar and Grill on my way.

"Where did you get the sandwich?" I asked.

"A friend of mine made it for me."

"Is he open for business?"

"Not yours."

I watched a couple of sparrows wrestle over a stray hot dog bun. Except for them, we had the shelter house to ourselves.

"I guess I'll wait and eat uptown then," I said.

Sean Ragan's hard blue eyes were neither friendly nor unfriendly. They were impassive. Not beyond seeing, but beyond reach. Soldier eyes. That's what Rupert Roberts called them. Eyes that could watch you die, and not care.

"I guess you will," he said, "have to eat uptown."

He started to leave. I shook my head no. "Not yet," I said. "I have some questions for you first."

He studied me. He could stay or he could go. It made no difference to him. The difference was to me. I hoped I looked convincing.

"I'm tired of your questions, Ryland," he said. "They don't get us anywhere."

204

I handed him the photograph that I'd found in Cheryl Loveless' dresser. It was the photograph of the four people sitting on the front bumper of the 1952 Chevy pickup. He studied the photograph, then turned it over and read what was on the back of it. Neither the photograph nor its inscription seemed to move him any.

"Interesting," he said, handing the photograph back to me.

"I thought so," I said. I turned the photograph over. "Did you notice the date beneath the inscription? July 21, 1971."

"Imagine that," he said.

"So not only was your carnival here twenty years ago. You were too." Sean Ragan was the fourth person in the photograph along with Clarkie, Cheryl Loveless, and Scott McBride. A cleaner, leaner Sean Ragan with long shiny black hair and a red bandanna tied around his head.

"What if I was?" he said.

"I just wondered what you were doing back here."

"You tell me," he said. "You're the one getting paid for this."

I started to tell him that no one was paying me. Then I realized what he meant. My payment, such as it was, would come when, and if, I found out the truth.

"Okay," I said, "here's what I think. I think that B and R Entertainment, which is now Sean Ragan Amusements, was originally Barnum and Ragan, or whatever. Your father once owned half the carnival. Now you own all of it. And one of your first acts as the new owner was to come back to Oakalla. Why? Because twenty years ago you saw something, or did something, that's been on your conscience ever since."

He shrugged as if to say, so what? Then he said, "What did I see, then? Now that you have my attention?"

"I don't know what you saw. I don't know if you saw Paul Samuel killed, or if you killed him yourself. But whatever happened, you couldn't forget it. Not even Vietnam could make you forget it. So it must have left a lasting impression."

"What it left," he said bitterly, "was a legacy of death."

"Meaning Scott McBride?" I said.

"Meaning Scottie," he said. "So all I've really accomplished by coming back here is to get my best friend killed."

"You can't blame yourself for that. Scott McBride came along for the ride. He had to know what might be waiting for him."

Ragan shook his head. "Scottie didn't have a clue as to what was waiting here. I never told him."

"Why don't you tell me?" I said.

Ragan almost smiled. It was as close as I would ever see him come to one. "In case something happens to me?"

"In case something happens to either one of us."

"It'll take some time," he said. "Do you have that long?"

"I have all the time you need."

"Then let's go someplace where we won't be interrupted."

"Do you have a place in mind?"

"Hidden Quarry."

"Fine with me," I said, regretting it the moment I said it.

We walked over to where Scott McBride's Firebird was parked. When we were inside, I noticed the keys in the ignition.

"I thought Clarkie had those," I said.

"He did. Until he gave them to me."

"When was that?"

"Sometime Tuesday afternoon. He said he thought I might want them."

"Did he happen to say anything else, like what his patrol car was doing hidden in the park late Tuesday night?"

Ragan shot me an angry look. "Who told you that?"

"One of your workers."

"Then he's a liar."

"You deny that it was here, then?"

Ragan's eyes bore into mine. I felt, rather than saw, the rage beneath them. "That's what I said."

He started the Firebird and we drove out to Hidden Quarry. It was strange to ride in a dead man's car beside a man I hardly knew and feared as much as trusted. It was stranger still when we made the last turn and drove down Hidden Quarry Road under a canopy of limbs and leaves thick enough to block the sun. I looked over at Ragan to see what he might be thinking. Whatever it was, it didn't bring a smile to his face.

Hidden Quarry lay just ahead. Ragan stopped the Firebird, sat for a moment, then got out of the Firebird and walked to the edge of the quarry where he stood for another moment, looking down into its waters. Then he took off his shirt and sat down on a slab of limestone. I sat in the shade of a white oak a few feet away. It was cooler there, and safer.

"You don't like the sun?" he said while pulling off his shoes.

"Not in July."

"You'd never make it in Florida, then."

"I don't intend to."

He lay back on the stone and closed his eyes. How he could relax on that slab of hot rock was beyond me.

"Where in Florida?" I asked.

"Ruskin. That's where we winter. It used to be a circus town. Now, with all the snow birds there, it's just a circus."

"Then why bother?" I said.

"It beats snow" was his answer.

He continued to lie on the rock. I continued to sit in the shade. "Scottie and Cheryl I can understand," I said, referring to the photograph. "And you as well. But where does Clarkie fit in?"

He opened his eyes momentarily, then closed them again. "Clarkie is the one who introduced us all to each other. First himself to Scottie, then Scottie to Cheryl, then Cheryl to me. It was strange at first, having this fat short-haired kid following us long-hairs around like a lap dog, but then I sort of got used to it. Everybody else either wanted to stay the hell away from us or spit on us. But not Clarkie. He didn't give a damn how long our hair was or what we smoked after the sun went down. He just liked us for who we were."

"And you? Did you like him?"

He turned his head to look at me. He didn't see the point of the question. "Clarkie didn't have a lot to offer in those days. He still doesn't as far as I can see. But he's a good guy, a good person. There's something to be said for that."

209

"Yes. But did you like him?" I was asking for Clarkie as well as for me.

Ragan turned away and closed his eyes. "I liked him. I don't know about Scottie. I don't think he thought much about Clarkie one way or the other. He was more interested in Cheryl."

A cloud covered the sun. I welcomed the breeze and the breath of coolness it brought. Then it moved on.

"I understand that Cheryl and Scottie became more than friends," I said.

"You understand right."

"Poor Clarkie," I said.

"Yeah. Poor fool. I don't think he ever really knew what was going on, or how many trips that Chevy pickup made out here without him."

"Was the pickup Cheryl's?" I asked.

"No. It belonged to her boyfriend."

"Where was he all of this time?"

"Away somewhere at camp. He'd left it with her while he was gone, since she had her license, but no car of her own."

"Trusting of him," I said, feeling the irony.

Ragan didn't say anything.

Another cloud covered the sun. I waited for it to pass. "What happened then?" I said.

"You mean with Paul Samuel?"

"Yes. That's what I mean."

"I knew the kid, if that's what you're asking. He had spent a lot of that week hanging around the carnival. He and that blond friend of his."

"Eddie Vincent?" I said.

"I don't remember his name. The only reason I remember Paul Samuel's name is because of what happened to him."

I waited for him to go on. When he didn't, I said, "But you say you did know Paul Samuel by sight?"

"Yeah," he said. "I knew him by sight. Kind of a gooney-looking kid. You know, a real ugly duckling, with a big nose and black horn-rimmed glasses. But a real bright kid, who never seemed to run out of questions." He opened one eye to look at me. "Sort of like you."

I let that pass. Instead, I thought of Paul Samuel, and how the ugly duckling often turned into a swan later on in life. His parents were both good-looking. There was no reason to think that he wouldn't be in time. At least that was what I always used to tell myself. And I hoped time hadn't proved me wrong.

"Did you see Paul Samuel the day he disappeared?" I said.

"I saw his bicycle, or what I took to be his bicycle, sitting in the back of a black Chevy pickup, leaving here."

"By here, do you mean Hidden Quarry?"

"Yes. Cheryl and Clarkie were supposed to meet us that morning at the park and go swimming with us. Sort of as a last hurrah. But they never made it to the park, so Scottie and I came out here by ourselves." He sat up. "That's when I saw the pickup leaving here with the bicycle in the bed of it."

"Did you recognize the pickup?"

"Yes. It was the one Cheryl had been driving."

"And its driver?"

He drew a blank, or pretended to. "I never saw who was driving it. Scottie was on the right side of the drive. I was on the left side. We split when we saw the pickup coming to get out of its way." We were interrupted by a noisy flock of Canada geese that glided in from the west and landed in the quarry. "It all happened so fast that I didn't get a look inside the cab. I just saw the bicycle in the bed and that was it."

"Did you know at the time that it was Paul Samuel's bicycle?"

"No. That came later, after he turned up missing, and I started to think about it."

I was tempted to believe him. But I couldn't figure out how Paul Samuel's bicycle could have gotten out to the quarry without him, since Paul, or who I believed to be Paul, was

212

walking out Colburn Road when Dick Samuel saw him that morning.

"What about Scottie, did he see the driver of the pickup?" I said.

The look on Sean Ragan's face said he wished he knew. "He said he didn't when I asked him about it later. But I don't know if he was shooting straight with me or not."

A second flock of geese flew in to join the first. We listened as they all honked their greetings to each other before they split up and went their separate ways.

"Then what happened?" I said.

"What was that?" His thoughts were somewhere else.

"What happened after you and Scottie saw the pickup?"

"Nothing out of the ordinary. We swam awhile, then went back to the carnival and went to work. That night after we closed down, we pulled up stakes and left."

"Did you ever see Clarkie or Cheryl again?"

"I saw Clarkie for the first time when he came by the park with you the other day. I haven't seen Cheryl Sims at all."

"It's Cheryl Loveless now."

If that meant anything to him, he didn't show it.

"What about the pickup, did you ever see it again?"

213

He was somewhere in the past, Vietnam perhaps. It seemed to be a place that I never wanted to go. "No," he said in answer to my question. "I never saw the pickup again. But we were in Tomah a couple weeks later when the word got out among our people that someone was on the grounds looking for Scottie. I thought it was probably a cop, since we'd had nothing but cops around ever since Paul Samuel disappeared." Sean Ragan's face had hardened without his realizing it. "But that turned out not to be the case."

"What was the case?" I asked when he didn't continue.

"I don't know. By the time I tracked him down, he had already left. All I saw were his taillights, leaving the grounds. But whoever he was, he left a bad taste in my mouth."

"Did he ever come back?"

"No. Not that I know of. A week before that Scottie and I had both enlisted, which was why he wasn't there when the man came looking for him. He was home taking care of business. Two weeks after that we were in Camp Lejeune, North Carolina. Three months after that we were in Nam—just in time for Christmas."

A long gander sailed in, dropped silently down into the quarry, and floated by himself out near the middle. If he had a story to tell, I didn't want to hear it.

"And the reason Scottie came back here to Oakalla with you, it was just to see Cheryl, or was it?"

Sean Ragan was watching the gander who seemed to be watching us. "Yes. It was just to see Cheryl. Scottie had never really gotten over her, I don't think. She had no place in his life. No one did. Scottie had room for only him. But if he could have made it with anyone, I think it would have been Cheryl."

"Now he's dead."

He didn't say anything.

"Doesn't that anger you?" I said, wanting to see some emotion from him.

He turned to look at me. His eyes were about as cold as eyes could be. "You just don't get it, do you, Ryland? I'm out of it now. I have been from the beginning. It's just an accident I'm here. Oakalla needed a carnival and I needed a gig. It's that simple. Don't try to make a hero out of me. I don't need it. Neither does Scottie." He turned back to the quarry.

"I don't believe you," I said. "Maybe you're out of it now. Maybe Scottie's life was more than you could pay. But you haven't been out of it from the beginning. And it's no accident you're here. You came because you left something unfinished here."

"Which is?" he asked. "Or are you going to

215

tell me that Paul Samuel is another MIA and that I've come back here to find him."

"Haven't you?"

He didn't answer. He wouldn't given me the satisfaction. Or so I thought until he spoke. "What if I did come back here to find him? What if . . ." He paused, as if searching for the reasons. "What if twenty years ago, when I was just a kid myself, I went to war in some God-forsaken hell-hole that nobody gives a shit about now. What if I left buddies there. Not just names on a list, but real guys . . . who got high with me, showed me pictures of their mothers and girlfriends, who, when Charlie was so close you could smell him, pissed down their legs like the rest of us, and never stopped talking about home. What if you figure you owe them one because you came back and they didn't. Not because you were any braver or any smarter or any better, but because when God, or whoever it was, rolled the dice, you came up seven and they came up snake eyes. What if there's no chance of ever going back there and finding them. But there's this kid, this goofy-looking kid who makes you his hero, who for a week follows you around everywhere you go, who gets in your way and under your skin and asks you a question every time you turn around. What if you come to really like this kid, in spite of yourself, and then one day he disappears, and you and your carnival are somehow blamed for it. What if, twenty years later, you finally get the courage, and the chance, to set things right. What if you come looking for the kid. Only to discover, like those other guys you left behind, he can never be found."

"He can be found," I said.

He turned my way. There was a familiar cast to his eyes. It was the look of a man betrayed by his own best intentions. "Not alive. Or don't you know that?"

"I know that. I've known it from the beginning. But don't you understand, Ragan, nobody rests until he's found. Not you, not me, not his friends, not his family, not even his murderer."

He rose to stand at the edge of the quarry. For a frightening instant, I thought he was going to jump. But he didn't.

"Sally Wampler," I said quickly. "How does she figure into this?"

"I didn't know that she did."

"Someone tried to break into her trailer the other night. You said at the time it had happened before."

He returned from the edge of the quarry to sit on the limestone slab. But he didn't look comfortable there anymore. "It's an occupational hazard with Sally," he said. "Somebody's always trying to break into her trailer. Usually it's a drunk with a hard-on."

"You don't think that this last time was any different?"

"It might have been a little different," he said. "But it still doesn't have anything to do with what happened here twenty years ago."

I wasn't so sure about that. "Sally was in Oakalla then. With your carnival."

"So what's your point?"

I thought for a moment and decided that I couldn't make one. "None, I guess. It seems strange, that's all, that the same day we find Scottie's body, somebody goes after Sally Wampler."

He didn't offer his opinion, or didn't have one, so we let it end there.

"I've got to get back," he said, rising. "Do you want a ride?"

"No thanks. I need to stay here for a while."

"I'd like to," he said. "But I have a carnival to run."

"I understand."

"I wish I did."

"Ragan?" I said before he could leave. "Cheryl Sims' boyfriend, whatever happened to him?"

He shrugged. "As far as I know, she married him."

I watched him leave, sat for a while longer,

then got up and went into the woods behind the quarry. Nothing was moving in there, not even a chipmunk's tail. Before long my clothes stuck to me like an extra layer of skin, and I was doing more standing than walking.

I didn't find Paul Samuel. Perhaps he was buried here in the woods behind the quarry. If so, he would likely stay here for all time. If not, and in any case, I was wasting my time looking for him.

As I stepped out of the woods, I saw Butch Loveless' Bronco II parked a few feet from where the Firebird had been parked an hour before. A moment later I saw Butch walking along the rim of the quarry with his head down, as if he were looking for something. Keeping his eyes on the ground the whole way, he stopped only once—to pick something up, examine it, then throw it away in disgust. Without ever raising his head to look my way, he left a few minutes later.

When I was sure he was gone, I walked over to where he had stopped, and found what he had picked up, then thrown away. An old hard brown leather shoe tongue, it looked like to me. I searched for the rest of the shoe, but didn't find it. Then I went home.

15

For supper Ruth and I had salmon patties and apple salad. Normally on a Friday evening we ate supper at the Corner Bar and Grill to celebrate the survival of another week. But because of the heat and the week that had just passed, neither of us felt much like going out.

"I still don't see why I have to make the phone call," Ruth said.

We sat at the kitchen table with our dirty supper dishes in front of us. We would get around to washing them when one of us found the energy to move.

"Because I'm afraid she'll recognize my voice," I said.

"So what if she does?"

"Then she might not tell me what I want to know."

Ruth sighed as she rose from the table. I knew what the sigh meant. It meant I owed her one.

"Thanks," I said.

"Don't get ahead of yourself. I haven't made the call yet." She went to the phone, looked up the number in the phone book, and dialed. A moment later, I heard her say, "Dorothy, this is Ruth Krammes. What time will Hayden be back tonight?" I tried not to watch as she waited for her answer. "Thank you." She hung up and returned to the table. "About ten, she thinks."

"Subtle," I said.

"It worked, didn't it?"

I had to agree that it had.

An hour later I left on foot for the hospital. As I crossed Jackson Street, I could see the sun setting in the west—a huge blood-red orb that flooded the landscape and dwarfed the sky. I had never seen the sun quite so large or so red. And when a long low cloud passed in front of it, like a ghost train, it never even cast a shadow.

I arrived at the hospital to find a state policeman sitting outside Clarkie's door. He was tall and lean, wore a gun, hat, and a badge, and looked like every speeder's worst nightmare.

221

"How's Clarkie doing?" I asked.

"Who wants to know?"

Very gingerly I reached into my back pocket, took out my wallet, and showed him my driver's license, then waited while he spent the next three hours examining it.

"Ryland, huh?" He seemed singularly unimpressed. "Captain Cavanaugh said you might be by one of these days."

He handed the wallet back to me and I pocketed it. "Well, here I am," I said. "May I see Clarkie now?"

He had his eyes on a blond nurse who was rolling an empty gurney down the hall. "Be my guest."

I went inside the room where Clarkie was sitting up in bed watching television. He had a bandage around his head, ugly bruises on his arms and face, one hell of a shiner around his right eye, and the general appearance of someone who had spent the past few hours in a clothes drier. He also had a hospital pallor about him that said he wasn't quite up to par and didn't yet know when he would be. Half-sick and half-scared, if his was anything like my last hospital stay, he had spent most of his time there thinking about his own mortality; or its corollary, his own vulnerability, which was even scarier to contemplate, since you could only die once, but you could be hurt

222

a thousand times in a thousand ways before then.

"Hi, Clarkie. How are you doing?" A dozen long-stem red roses stood in a vase in his window sill. I looked for a card that should have accompanied them, but didn't see it.

"Not bad," he said. "Under the circumstances." He used his remote control to turn off the television. "Except my neck hurts like hell."

"Your neck? I thought it was your head that was cracked."

"So did I."

I pulled the lone chair in the room up beside his bed, then extended my hand. He slowly raised his arm and shook my hand, but there was no strength in his grip, and I could tell that every little movement hurt him.

"Had many visitors?" I said.

"Not many," he said. "Cheryl Loveless and her dad stopped by early this morning to bring me the roses. Aunt Norma stopped by to give me hell for not taking better care of myself. And Danny Palmer and Sniffy Smith dropped by after they closed up the Marathon last night. But that's about it. Except for Fillmore Cavanaugh, and he doesn't count." Clarkie sounded a little hurt and a whole lot lonely.

"Well, at least you're catching up on your rest."

"Yeah. That's something I really need right now. Rest."

I couldn't tell if he were serious or not. With Clarkie you never knew. His sense of humor was, like modesty in a locker room, not something you came to expect.

I looked out the window where dusk had started to fall. Soon it would be dark. Then it would be night.

"Clarkie, we need to talk," I said. "And we need to talk now because I'm running out of time."

"So talk," he said, staring at the blank television screen. "I'm listening."

"About Cheryl Loveless. We need to talk about Cheryl Loveless and Scott McBride and where you were when the lights went out."

Clarkie's face, what I could see of it, had turned to stone. Apparently I'd said the magic words. Now how did I reverse the spell?

"Clarkie," I continued when it became obvious that he wasn't going to answer, "I've already talked to Sean Ragan. I know all about you, him, Scottie, and Cheryl, and what you all once meant to each other. What I need to know is what happened to you and Cheryl on that Saturday morning twenty years ago when you were all supposed to go swimming together out at Hidden Quarry?"

"I don't know what happened to Cheryl," he said. "She never came by for me."

224

"Then what happened to you? Why didn't you go with them?"

He stared out the window at the fast-approaching night. He didn't want to tell me because it was too painful for him to relate. But I had to know, so I waited him out.

"My mother wouldn't let me go," he said woodenly. He turned to me. There were tears in his eyes. "Now, are you satisfied?"

"Clarkie, there's no crime in that."

"I was sixteen-years-old!" he shouted. "Sixteen-years-old, for Christ's sake! There is a crime in that, Garth. I had every right to go where I wanted. I just didn't do it." He raised his right arm, then let it fall with a gesture of futility. "Because I didn't have the guts."

"How would that have changed anything, then or now?" I said.

"Now? I don't know. Maybe I would be a different person today if I'd gone to Hidden Quarry instead of staying home. Maybe I'd be a little braver, a little stronger, a little better able to like myself." He looked away, unable to face me any longer. "I don't know, Garth."

He was in such anguish that it hurt me to see the pain on his face and to hear the pain in his voice, and still not understand. "Help me in this, Clarkie. What was at stake for you then, besides standing up to your mother?"

"That was my stake, Garth," he said quietly.

"Not my mother herself, but her values and my father's values and this little jerkwater town's values that judged someone by the length of his hair and the cut of his clothes. When I didn't have the guts to say, 'These are my friends and I'm going with them, no matter what you think.' Then that made everyone else right and me wrong. And that's the way I've lived ever since."

"Can we back up a minute, Clarkie? How did your mother know what you were up to that morning, if you didn't tell her ahead of time?"

He looked puzzled. "What does that have to do with what we're talking about?"

"I'm not sure. I'd just like to know."

"I don't know," he said, losing interest. "She just knew, that's all, the way she seemed to know everything else about me."

He was withdrawing into his shell again. I had to find a way to keep him out in the open.

"It's like this, Clarkie. If she knew, then someone told her. If someone told her, then he had a stake in you, too. Probably a lot of people did. That's the way it was in small towns back then. To go against the grain, you had to have more courage than most of us did. It doesn't make you a coward. It just makes you normal."

"You never went against the grain when

you were a kid?" he said. "Somehow I find that hard to believe."

"Not in any obvious way," I said. "Not in the way I dressed, or the way I wore my hair, or the way I went about doing things. Only in the way I thought. And I usually kept those thoughts to myself, safe for a later day when I was on my own." I rose and went to the window. Clarkie was right. He had more at stake back then than I had first realized. "Don't you see, Clarkie. Most kids don't have any real power. Not unless you put a gun or a knife or a bottle or a pill in their hands, and then that's just the power to destroy. So most of us go with the flow. There's no shame in that."

"There is twenty years later," he said.

I smiled at him. "Clarkie, and please don't take this wrong, but you're about as far from the mainstream as a person can get. You're your own man. You sure as hell aren't anybody else's."

He didn't return my smile. His eyes said he wanted to, but he wouldn't let himself. "I might be my own man, Garth, but what kind of man am I? That's what I'd like to know."

"You're a man in motion, Clarkie, as we all are. The final die's not been cast yet."

"It has for Scottie McBride," he said.

"And Paul Samuel." Who never even got his chance to be a man.

227

"You've found him, then?"

"No. But I'm working on it."

"So what's your point, Garth?"

"My point is, to paraphrase Robert Frost, we're not the ones dead. We still have a life to live, and everything that implies."

Clarkie looked past me, out into the night. "Sometimes it's a hell of a life."

"Yes, Clarkie," I said, returning to my chair. "Sometimes it is."

We didn't speak for a while. Clarkie lay back on his pillow and closed his eyes. I thought about the dead, those whom I had loved and lost, whose lives had stopped forever. I really hoped there was a heaven, because I couldn't imagine not seeing them ever again.

I looked at my watch. Nine-fifteen P.M. In just a few minutes, I had to be on my way. "Clarkie, there's still the matter of where you were Tuesday night and why."

He didn't say anything. I hoped he wasn't asleep.

"Clarkie?"

His eyes opened. "I heard you the first time," he said. "I'm just trying to decide if I want to tell you or not."

"It's important, or I wouldn't ask."

"I know it's important," he said, showing some of his old spirit. "That still doesn't make it any easier for me."

While he was deciding whether to tell me or not, I was watching the clock. I soon had to leave, no matter what he decided.

"I was watching Cheryl's house," he said. "I'd parked my patrol car in the alley that runs along behind it, and I was watching her house."

"Why?"

"Because I wanted to catch Butch Loveless in the act."

"The act of what?"

He sat up. He was both angry and frustrated—angry at himself, frustrated with me. "I don't know," he said. "The act of something. Beating Cheryl up or trying to kill her, something like that. I wanted to be her hero. I wanted her to look at me just once with love in her eyes."

"So you just happened to pick Tuesday night to do that?"

"No," he said, his frustration growing. "I picked Tuesday night because we found Scottie on Tuesday morning. I thought that Cheryl might blow once she found out about it. Or that Butch might blow if Cheryl said something to him about it. You know, accused him in any way. So I wanted to be there in case anything like that happened." He saw that I wasn't showing much sympathy for him. "I'm sorry, Garth. My feelings for Cheryl got in the way of my better judgment. Don't tell me that's never happened to you."

He had me there. "Let me count the ways," I said. "But that still doesn't excuse either one of us."

"I didn't say it did."

"But nothing happened to give you your chance to be a hero, or did it?" I said.

Up until then he had been more than holding his own, which was remarkable, considering how he must have felt. But that question seemed to let all of the air out of him. He lay back on his pillow and closed his eyes. I wasn't sure that he was going to open them again.

"No," he said. "Nothing happened to give me a chance to be Cheryl's hero."

"What did happen?"

I waited for his answer, watched the clock, then waited some more. A couple minutes passed. Another minute, and I would have to leave.

"I don't remember what happened," he said. He lay looking at me, but I couldn't be sure that he was seeing me. "I was there behind the bush beside their house, looking in the window, when someone puts his arm around my neck and bam! I'm out just like that. The next thing I remember is waking up here in the hospital."

"You don't ever remember being in the park?"

"No. Who says I was there?"

"One of the carnival workers. But Sean Ragan denies it."

"I could have been there, I guess. I could have been anywhere, for that matter."

"You don't remember crawling out of the patrol car, or any of your ride down Hutchinson's Hill?"

He tried to shake his head. It was painful just to watch him. "No. I don't remember any of it."

"What about the guy who put you out? Do you have any idea who he was?"

"No. I never even heard him coming."

"Could it have been Butch Loveless?"

"I don't see how," he said. "Butch was in the house at the time."

"In your sight?"

He took a moment to think about it. "No. Not in my sight. He'd moved to another part of the house from where I was."

"But the odds are good that he was still inside?"

Clarkie's face said he wasn't sure. "I don't know about the odds, Garth. He was inside the last time I saw him, and I never heard him come out. That's all I know."

"What about Cheryl? Where was she?"

He didn't want to answer that question. But I already knew that. "I don't know where she was. Probably with Butch." That admission hurt him more than any of his injuries.

"So I take it they weren't still fighting?"

"No. They weren't still fighting. But they weren't lovey-dovey either, if that's what you're saying." Whatever they were, Clarkie's reaction made it obvious that they weren't what he expected them to be. "It's funny, Garth," he continued, "I've spent my whole life, or most of it anyway, trying to get Cheryl to notice me. You know, to see me as a man and not just as a listening post. Now I realize I've been wasting my time."

I stared at the dozen long-stem roses that Cheryl Loveless had brought to him that morning. "Maybe it hasn't been a complete waste of time," I said.

Clarkie's smile wanted to hope, but refused to. "No, Garth. I know what you're thinking, but you're wrong because that's the way I've been thinking all these years. If it wasn't Butch, it would be somebody else like him, not me. Cheryl wouldn't know what to do with someone who treated her right. At least that's my opinion." Clarkie's eyes were sad, but not defeated. "I mean she's thirty-six years old, the same as me. You'd think she would have learned something by now, if she was going to."

"For some of us it takes longer than others," I said. "So don't count her out just yet."

"Oh, I'm not; I'm not," he said, sounding for all the world as if he already had. "I'm just not putting all my eggs in her basket anymore."

"That's probably a good idea, in any case."

He smiled and closed his eyes. I thought he was off to sleep.

"Garth," he said on my way out. "You know what else is funny. When I saw Scottie down at that race in Atlanta, he didn't even remember that Saturday morning when we all were supposed to go swimming together. Here I had spent all those years rehearsing my apology, and he didn't even remember it." Or me either, Clarkie's voice seemed to say.

"It appears he remembered Cheryl," I said.

I knew Clarkie was on the mend when he said, "Who wouldn't?"

16

Twenty minutes later I stood sweating in the alley that ran east to west behind first Dick and Goldie Samuel's house, then Hayden and Dorothy Sims' house, and then, four houses to the west, Butch and Cheryl Loveless' house. It was also the same alley that started at School Street in the heart of town, ran under the water tower, and behind the City Building, and ended at Beaver Street on the west side of town. The same alley where Clarkie had been attacked; the same alley that Paul Samuel had taken to Eddie Vincent's house on the last day of his life.

In the south one lightning flash followed another, but without thunder, like the flickers of a silent movie. Some called it heat lightning, since it usually occurred on hot, still nights such as this one and seemed to be a thing unto itself. But it was simply lightning whose thunder was too far away to hear.

Closer and more vivid had been the sights and sounds of the fair, as the next to the last day wore down to its last hour. The whirling colors had seemed brighter tonight, the screams sharper as they punctured the quiet with an urgency they didn't seem to have before. Perhaps the kids were trying too hard to get their thrills before the carnival moved on and left them behind.

A car turned into the east end of the alley and came my way with its bright lights on. I stepped back into the hedge that lined the alley and tried to plan my next move. That, I decided, depended on Cheryl Loveless. If she went into the house with Hayden, then I would have to knock on the front door and ask for her. If she went down the alley toward home, which I hoped she'd do, I'd follow her and stop her at the first opportunity. What I hadn't planned on was her jumping out of the car and running as soon as it stopped in front of the garage door. I almost didn't catch up to her before she reached home. Then I had to tackle her to get her to stop.

The impact with the hard ground knocked

the wind out of both of us. I rolled off of her so that she could breathe. She rolled away from me and then rose to her knees to face me. She was ready to bite, spit, scratch, or scream, whatever it took to save herself.

"It's Garth Ryland," I said. "So don't do something we might both regret."

She just glared at me. She still couldn't get her breath. Her breathing was shallow and rapid, almost a pant.

I crawled over to her. "Relax," I said, taking her by the shoulders and forcing her to bend down and then back up again. "I'm not here to hurt you."

"You have a funny way of showing it," she said when she could talk again.

We sat for a while in the dark alley. By now the carnival would be winding down, the rides blinking out one by one, and then there would be the long parade of red taillights along Gas Line Road as the carnival goers returned home. One more day, I thought. One more day and then it would all be over for another year.

"I'm sorry about tackling you," I said. "But I had to stop you before you got in the house."

"Why?" she said, taking a deep breath. "What have I ever done to you?"

"It's not me I'm worried about," I said. "It's you."

"Yeah," she said, not believing me. "Which is why you tackled me in full sight of my house, where Butch can look out and see us, then make up his own mind about what's going on."

I glanced up at her house. There was a hedge between us and it, along with several bushes, but there was no sense in taking any chances. "Where would you like to go?" I said.

"Anywhere but here."

"How about your parents' house?"

"Not there either," she insisted. "That house has big ears."

"How about my house?" I said.

"Fine with me."

Good, I thought. Ruth is going to love this. So would Butch Loveless, if he found out.

I rose, then held out my hand to help her up. She took my hand, but dropped it immediately on reaching her feet again. "No offense," she said. "But this isn't exactly a date."

"None taken," I said.

We walked on down the alley to where Hayden Sims' white Lincoln Continental was still parked outside the garage. The garage light was on, and I could see Dorothy Sims' old Dodge Dart parked inside. I wondered what Hayden was up to until I heard the hose and saw him watering a rose bush a few feet away. Intent on what he was doing, he didn't see us pass.

I walked a few more feet down the alley and stopped. "What are you doing?" Cheryl whispered. "Somebody's going to see us."

I was staring at Dick and Goldie Samuel's house, which was dark, inside and out. Was Goldie in bed, or sitting on her front porch swing, or standing at a window, looking out into the night? I wished I knew. More to the point, I wished I knew why it mattered to me.

We walked on. Four blocks later we were home.

Ruth laid down her magazine and watched first Cheryl, then me enter the living room through the front door. She didn't say a word, but the look she gave me said it all.

"We'll be in the kitchen," I said to Ruth. "That's all the farther we're going."

"I didn't say anything," she said, returning to her magazine.

Cheryl wore pink cotton shorts, a pale green tank-top shirt, tennis shoes with pink laces, and pink socks that barely showed above the top of her shoes. She wore no lipstick and just enough makeup to help hide the bruise on her face. As I glanced at the bruises on both of her shoulders, where Butch had evidently grabbed her, my eyes strayed to her breasts, which gave the tank-top a pleasing lift. Then she noticed that I noticed and we both looked away.

"Would you like something to drink?" I said.

"What are my choices?"

"Water, coffee, tea, beer, or bourbon."

"No wine?"

"No wine."

"Then I'll have a beer."

"Is Old Style okay? We're out of Leinenkugels."

"Old Style will be fine."

I poured us each an Old Style into the frosted mugs that Ruth kept in the freezer. "Ruth, how about you?" I said, knowing that she was listening to every word.

"No, thank you" came her answer from the living room.

"I don't think she likes having me here," Cheryl whispered as we sat down at the table.

"She doesn't like having anyone here." I didn't whisper. "Not unless they're approved."

"Aren't I approved?"

"By her, I mean."

"Oh," she said, as if she really understood.

We each took a drink of beer at the same time. I didn't know about hers, but mine hit the spot.

"So," she said, "why is it you're so worried about me?" Cheryl Loveless had beautiful green eyes, the kind you could get lost in and not care.

239

"I'm afraid that someone might want to kill you."

"Why would anyone want to kill me?" If she were worried about it, she didn't let it show.

"Because you might know who killed Scott McBride."

"Says who?" she said, coloring a little, but still well under control.

"Clarkie for one. Sean Ragan for another. They both told me the same story about you and Scott McBride."

"Then they're both liars."

"I don't think so, Cheryl."

She pushed her chair away from the table and stood up. "I don't think this was a good idea, Garth. I'm going home."

"To what?" I said. "Another beating? Ignoring the truth won't change it. Scott McBride is dead. And as much as you don't want to admit it, you're partly responsible for it."

She stared numbly at me, as her mouth opened in protest, but no words came out. Then she began to shake uncontrollably. I stood and held her until Ruth came into the kitchen and took over for me.

I went outside to look at the stars. Nothing made me feel more helpless than someone in tears. Ruth knew that, so she had come to both Cheryl's and my rescue

When I went back inside several minutes later, Ruth had returned to the living room, and a composed Cheryl sat at the kitchen table drinking her beer. "I'm sorry," I said, sitting down.

"So am I," Cheryl answered, "for lying to you. If I hadn't, then maybe Clarkie wouldn't have gotten hurt and someone wouldn't have tried to kill you."

"Who told you that?"

"Ruth did, among other things."

"Okay, let's start over," I said. "What happened last Monday after Scott McBride came into the insurance office, looking for you?"

She took a deep breath, then said, "I was there sitting at my desk, lost in my own little world, when in Scottie came." She raised both hands in a gesture of helplessness, then put them down again. "I was so shocked I didn't know what to do." She smiled at me. "You thought you took my breath away tonight when you tackled me. You should have seen me then. I thought I would die before I could get that first word out."

"How did Scottie react?" I said.

"Cool as a cucumber, as always. Except for his eyes. They were on fire." I envied Scott McBride. She spoke about him with a passion that any lover would like to be spoken about by his beloved.

241

"After you got over the shock of seeing Scottie, what happened then?" I said.

She made a face as if to say she wasn't yet ready to move on. "Let's go for a ride, he said. I told him I couldn't. People would talk. When did that ever bother you before, he said. I told him I wasn't married before, or the head of an insurance office. Fine, he said, then I'll meet you at Hidden Quarry in a half hour. And he left."

"And you did what?"

She shrugged as if there was never any doubt. "I met him at Hidden Quarry within the half hour."

"What time was that, do you remember?"

"Sometime between one and two. I don't remember exactly."

"What happened then?" I felt it necessary to ask.

Her smile was bittersweet. "The same thing that always happened when we went to Hidden Quarry. We made love. Wild, crazy, wonderful love. It was always like that with us. We couldn't wait for it to begin. We cried when it was over."

I didn't remind her that "always like that" was at most a week twenty years ago. I didn't remind her because I had my own cherished myths that I kept in a nutshell in a corner of my mind. Myths that rang like truths over time.

"So I take it not much was said your first few minutes there?" I said.

"Hardly a word. Until afterwards." She bit her lip to keep from crying. "Then he told me he loved me. That he'd always loved me. That he'd never loved anyone else."

I believed her. I also believed Sean Ragan who had as much as said that Scott McBride had never loved anyone in his life. If truth and beauty were in the eyes of the beholder, then so was love.

"Then what happened?" I said.

"I left. I told Scottie I had to get back to work, or someone might put two and two together, if they hadn't already."

"Which was what time?"

"I don't know when I left Hidden Quarry. I got back into the office about three-thirty or so. I stayed there until a little after five, then went home. A few minutes after that Butch came home. That's when the shit hit the fan."

"What was Scottie doing when you left?"

"Sitting on a rock, looking down into the quarry." Her eyes were there with him. "We'd agreed that if I could get away that evening, I'd meet him at the park and we'd do it all over again. If not, I'd meet him at Hidden Quarry at noon on Tuesday." She smiled at her own daring. "I know it was wrong, that there was no future in it. But that didn't change anything."

243

"Maybe that was its attraction," I said. "That there was no future to it. Maybe that's always been the attraction."

"Maybe," she said, not really wanting to talk about it.

"So then when you got home, you and Butch had a fight, and he beat you up."

"He didn't exactly beat me up," she said. "He grabbed me by the shoulders and shook me." She touched the bruises on her shoulders. "Which is where I got these. Then he slapped me." She touched her left cheek. "Which is where I got this."

"If that's not getting beat up, then what do you call it?" I said.

"He didn't hit me hard, or with his fist," she said. "It's just that Butch is so strong, that he sometimes doesn't realize his own strength." She seemed to both fear and admire him for that.

"All the more reason for him not to do it," I said.

"Perhaps," she said, not sure that she agreed with me.

"What started the fight anyway?" I said.

"Butch called me a whore. That's what started it. He knew where I'd been and what I'd been doing. He even knew the kind of car that Scottie was driving. But he didn't know it was Scottie, not until you and Clarkie came to the house the next day."

"How could he have known that unless somebody told him?"

"He couldn't have," she said.

"Do you have any idea who might have told him?"

"It could have been anyone in the insurance office," she said. "I don't want to speculate."

"Even your mother?"

She didn't answer. She seemed to be wondering that herself.

"Then let me ask you this question," I said. "Who took all your stuff, including Scottie's poster, down from your bedroom walls?"

"Mom did. She took it down and put it in mothballs under my bed." Her look said she was still angry about it.

"Did she say why?"

"No. She didn't say why. Only that in time I would understand."

"Have you understood?"

"Not yet I haven't. But there are a lot of things about my mother that I don't yet understand."

"Unlike your father?"

"Yes," she said without enthusiasm. "Unlike Dad, who is perfectly clear to me."

I rose and took the last Old Style from the refrigerator, divided it evenly between us, and sat back down at the table again.

"I really should be going," she said, making

245

no move in that direction. "Butch is going to be pissed enough the way it is."

"Just a few more questions."

"Okay," she said, as she took a drink of beer. "Just a few more."

Again I looked into her green eyes. In them I saw what Clarkie must have seen way back in seventh grade. Cheryl Loveless wouldn't be hard to love, if you once let yourself.

"This has to do with twenty years ago," I said. "The day you, Clarkie, Sean Ragan, and Scottie were all supposed to go swimming together out at Hidden Quarry."

She blushed. With her fair skin, she was a natural. "The day we were all supposed to go *skinny-dipping* together," she corrected me. "How could I ever forget that?"

How could Clarkie and Sean Ragan have forgotten that, unless out of respect for her? "I just wondered why you never showed up?" I said.

She frowned. It made her look hard. I liked her better when she smiled. "You can thank Butch for that. He was there at my house waiting for me when I came home on Friday night. We had a fight, our first real one, and he hit me in the face with his fist. It turned out that he broke my cheekbone, but I didn't find that out until about a week later."

"Why was he there waiting for you? I

thought he was supposed to be in camp somewhere."

"He was. In wrestling camp until Sunday."
She seemed as puzzled by Butch's sudden
appearance as I was. "I don't know what he
was doing there."

"You never asked him?"

"I never thought to, since I was in the
wrong."

I didn't argue with her. Right and wrong,
like love, left a lot of room for interpretation.
"What happened then?" I said.

"I went up to my room and stayed there for
the better part of the next two days," she said.
"When I came down again, the carnival had
left town and taken Scottie with it."

She fought back the tears as long as she
could, then let them have their way. I got up
and went into the bathroom, grabbed a box
of Kleenex off the top of the stool, grabbed the
kitchen wastebasket on my way back into the
kitchen, and sat back down at the table.

She nodded her thanks and then proceeded
to fill the wastebasket with Kleenex. "We have
more wastebaskets," I said. "So don't worry
about it."

She was laughing and crying as she said, "I
have a lot of crying to catch up on."

"I know you do."

But her look said I couldn't possibly know.

"Did you ever see Scottie again?" I asked when she was ready to answer.

"No. I got a couple letters from him when he was in Vietnam, then that racing poster several years later, which was after Butch and I were married. Then another letter about three years ago, just after he'd gotten off drugs and started his comeback. He said for me not to be surprised if he showed up at my door someday."

"Which also prompted a fight between you and Butch, if Clarkie told me right."

"He's right. It did," she said. "It seems that every fight that Butch and I have ever had has been over Scottie."

"Sorry to keep asking," I said, "but how did Butch know about the letter? Was he there at home when it came?"

"No. It was put in my parents' box at the post office. Mom brought it to me at work."

"Summer or winter?"

"Summer, I think. Why?"

"I just wondered." But what I wondered, I wasn't sure. Maybe my brain knew something it wasn't telling me. "If your mother brought it to you at work, then how did Butch find out about it?"

She thought a moment, then shrugged her shoulders. "I don't know. Unless Mom told him."

248

"Why would she do that?"

Cheryl's face hardened. "Why wouldn't she do that, if she would tell him that we went out to Hidden Quarry together?"

"She didn't tell him that you and Scottie went out to Hidden Quarry together," I said in Dorothy Sims' defense. "Whoever told him didn't mention Scottie's name."

She lost some of her anger. "That's right. They didn't. But it still could have been Mom," she said.

I nodded in agreement, although, unless it was for spite, I didn't see the sense in it, or what Dorothy stood to gain. "One last thing, Cheryl. The black Chevy pickup that you were driving the week Butch was in wrestling camp, did it belong to him?"

"Yes. It did belong to him," she said with regret.

"Do you know what happened to it from the time you parked it Friday night until you left Sunday to go to the park?"

"No," she said, "I don't. But I would assume that Butch took it."

"But you don't know that for sure?"

"No. I don't know that for sure. Why?"

"Never mind. I'll need to talk to Butch about that."

"Now?" Her look said I must be crazy.

"Can you think of a better time?"

249

"Then I want to be there. I want to hear what he has to say."

I didn't like the idea. Butch had a violent streak in him, and there was no telling what he might do once I confronted him. Besides that, his and Cheryl's anger seemed to feed off the other's, almost seemed to require the other's to survive. It would be a lot simpler and perhaps safer if I went alone.

"I'd rather you stayed here," I said.

"I don't care what you'd rather I do," she said. "I'd already be there now if it weren't for you."

I thought it over and didn't see how I could keep her here. "Then let me handle it if you have to be there. Be seen and not heard."

Her tight-lipped silence said I should prepare for the worst.

17

"Where in the hell have you been?" was the first thing Butch Loveless had to say. "I just called your mom, and she said you should have been home two hours ago." Already we were off to a good start.

We had borrowed Ruth's Volkswagen, since Jessie was still at the Marathon and I didn't want to walk because of the lateness of the hour. On our way past the Sims' house, I saw Hayden Sims still outside watering his roses. On our way past the Samuels' house, I saw no one.

Butch Loveless had met us at the door. He wore grey sweat pants, a grey half-shirt that said "Oakalla Wrestling" on it, and a scowl nearly as big as Butch himself.

"I've been talking to Garth," Cheryl said, taking my hand and leading me past Butch into the house. "And it's time you talked to him, too."

"What about?" Butch wasn't in the mood to talk to anyone, especially me.

"A lot of things, Butch," she said.

Butch looked at Cheryl, then at me. Then he turned and walked past us into the living room. We followed him in there where Cheryl sat beside him on the couch, and I sat on a bean-bag in front of the hearth. A newspaper lay on the floor beside me. Last winter's ashes lay in the fireplace. Dust lay in windrows along the edges of the room.

"I'll get right to the point, Butch," I said. "I saw you out at Hidden Quarry today. You appeared to be looking for something."

His mouth twisted as he started to deny it, then changed his mind. "Okay, I'll admit I was there. There's no crime in that. And I'll admit I was looking for something. My billfold. I must have lost it when I went swimming there last weekend."

"You must have lost it when you were out there this Monday afternoon," I said.

"I don't have to listen to this crap all over again. Once is enough." He started to rise from the couch. Cheryl pulled him back down again. She didn't do it gently either.

"For once in your life, be a man," she said.

"Or don't you know how to except around women and children?"

Butch shook loose from her and drew back his hand as if to hit her.

"Go ahead," she said defiantly. "But this time I've got a witness. And you can bet your happy home that I'll use him."

"If he's still around when you need him," Butch threatened.

I didn't fear his threat. Butch Loveless, I was starting to believe, was a classic schoolyard bully, who had never grown up. He would push you as far as you'd let him, but once you called his bluff, he'd have to stop to think about it. Truly dog-dirty mean meant that you never stopped to think about it. You broke whatever was necessary and then worried about it later. That didn't mean that Butch Loveless wasn't dangerous. But I'd be safe as long as I didn't turn my back to him.

"Butch," I said, still needing answers and not wanting him to clam up on me. "I'm not accusing you of anything. Neither is Cheryl. But if you were out at Hidden Quarry on Monday afternoon, it doesn't do either one of us any good for you to deny it."

"Why doesn't it?" he said. "If I admit I was there, then you're going to try to pin golden boy's murder on me."

"That's what he's always called Scottie," Cheryl explained. "Golden boy."

253

"And the name fits, too," Butch said. "Golden boy can do no wrong. Unlike the rest of us."

They exchanged looks. Each wanted reassurance from the other, but neither one was willing to offer it.

Then I said, "I'm not trying to pin anything on you, Butch. You're doing a good enough job of that yourself. What I'm trying to do, is get to the truth of the matter."

"Which is that I killed golden boy," he answered.

"At least have the decency to call him by his real name," Cheryl said.

"Cheryl, take a hike," I said. "Either that or shut up. I can't talk to Butch and you both."

"I'll be quiet," she promised, then buttoned her lip to show me how sincere she was.

I had to smile at her. I liked Cheryl Loveless.

"Nobody's out to get you, Butch," I said. "But if you don't talk to me, then you'll have to talk to somebody else. And he might not like your answers anymore than I do."

Butch didn't say anything. I could tell that he was debating on whether to call my bluff or not. Except it wasn't a bluff, and he was smart enough to know that.

"What's in it for me?" he said. "Tell me that. And don't give me any crap about it being the right thing to do. I've done the right thing all of my life and it's never gotten me anywhere."

He looked at Cheryl, who looked away. This was his answer to her infidelity, aimed directly at her heart. If I were to judge by her reaction, he'd scored a bullseye.

"What's in it for you, is no jail time, if you're lucky. But the way you're going, I can't even promise that."

That sobered him. "Jail time for what?" he said, not sure he believed me.

"Obstructing justice. Withholding evidence. Both are felonies in this state. You could do time, Butch, particularly if Scott McBride's murderer gets away because of you." All of which was true, but not likely to happen, unless Butch was somehow directly involved with Scott McBride's death.

He looked at Cheryl to get her opinion. Bless her heart, she sided with me.

"Okay," he said, still not sure he was doing the right thing. "Say I was out at Hidden Quarry Monday afternoon, that doesn't mean I saw or did anything."

"It doesn't mean you didn't either. Not unless you tell me why you went out there and what you did once you got there."

While he sat there on the couch debating with himself, I glanced over at Cheryl. But her eyes were on Butch, eyes of love it seemed. I thought of Clarkie and began to see what he had been going through all these years.

"I got a phone call," he said. "In my office at

school. The guy on the other end said that he'd seen Cheryl out at Hidden Quarry with a guy in a silver Firebird. And if I hurried, they might still be there."

"What time was that?"

"Sometime between four and four-thirty Monday afternoon. I'd finished lifting at four, like I do every day, and taken a shower. I'd just gotten out of the shower when the phone rang."

"*Guy*, you said. Are you sure that the person who called you was a man?" I asked.

"Pretty sure. He whispered, so it was hard to hear him. But he sounded like a man to me."

I'd think about that later. "Were you the only one in the school at the time? Or did somebody else take the call and relay it to you?"

"The call came directly to me," he said. "The school closes down completely in July, so the principals and superintendent can take their vacations then. The only one in the school is the janitor, and he usually leaves at four."

"Is the school locked?" I said.

He shrugged. "Sometimes it is. Sometimes it isn't. It all depends on who's in there, and if they remembered to lock up or not." He looked sheepish. "Me, I'm not good about it. I never remember to lock anything, unless someone reminds me."

"It's true," Cheryl said. "He even leaves his keys in the ignition half the time."

"So anybody could have come into the school to see if you were there, and then called you from there, if he wanted?" I said.

"He could have," Butch said. "I don't think he did, but he could have."

"Why don't you think he did?"

"I just don't think he did," he said, as if that were all that mattered.

"After you got the phone call, did you go out to Hidden Quarry right away?" I said.

"As fast as I could get out there. But when I got there, no one was around. I saw the Firebird sitting there, and somebody's clothes, but no Cheryl and no golden boy, as it turned out."

"How long did you stay?"

"A few minutes. Long enough to convince myself that there was no point in staying any longer."

"Is that when you lost your billfold?"

He gave me a helpless look. "That's when I think I lost it. All I know is, I didn't have it after that."

"When did you discover it was missing?"

"The next morning when I went to buy some gas at the Marathon. I figured I must

257

have lost it crawling up and down those rocks out there."

"While looking for what?"

"Cheryl. Like I said before. I figured she might have been hiding from me."

I wondered if the same kids who had found Scott McBride's body had also found Butch's wallet. If so, it would probably turn up eventually. "You say you saw some clothes and the Firebird," I said. "But you never saw Scott McBride?"

"No. I never saw him. In the water or out of it."

"By in the water, you mean swimming, I take it?"

"What else would I mean?" he said. Then he realized what I meant. "Oh, you mean floating face down." He turned to grin at Cheryl. "No. I never had that pleasure."

Cheryl rose and left the room without a word. A moment later the kitchen light went on. A moment after that I heard her sob. So did Butch, but he made no move in her direction.

"She'll get over it," he said. "She always does."

I got up and walked to the front door for a breath of fresh air. Butch Loveless still sat on the couch when I returned to the room.

"I was hoping you'd left," he said.

I sat back down on the hearth. It hadn't

softened any in my absence. "I still need to talk to you about Paul Samuel," I said.

"Paul Samuel?" Butch seemed genuinely puzzled. "Who's he?"

"A boy who lived just down the street from here. He disappeared twenty years ago and hasn't been seen since."

"I remember him now," Butch said. "Skinny kid. Big nose and ears. I used to see him riding his bike around town. Him and Eddie Vincent, I think it was." He gave me a curious look. "But what does that have to do with me?"

Cheryl returned from the kitchen, carrying a glass of wine, and sat cross-legged on the floor at Butch's feet. He reached down and playfully tousled her hair. Apparently all was forgiven.

"Paul Samuel," I said to Butch. "Do you remember the day he disappeared?"

If he did, it didn't register. "Vaguely," he said. "But if I remember right, I was out of town when it happened."

"No, you were here, remember?" Cheryl said, turning to look up at him. "You'd come home early from wrestling camp."

Butch looked as if he'd just as soon forget. "I remember that night," he said. "Too well. It was probably the worst night of my life."

"What happened?" I said.

259

He looked away. "I don't want to talk about it."

"It's okay," Cheryl said. "Garth already knows some of what happened."

"Then he knows why I don't want to talk about it."

"I don't care what happened between you and Cheryl," I said. I did, but that was beside the point. "I'm more interested in what happened before and after, and why you came home from camp early."

"Cheryl can tell you why I came home early," he said. "Somebody called me at wrestling camp and told me that she was fooling around with some carny. So as soon as camp was over that day, I hitched a ride home."

"Who's the one who called you?"

"I don't remember," he said. "Probably one of my buddies here in town. I told them to keep an eye on Cheryl while I was gone."

"And after the fight with Cheryl, what did you do then?"

"I don't remember," he said. "Went home, I guess. I was pretty shook up about the whole thing."

"Did you drive your pickup home?"

"I must have," he said. "The way I felt, I wouldn't have left it there." Then he thought about it some more. "I take that back. I didn't drive it home because then Cheryl's dad, who was my coach, would have known I'd cut out

260

of wrestling camp. So I left it there, hoping that Cheryl wouldn't tell him what happened."

"Did you tell him what happened?" I asked Cheryl.

"No. I never did."

"Didn't he ask?"

"No. Not that I recall."

"Did anybody in your family ask?"

Cheryl smiled at my frustration. "Mom, I think, said something about it, but I told her that I was practicing a cheer and hit my face on a chair."

"And she bought it?"

Cheryl was no longer smiling. "Why wouldn't she? She's bought a lot worse in her lifetime."

I would have asked for an explanation, but it was already two A.M. "But Paul Samuel *was* your next door neighbor then?" I said to Cheryl.

"Yes. Paul was my next door neighbor."

I looked up at Butch, who yawned, looking bored now that he was no longer the center of attention. "What did you do after you went home that night?" I asked him.

"Laid low, hoping no one would see me."

"And the next day?"

"The same thing. I didn't leave the house until Sunday afternoon, when I would have been home anyway."

261

That made sense to me. Whether it was true or not, I didn't know. "Did you go out looking for Scott McBride a couple weeks after that?" I said.

"Why would I do that?" he said, apparently puzzled by my question. "I didn't even know the guy's name at the time. What would be the point in going out looking for him?"

"To settle a score."

"I didn't know at the time how big the score was," he said. "If I had, then name or no name, you can bet I would have gone out looking for him."

"And when you found him?"

Butch smiled at me. It wasn't a pleasant smile. "You can figure that out."

A couple minutes later Cheryl walked out to the Volkswagen with me. Butch stayed on the couch. I didn't remember either one of us saying goodbye.

"Thanks for all your help," I said to Cheryl. "I appreciate it."

She was looking at Butch who by then stood at the front door looking at us. "He's not a bad person really," she said. "A little moody at times, but then who isn't? I know I have my faults, too."

"Your faults don't leave other people black-and-blue."

"Sometimes they do," she said. "On the inside."

I didn't argue with her. I got in the Volkswagen and started it. "Hang loose," I said. "I might need to talk to you again."

"I plan to. And say hello to Clarkie for me the next time you see him."

"He really cares for you. You know that, don't you?" For Clarkie's sake, I felt I had to tell her.

"I know that. And I really care for him. As a friend," she emphasized.

"No bells?" I said.

"No bells."

"We can't all be lovers, I guess."

"Lovers are a dime a dozen. Friends, real friends like Clarkie, are hard to come by. I just wish," she glanced at Butch who still stood in the doorway, "that he was a little more like Clarkie."

"Or that Clarkie was a little more like Butch?"

"That too," she said. Then she kissed me on the cheek. "I'd better go."

"Me too."

I put the Volkswagen in gear and started home. On the way I remembered the question that I had forgotten to ask her. When I was chasing her down the alley, why was she running and what was she running from?

263

18

I was sitting up in bed with my back resting against the headboard. I knew it was morning because the street light on Fair Haven Road had just shut off and Ruth had just turned on the vacuum cleaner. I itched. I didn't know in how many places, but enough to keep me out of bushes and hedges for the rest of my life.

Rising, I went to my east window and stared outside. Though the sun wasn't yet up, the morning was taking shape in various shades of blues, browns, grays, and greens. Already my neighbor was mowing his lawn, trying to beat the heat. I sighed. As a kid and for most of my life, Saturday had always been my favorite day of the week. But not lately.

On my way downstairs, I waved at Ruth who was vacuuming her way down the hall with a vengeance. But she ignored me. Ruth didn't like distractions in any form, particularly on Saturday morning.

Downstairs, I called Fillmore Cavanaugh and brought him up to date on what I knew. I had gotten him out of bed, but he didn't seem to mind.

"Anything else I should know?" he said.

"No. That's about it for now."

"What do you have planned for today?" The question seemed innocent enough, but I thought I detected a note of concern.

"I don't have a plan," I said. "But if I don't find our killer today, I don't think I will."

"Why not?"

I didn't have an answer for him, only a gut-feeling. "Because after today, Jupiter no longer aligns with Mars."

"Whatever you say, Garth." He hung up on me.

"What *are* your plans for the day?" Ruth had turned off the vacuum cleaner and come downstairs.

"I don't know, Ruth. I really don't."

"You're not going to the parade?"

"I don't know that even. We'll see how things work out."

The Homecoming parade would start at eleven at the Lutheran Home, wind its way east along Jackson Street to Park Street, and end up at the park where that afternoon there would be a flea market along with the carnival, then a fish fry, and a variety show that evening. Bill Nicewander, Oakalla's long-time jeweler and his wife, Mary Catherine were the grand marshals this year, and Ruth and I were supposed to be in the parade, representing the *Oakalla Reporter*.

"Did you want to go?" I asked.

She did, but wouldn't admit it. "Not without you, I'm not. I'd look stupid, riding in that car by myself."

"Or pushing it, if the car turns out to be Jessie."

"I'd rather ride in a hearse."

I smiled. We both knew she wasn't kidding.

While Ruth put on a pot of coffee, I poured us each a glass of orange juice and set the milk and Cheerios out. Saturday mornings could either be leisurely or busy, depending on our mood. But this one had no shape to it.

"What are your plans for the day?" I asked Ruth as I sat down at the table.

"I plan on cleaning the house."

"After that?"

"I don't have any."

I drank my orange juice, then poured some

Cheerios into a bowl and added milk and sugar. Then I handed the box of Cheerios to Ruth, who set it on the counter. She ate cold cereal about once a year, which was about as often as I ate hot cereal. Apparently this wasn't the day.

"Well, if you don't have any plans, we'll try to make the parade, then," I said for something to say.

She stared at me for the longest time. Then she said, "You're up to something. What is it?"

"I thought I might go talk to Rupert," I said. "I know he wasn't sheriff yet, but still he was around here when Paul Samuel disappeared, so maybe he knows something I don't."

She turned down the fire under the coffee, which had started to perk, and sat down at the table. "It's about time. That's all I can say."

"Yeah," I agreed. "It's about time."

Rupert and Elvira Roberts lived in the triangle between the junction of Ferry Street and Colburn Road in the southeast corner of town. I had passed their small white frame house almost every day that week on my way to Hidden Quarry. I had passed their garden, their ragged yard, which looked about as brown and dead as mine, their small white one-car garage, and their windbreak of stately white pines that grew along the west side of

267

their property and gave them shade all afternoon long.

I had passed as if with blinders on, thinking that if I didn't look, then I wouldn't have to see Rupert and feel guilty for not stopping by. But it hadn't worked because even though I didn't see him, I still felt guilty anyway.

"They say you're supposed to do that in the evening so that the ground has all night to soak it up."

Rupert was outside watering his garden. He looked about as contented as a man can look.

"Is that what they say?" He spat a stream of tobacco juice in the general direction of the garden.

He switched the hose to his left hand and offered me his right hand. I shook it. It was good to feel its bone-hard grip again.

"How are you, Garth?" he asked.

"Not bad. How are you?"

He switched the hose back to his right hand, then patted his stomach. "Not bad. Except I'm afraid I'm putting on a little weight."

It didn't look to me as if he'd put on any weight. He looked as lean and lanky as ever. And as strong and wise. He looked even better than the last time I'd seen him—tanner and fitter. Retirement must have agreed with him.

"How's your garden doing?" I asked. From where I stood, I could see tomatoes, sweet corn, cucumbers, and yellow squash. In contrast to his yard, his garden was thick, green and healthy looking.

"It was doing a lot better until the drought hit. We had lettuce early on, and all the green beans we wanted. But now I have to water it twice a day just to keep it going."

I glanced up at a cloudless sky. "Maybe it'll rain soon."

"Do you suppose?" He didn't believe it any more than I did.

We didn't talk for a while. He was content to water his garden, and I was content to watch him. I usually felt content in his presence, calm and secure, the way I had felt when following my father around his dairy. As always, I was on his time, whenever I was around him, and except on rare occasions, always his subordinate. But I was willing to give him that in exchange for his company.

"I hear you're working on the Samuel boy case," he said.

"How did you hear that?" I asked, though I had a good guess.

"Ruth called me a couple of days ago to pump my brain. But I had to tell her that I couldn't add much beyond what you already knew."

I felt myself sag. If Rupert couldn't help me, I was at a dead end.

"Since then, though," he continued, "I've had a little time to think about it. There *was* a woman who claimed that early that morning on the day that Paul Samuel disappeared, she talked to a boy who she said was Paul Samuel. No one paid much attention to her because she was senile and blind as a bat. Besides, she lived in the opposite direction of the park where Paul Samuel was supposed to be headed. She could have been talking to a fire hydrant for all anyone knew."

"Who was it?" I felt my hope return.

"Nellie Pyle, but she's dead now."

"Edna Pyle's mother?"

"The same. They made quite a pair in their day."

"Then maybe I should talk to Edna," I said, feeling less hopeful. "I need to see her about something else anyway."

I stood for a moment longer, listening to the water spatter the sweet corn, smelling the early morning smells of mint and clover that would evaporate in the heat of the day. I was reluctant to leave, reluctant to be on my own again.

"There is one thing I should mention," Rupert said. "My brother, William, who, as you know, was the newspaper publisher here in town at the time, put up a five thousand dollar reward for the person who found Paul

Samuel. It's been in the bank collecting interest all these years. With it, you might be able to buy that new press you've always wanted."

Not on your life, I thought to myself. Outloud I said, "I don't want it. Not for this. But I'll tell you what you can do with it if I do find Paul Samuel. You can give it to the Town Board in exchange for their written promise not to pave the alley behind my house. At least not in my lifetime."

He spat at a flying grasshopper that had landed at his feet. "That's not much of a trade," he said, watching the grasshopper fly away. "I don't think they've got the plans or the money to pave that alley anyway."

"Still, I don't want to take any chances."

"Suit yourself," he said. "The money's there for the taking. Or it will be until January, when it goes back into my brother's estate."

"Who gets it then?"

He spat in disgust. "My sister-in-law."

"Well, maybe she needs it."

"Yeah, like we all need another depression."

I glanced at the sun that had just cleared the trees in the park. Already I could feel its heat. "I'd better go," I said. "The morning's getting away from me."

I had meant to ask him how he liked his retirement, and if he missed being sheriff at all. But that seemed pointless now. Whatever regrets he had, had to be small ones. And whatever I might say to him, about just how much I missed him, and how I felt that Oakalla was tearing apart at the seams without him on the job, would serve no purpose except perhaps to make him feel bad. Like it or not, I was on my own.

He offered his hand again and I shook it again. "Don't be a stranger," he said.

"I won't," I said, and meant it.

Edna Pyle was a small nervous woman with thin grey hair and a bark like a toy terrier, who lived in a two-story, dark-red brick house just south of the school. I'd been talking to her for the past couple minutes, but hadn't learned very much. She was trimming the grass around her house, the shears keeping time to the click of her false teeth.

"You say your mother spoke to Paul Samuel, but no one believed her?" I said.

Her shears went even faster than before, as grass flew in all directions. "I didn't say that. You did. But that's what happened."

"What was your mother doing at the time?"

"Pulling weeds from between the cracks in the sidewalk. If there was anything Mother hated, it was weeds. Weeds and whiskey—to her they were the scourge of man. To me, *men* are the scourge of man." The shears brushed the leg of my jeans. I backed up a step.

"How did your mother know it was Paul Samuel?"

"She didn't. Mother couldn't even see to tie her shoes. Cataracts. But she recognized his voice. She'd talked to him before when he was in the neighborhood. She talked to him regular, she said. He was one of the few people around town, young, old, or otherwise, who would take the time to talk to her."

I put that into the bag of facts that I had on Paul Samuel, even though I doubted that it would do either Paul or me any good.

"Anyway," Edna Pyle continued, "Mother put two and two together and came up with Paul Samuel."

"What did Paul say to her?"

She momentarily stopped trimming to glance sharply at me. "So now it's Paul Samuel she saw when for the past twenty years it's been nobody."

"I wasn't here twenty years ago."

"You don't look like a teenager to me."

"I mean I didn't live in Oakalla."

"Pity. It'd saved Mother a lot of grief." She resumed trimming. "To answer your question, Paul Samuel hardly said a word to her. He was crying, she said. He'd tried to take the corner too fast on his bicycle and hit that tree over there." She pointed with her shears to show me the tree. "Mother went over to him and tried to help him out, but he'd have none of it. So she brushed him off as best she could and sent him on his way."

"Was he still riding his bicycle when he left here?"

"I don't recall that Mother ever said." She rested the trimming shears on her knee. I felt safer with them there. "You see, most people thought Mother was senile because she didn't see well and would end up talking to things like stop signs and juniper trees. Mother did love to talk, that's true. But until the very end her mind was as sharp as a darning needle, so when she told me something she *heard*, I knew it was gospel."

"Did she say which way Paul Samuel went from here?"

She waved her hand for me to be quiet. She was thinking and needed total concentration. "Now that I think about it, Mother did say something about the bicycle. She asked me a couple days later what had happened to it. I told her I didn't know, that I'd never seen it to begin with."

"So it's possible that Paul Samuel left here on foot?"

If so, then that seemed to confirm Dick Samuel's story that he had seen Paul walking along Colburn Road. But how had Paul's bicycle gotten out to Hidden Quarry in Butch

274

Loveless' pickup, unless someone picked it up along the way? If that were so, then someone had to be on Paul's trail from the moment he left home. Which left one final question: Why was Paul followed and why was he killed?

"It's possible he left here on foot," she said. "Otherwise, why would Mother ask about the bike?" She thought some more, then said, "East. She thought Paul Samuel went east from here."

Which, depending on his next turn, could take him either to the park or out Colburn Road to Hidden Quarry, or any place in between. But I was betting on Hidden Quarry.

"One other question, Edna, about another matter. What time did Butch Loveless drive by here last Monday?"

"Four-thirty. Just like I told that state trooper. I was watching Oprah and had just stepped outside to get my evening newspaper during the station break when here he came hell bent for election down the street." She clicked her tongue in amazement. "It's a wonder he ever made that corner there. He was on two wheels the whole way around it."

"Headed east?"

"East, then south on Colburn Road. I could hear him all the way out of town." She was still angry about it. "I missed five minutes of Oprah because of him."

I nodded sympathetically. She'd told me what I'd wanted to know, which was that Butch Loveless had been telling the truth—at least as far as I could tell. What he had done once he arrived at Hidden Quarry still remained in doubt.

"Thanks, Edna. You've been more help than you know."

She seemed neither pleased nor displeased. She shrugged and went back to work.

19

I was the first customer at the door at the First Farmers bank that Saturday morning. Because of the Homecoming parade and the bank's float in it, only one teller was working. The rest were probably riding on the float.

There was only one other person besides the teller in the bank that I could see, and that was the person I'd come to see. Eddie Vincent sat inside his glass office with his head down, reading a magazine. Or looking at the pictures, since what I saw in the magazine was mostly skin, and little else.

"Morning, Eddie," I said, surprising him. "I thought you might be out getting ready to ride in the parade."

Eddie looked up at me. His expression went from startled to embarrassed, as he slid the magazine from his desk onto his lap, and then when it wouldn't stay on his lap, onto the floor. Eddie's right arm was still in a sling and his pink cheeks were even pinker than usual. But their color went well with his light blue suit and platinum-blond hair.

"No, Garth," Eddie said, regaining some of his composure. "After what happened to Paul, I'm not real big on Homecoming."

"What did happen to Paul that day, Eddie? You've never told me."

He squirmed, looking trapped. "I don't know what you're talking about, Garth. I don't know what happened to Paul that day."

"You know more than you've told me, Eddie. A lot more. And I'd rather hear it from you than have you hear it from me."

I noticed that the teller was giving us a curious look. I turned, closed the door to Eddie's office, then pulled one of his big blue comfortable chairs up to his desk. But unlike the first time I talked to him, I didn't feel at all sleepy.

"What do you know?" Eddie said, not yet ready to commit himself.

I stared at him, biding my time. I'd had a chance to think on my way from Edna Pyle's to the bank. Mainly what I thought about were fifty dollars, a *Playboy* magazine, a scream in the night, a white balloon, and a Trojan condom.

"As I said, Eddie, I'd rather it came from you."

"You're bluffing, Garth," he said, not at all sure that I was. "If you aren't, you'd have already showed me your cards."

I let him squirm for a while longer. Then I said, "It's this way, Eddie. You and Paul were on your way to the carnival, but it wasn't to ride the rides. You were on your way to see Sally Wampler and maybe buy yourselves some manhood. It didn't matter that you had just been grounded, or that both you and Paul had lied about what you were up to, you were determined to get yourselves laid that day." I stared at him. He had to look away. "Am I right so far, Eddie?"

He didn't answer. He would have bolted from there rather than hear the rest of what I had to say, but with the lobby filling up with customers, he had nowhere to go.

"Except it didn't quite work out the way you planned," I said. "In the first place, Paul forgot his wallet and had to go back after it. Then something happened there at his home to completely upset him, so much so that he forgot about his wallet, and left on the run without it. Or on the ride, I should say, since at that time he was still on his bicycle."

Eddie's face was as pale as his hair. He looked green around the gills, as if he might vomit at any moment. I wished then that I'd brought a paper bag along.

"Are you going to be okay?" I asked.

He nodded, but not very convincingly.

"Should I go on?"

He nodded his consent. If for nothing else, I had to admire him for that. A lot of people would have done what Eddie felt like doing, which was to cut and run.

"So when he returned to your house, Paul didn't even stop. Or if he did, it was a flying stop to say that he wasn't going to the park with you after all." I smiled at him, trying to look reassuring. "Okay, Eddie, why don't you take it from there?"

"I can't!" His voice was hoarse with emotion, barely a whisper.

"You can, Eddie. If I can face Paul Samuel, so can you."

"But you weren't his best friend," Eddie pleaded, as tears came into his eyes. "You didn't betray him like I did."

"By going to the park without him?"

"No. By not going with him, wherever he went."

"He went to his death, Eddie. I don't think anyone would expect you to follow him there."

"You don't know that!" he yelled so loudly that a couple of the bank's customers looked our way.

"I do know that, Eddie. So do you. It's what you've been hiding from for the past twenty years."

"No!" He cried out. Then he lowered his head and buried his face in his sling.

I got up and closed the curtain around Eddie's glass cage. I owed him his dignity at least, if there was any of it left after I got done with him. Then I locked his office door to make sure no one came in. Let the people in the lobby think what they would. Whatever they thought, they wouldn't come within miles of the truth.

"Sorry, Garth," Eddie said, raising his head to look at me. Then he took a white handkerchief from his hip pocket and blew his nose. "I don't usually lose it like that, especially with people around."

"You don't usually come face to face with a ghost," I said. "That'll unnerve anybody."

"You seem to be handling it well."

"My time is yet to come." When I really and truly come face to face with Paul Samuel, which finally looked as if it were going to happen.

Eddie took a deep breath and tried to compose himself. But I knew he would be walking a tightrope from here on.

"You're right about everything, Garth," he began. "Paul did forget his wallet, and he did go back home after it. He wasn't gone very long when here he came racing up the alley on his bicycle. I practically had to jump in front of him to get him to stop. 'Leave me alone' he said when I asked him what was wrong. 'Just leave me alone.'"

Eddie's phone rang. He answered it, then said in his best banker voice, "I'm fine. And Marcie? Please hold all of my calls until Mr. Ryland leaves."

As he hung up the phone, I noticed that his hand was trembling. We took a short break while he found the will to go on.

"I should have stopped him right there," Eddie continued, "and made him tell me what was wrong. But I was more interested in getting to the park and getting laid than in any problems Paul might be having."

I wanted to tell him that at that time in my life, I would have been more interested in getting laid than in hearing any problems Paul Samuel might be having. But I didn't.

"So when Paul wouldn't tell me what was wrong, and I got tired of holding him there by his handlebars, I let go and he rode off. South, if I remember right. Toward the school."

"Until he wrecked at Edna Pyle's corner," I said.

"How do you know that?"

"Never mind. I just do."

Eddie's eyes searched the grey curtains that covered the glass walls. What he saw there gave him no consolation. "You know the rest of it," he said. "I went on to the park alone, where, as the saying goes, Sally Wampler and I got it on."

"Then you came home and got sick?"

"Sicker than a sonofabitch," he said. "I don't know if it was from guilt, or fear, or the corndog I ate at the park, but I couldn't keep anything down for two days. I was so sick I didn't even realize Paul was missing until my mother told me sometime that next week. Then I was really sick."

"You can't blame yourself, Eddie."

"I do, though, Garth. That summer was nothing but a waste from beginning to end. It seems like every plan that Paul and I made fell through. And if we weren't mad at each other about that, we were fighting about something else."

"Some summers are like that," I said, remembering one in particular from my own boyhood.

"Not all summers, though," Eddie said, giving me his first smile of the day. "The summer before that was one of those once-in-a-lifetime summers. You know the kind. Magical. When you're up with the sun and out way after dark, and never seem to run out of things to do." Then a shadow crossed his face and stayed there. "Remember the line from the song, *Puff the Magic Dragon*? 'A dragon lives forever, but not so little boys.' Whenever I hear that song, I think of Paul and me."

"That was a long time ago, Eddie," I said. "There's still a long time to go."

"I hear you," he said. "I'm not sure I believe you."

I shrugged. I wasn't sure I believed me either.

"Especially when one of us is impotent," he said.

It was hard for me to look at him. If ever I had seen anyone totally disarmed and at my mercy, it was Eddie Vincent. "I take it you're not talking about me," I said.

"You take it right."

Then I thought I understood something that had been puzzling me. Before, I had known whom. I just hadn't known why.

"Sally Wampler," I said. "Then it was you who tried to break into her trailer the other night?"

He raised his right arm, the one in the sling, the one he hadn't hurt playing tennis. "It was me," he said.

"Why did you do it?" I said. "Was it to get even for Paul?"

284

"No, Garth. It wasn't like that at all."

He almost lost it again. While I waited for him to blow his nose, I glanced down at my watch. Nine-thirty. It seemed a lot later.

"Tuesday night we had a JAYCEE meeting up at the City Building," he said. "Glen Hunter cornered me afterwards and said I'd never guess who was back in town. Who? I said. Sweet Sally, he said. Surely I remembered her from the first time she was here. Vaguely, I said, all the while feeling my heart going a hundred miles ah hour. Well, he remembered her if I didn't, he said. She was the best damn lay he'd had before or since, and he just might treat Billy to a ride on her." Eddie had slumped in his chair. He looked exhausted. "I should have let it go at that," he said. "I should have gone home to Mother as I always do. But I didn't."

While Eddie rested a moment, I glanced at the plaques on his one wooden wall. For someone who was so hard on himself, he had done a lot of good for the town of Oakalla.

"So from the City Building I walked to the park. I didn't have any plan in mind. I just wanted to see Sally again, maybe talk to her if I got the chance. About what I don't know. Maybe to have her convince me that what I did wasn't such a terrible thing after all. So I waited for the carnival to close down, then hung around the park until I thought it was safe to go to her trailer. About that time the door opened, and here came Billy Hunter out of the trailer." Eddie no longer looked exhausted. With his flaming red face and fiery red eyes, he looked like a man possessed. "Buckling his belt. Feeling smug as hell, just the way I did twenty years ago. I lost it, Garth. I remember yelling something at Billy, like get the hell out of here, you little bastard, then charging the trailer. I didn't know what I was doing. All I do know is that when she screamed, I ran. Home to Mother." His voice was filled with self-loathing. "I ran home to Mother."

Where he would likely stay, I feared, until one of them died.

"I'm sorry, Eddie," I said. "I know this hasn't been easy for you. But it was time to get the monkey off your back."

"It's not easy, Garth," he said, still angry at himself. "This monkey has boots and spurs, and believe me, he loves to ride."

"But do you like to be ridden?"

He waved his hand feebly, as if at a natural disaster, as if what he liked or didn't like was of no consequence.

"One last question, Eddie. While you were at the park, did you see Clarkie's patrol car anywhere around?"

286

"Not that I remember, Garth. And I was all over the park."

"Do you remember seeing Sean Ragan around?"

"Who's Sean Ragan?"

"Never mind. It's not important now."

When I left a few minutes later, he still sat at the desk with the curtains closed around him. No one seemed to notice my going; or that I locked his office door on my way out.

20

On my way to see Goldie Samuel, I met a group of kids on their way to watch the parade. I envied their high-tops and high-fives, their unbridled enthusiasm as they danced along the sidewalk and made the street their playground. But I wouldn't have traded places with them. Not even today.

When Goldie Samuel didn't answer my first knock on her front door, I thought she might be out back sunning herself. I'd started that way when the front door opened.

"Good morning, Garth," she said.

Goldie Samuel stood behind the screen door. She wore light-brown slacks, a dark-brown blouse, and carried what looked like a small caliber pistol in her right hand. The pistol was pressed flat against her leg, as if she didn't want me to see it. She didn't seem glad to see me.

"I need to talk to you," I said.

"Now's not a good time, Garth. I'm meeting someone in just a few minutes."

"Here?"

She hesitated. "No. Away from here." She wasn't going to tell me any more than necessary to get me to leave.

"Then call whoever it is and tell him you'll be a few minutes late. I'll wait out here while you make the call."

The lines of her face stiffened and hardened. She looked as brown and brittle as November's last leaf. "What gives you the right to tell me what to do?" she said.

"I know what happened to Paul," I said. "I thought you might want to know, too."

She stood there a moment, then closed the door in my face. When she opened it again in a couple minutes, she carried a glass of ice water in her hand in place of the pistol.

"Where's your gun?" I said.

"What gun?"

"The one you were carrying the first time that you came to the door."

"You must be mistaken, Garth." She lied so smoothly that I hardly noticed. "There was no gun."

We went into the kitchen. I sat down at one end of the table. She sat down at the other. I looked for the pistol, but didn't see it.

"You say you know what happened to Paul," she said. "Or was that just a ruse to get you inside?" She seemed to think it was.

"It's not a ruse," I said.

"Then let me hear it." Her blue eyes were small and hard. They reminded me a lot of Sean Ragan's eyes. Soldier eyes. Survivor eyes. Eyes that had hardened from too much exposure to life. "Or do you need music?" she said.

"I don't need music," I said. "And you don't need to play the bitch for my benefit."

"It's not for your benefit, I can assure you," she said.

"Then for whoever's benefit, forget it for now. It doesn't do either one of us any good."

"You're wasting time," she said coldly. "My time. Your time. It's all precious, not to be wasted. Ask Paul."

I studied her and caught a glimmer of what was wrong. On her own, Goldie had come to much the same conclusions as I had.

"I do know," I said.

"Then tell me."

I told her. She seemed surprised.

"You amaze me," she said quietly, losing none of her anger. "I didn't think you or anyone else would ever figure it out."

What I had told her was that, when Paul Samuel returned for his wallet, he had found his mother making love to someone other than her husband, and thus he had begun the flight that ended in his death.

"Actually Hayden and I were on the kitchen floor when Paul walked in on us," she said. "We couldn't even wait to get to the bedroom . . . if you can believe that." Twenty years, a privacy fence, and a mountain of guilt and hatred later, Goldie Samuel could no longer believe that.

"It is hard to imagine," I said. "But I didn't know Hayden then."

"Hayden then is Hayden now," she said. "Insensitive, intractable, and insufferable. I just found it attractive then. I don't anymore."

"Did you and Hayden meet at school, or was it a neighborhood thing?" I said.

"A little of both. Probably more school than neighborhood. Paul was the one who really brought him to my attention. He was Paul's scout master and Little League coach. Paul thought the sun rose and set on Hayden Sims."

I felt the irony all the way down to the tip of my toes. It made me shudder, despite the heat.

"Then that wasn't the first time that you and Hayden had been together?" I said.

"No. Not the first. More likely the fifty-first, or the hundred-and-first. With Dick on the road . . ." She shrugged as if it were inevitable. "We had a lot of opportunities."

"Even with Paul around?"

"Even with Paul around. You'd be surprised with what you can get away with if you have the guts."

Even murder, I thought.

"But that day ended it," she continued. "I never wanted to have anything to do with Hayden after that."

"And he with you?"

She smiled wickedly. I wished I knew what it meant. "Oh, he called me after that. He even asked if he might come over. But his heart wasn't in it anymore than mine was." Her eyes met mine. I could feel their heat all the way across the table. The heat of dry ice. So cold it burns. "Or rather I should say his groin. Hayden doesn't have a heart, not like other people."

"Let's go back to that day again," I said. "After Paul found you and Hayden out, exactly what happened then?"

She looked down at the floor where she and Hayden must have been lying. Suddenly her eyes filled with tears. But she blinked them back. "I don't know exactly," she said. "I heard the back door slam and looked up to see Paul standing there." She closed her eyes, as some of the tears escaped and ran down her cheek. She made no move to wipe them away. "That's my last memory of him. His look of total bewilderment and betrayal. I'll carry it to my grave."

I glanced at my watch. Ten-thirty. In another half hour the parade would start. It didn't appear that I was going to make it.

"Did you and Hayden go after him?" I said.

"Hayden did. Once he got dressed. About an hour later he came back and said that he couldn't find Paul, but that he would keep on looking if I wanted him to. I said no. It would be better if Paul came home on his own. But then, of course, he didn't." She sat back in her chair with a look of absolute loss on her face. It was the same look that I'd seen on Eddie Vincent's face when I left him earlier that morning. It told me that Paul Samuel's wasn't the only life lost that day. "That seems a little steep, doesn't it, Garth? To have to pay for your adultery with your son?"

"If payment is required. I don't believe it is."

"You don't believe in justice?"

"I don't believe in vengeance."

"Somebody does," she said.

Her eyes had lost their glow. The cold fire that had just burned there a moment ago had burned itself out. In its place was a deadness, of soul and purpose, that could look death in the face, and smile.

293

"But what are we going to do about it?" she said. "That's what I want to know."

"We aren't going to do anything," I said. "You leave the doing to me."

"Then what are you going to do?" she said dully, as if she really were leaving it up to me.

"The first thing I'm going to do is search the Sims' house. Once I'm sure there's nobody home."

"You won't find anything," she said with certainty. "I know because I've looked."

"For Paul?"

"For anything," she said. "For anything that might tell me where he was or what happened to him."

I unbuttoned my shirt and handed her the envelope that contained the clipping that had come in Monday morning's mail. The envelope was slick with sweat, but she didn't seem to notice.

"Then you didn't send me this?" I said, certain that she had.

She opened the envelope and took out the clipping. "No. I didn't send you this," she said. Then she turned the clipping over and read what was on the other side. She froze for just an instant, as if everything within her had suddenly stopped, before she handed the clipping back to me.

"Then who did send it to me?" I said. "Do you have any ideas?"

"No. None whatsoever."

"Strange," I said for want of a better word.

"Yes, it is. Isn't it?"

"And you haven't been out to Hidden Quarry at all this week?"

I was thinking about the two sets of small fingerprints that Clarkie had found in Scott McBride's Firebird. Up until now, I had thought that one set might belong to her, and the other, of course, to Cheryl Loveless. That is, if Clarkie had read his fingerprints right.

"Not yet," she said with a disarming smile. Then she looked at the clock above her kitchen door. "The parade will be starting soon, won't it?"

I studied her to gauge her meaning, but couldn't read her. "In just a few more minutes, if it gets off on time."

"Oh, it will," she said cheerfully. "I've never known it not to."

"Did you cancel your appointment?" I said.

"With whom?"

"Whoever it was you were going to see when I came to your door."

"Yes," she assured me as if it were a foregone conclusion. "I cancelled it. It wasn't all that important anyway."

"Goldie, are you all right?" I mistrusted the bright light in her eyes, the bright edge to her voice. I knew them both well from my opening days of hunting season.

295

"I'm fine, Garth. Just fine."

I doubted that, but it was time that I was on my way. "Do you know if the Sims are home now?" I asked.

"I saw Dorothy leave earlier," she said. "Dear sweet soul she is, she's probably helping out with the insurance company's float. As for Hayden, I don't know. You might call him and find out."

"I'd rather not do that," I said. "For obvious reasons."

"Then I guess you'll have to try to wait him out."

"I guess I will," I said.

21

Wearing white shorts, tennis shoes, and a kelly green golf shirt, Hayden Sims left his house by the back door at exactly ten fifty-five A.M. and walked west down the alley to its end. When he turned north toward Jackson Street, I figured he was on his way to watch the parade. That gave me at least forty-five minutes, maybe an hour, before he might return. Not much time to find someone who had been missing for twenty years.

At exactly eleven A.M. I knocked on the back door of the Sims' house and hoped no one would answer. When no one did answer, I went inside.

The house hadn't changed in my absence. It

still was neat, clean, sterile. It still felt as cold as a meat locker.

Downstairs, starting in the basement, I went from room to room, looking for anything that I might have missed. At eleven fifteen I gave that up and went upstairs where I had the same luck in finding nothing. So I went outside and into the garage.

Parked side by side in the brick two-car garage were Hayden's late-model white Lincoln Continental and Dorothy's old blue Dodge Dart. Like the house, the garage was as neat as the proverbial pin with every tool (what tools there were) hung on pegboard at the front of the garage or on hooks along each side. Most of Hayden's tools were lawn and gardening tools—rakes, shovels, hoes, trowels, and trimmers, but he did have a claw hammer, handsaw, adjustable wrench, and screw driver hanging on the pegboard. All the tools were well-oiled and well-kept, and like the Lincoln Continental, all top-of-the-line.

I had turned on the overhead light on my way inside. I then turned on the fluorescent lamp above the workbench at the very front of the garage and stood on a stepladder to see what Hayden kept in the loft above. Not much that I could see. Nothing but a few old rose trellises, a pair or two of handprints, and some small bare footprints in the dust.

Hoisting myself up into the loft, I followed the footprints to the front of the loft where they turned, ran along the wall for a few feet, then circled and returned to where they began. They puzzled me. So did the wall of the loft, which, unlike the rest of the garage, was brick paneling and not brick itself.

I wished Hayden's garage was more like mine at home. Then there would have been any number of things, like quarter-round, two-by-fours, binder twine, electrical wire, copper tubing, iron pipes, and boat oars to use to measure the distance from the ladder to the front wall of the garage, and then the distance from the ladder to the front wall of the loft. The way it was, I had to use a hoe.

The loft ended approximately two feet short of the brick wall of the garage. I measured it again just to make sure and came up with the same result. That gave me pause for thought. But my thoughts were interrupted by the boom of a bass drum. The parade was already under way.

I grabbed the claw hammer and went up the ladder into the loft. If I was wrong about this, I'd hate myself in the morning. But regrets were something that I'd learned to live with.

The first blow of the hammer tore a hammer-sized hole in the paneling and nearly broke my wrist. The second blow enlarged the hole. After that, I used my hands to tear the paneling away.

But once I'd crawled inside the hole I'd made, I couldn't see my hand in front of my face. Or as my cousin once said about Grandmother Ryland's middle bedroom upstairs, it was so dark you couldn't tell whether your eyes were open or not. Then my claustrophobia kicked in and the farther I got from the hole and the light, the worse it got, until in sheer panic, I wanted to kick a hole in something just to have some space.

So I stopped. Gathered my thoughts. Listened to my sweat drip, drip, drip on the floor of the loft. And went on.

After working my way to the west side of the loft without finding anything, I rested there a moment with my face against the eave, trying to suck in a drop of fresh air. I could no longer hear the parade, but I could hear some baby birds cheeping in a nest somewhere close by. Probably sparrows.

Time to move. But when I tried, I found myself sweat-stuck to the floor. It took all I had for me to roll over, turn around, and head back the other way. It took even more for me to keep on going once I reached the hole and the light again.

At the east end of the loft I found what I was looking for. It was a high heavy box, jammed up against the eave.

When I first tried to move it, I had no luck. Only by hugging it and inching it toward me, could I move it at all. But once I dislodged it and could squeeze behind it, I put my shoulder to it and crabbed it all the way to the opening. A couple hammer blows enlarged the hole. Then I pushed it out into the light.

It was an old wooden seaman's chest, shaped like a treasure trunk, with two leather straps buckled across its lid and a brass handle at each end of it. It also had a heavy brass clasp, a thick brass ring, and a large brass padlock fastened over the clasp and through the ring.

I picked up the hammer and thought about using it on the trunk to try to get inside. Then I put the hammer down. It would take too long for one thing. For another, I didn't want to take a hammer to Paul Samuel's casket.

I climbed down from the loft and went outside. The hot July breeze felt cool to me as I stood in the yard a moment to catch my breath. Hayden Sims had neither a hacksaw nor a bolt cutter in his garage. But maybe Dick Samuel had one or the other.

As I stepped out into the alley, Goldie Samuel almost ran over me on her way past. She was driving what I later learned was a lime-green Ford Torino, and she was in a hurry to get wherever she was going.

301

Dick Samuel's garage was a poor man's version of Hayden Sims' garage. Instead of brick, his was made of wood. Instead of pegboard and hooks for hanging his tools, he had rafters and nails. And what tools he had were either rusted or broken or both. His hacksaw had no blade that I could find. His large rusty coal chisel had a pencil-sized V in its edge where someone had tried to cut something that wouldn't be cut. His axe had no handle on it.

From there I ran the two blocks to the City Building where I saw the tail end of the parade go by on Jackson Street. Already I was out of time. I couldn't find bolt cutters and get back to the garage before either Dorothy or Hayden Sims might come home. But I couldn't see stopping now.

One of Oakalla's two fire trucks was out of its bay and likely in the parade, as it was every other year. Under the seat of the passenger side of the other one, I found a pair of bolt cutters. How I knew that they were there, I didn't remember. I just knew that they were.

Back at the Sims' garage, I stopped in the alley to rest a moment and to make sure that no one had come home. The lights in the garage were still on. The side garage door was still open. All seemed as I had left it. But when I went around the corner and into the garage,

302

I thought I saw someone's face through the back door window of the house. I looked again from inside the garage; the face was gone.

Sweat ran out of every one of my pores as I bent over the chest to cut the padlock. It ran down my forehead and into my eyes; it dripped from my elbows and chin and made a puddle on the dust there on the floor of the loft. It blinded me momentarily and gave me one more chance not to cut the padlock. But in the end I did cut the padlock, then opened the truck to see what was inside.

The first breath of air that came from the truck was sickeningly sweet, so thick that it seemed to take my own breath away. For a frightening instant, I thought that I was going to suffocate, until I scrambled far enough away to escape the smell. There, against the eaves with fresh air at hand, I waited until the smell filled the loft, and I got used to it.

Paul Samuel was inside the trunk, or what was left of him. A skull and half a skeleton lay on the top of the chest in a bed of lime. Beneath them, as if his body had been cut in two, then folded under to fit the chest, lay the other half of the skeleton.

Reaching through it down into the lime, my hand brushed the long sharp steel edge of something. I felt for its handle, found it, then

303

pulled the corn knife out of the chest. Its blade was spotted with rust—blood spots perhaps that had rusted over time. Since Paul Samuel had been too big to fit all at once into the chest, Hayden Sims evidently had chopped him in half and stacked him on top of himself. A nice neat job by the looks of it—as neat as you could be with a corn knife.

Further down in the chest I found Paul's clothes—blue shorts, red-and-black Led Zepplin T-shirt, white tennis shoes, white socks, and white underwear. As I stared at the shape of the clothes on the loft, they looked like a flag lying there.

A few minutes later I folded the clothes, put them back inside the chest, closed the lid of the chest, and sat down. Tried to think, but no thoughts came. No tears either, though my eyes burned and my heart ached. No solace was to be found that day. Nothing but complete, rock-bottom desolation. And that was just the beginning.

22

I sat at Goldie Samuel's kitchen table, drinking my third glass of ice water and wondering where she had gone. She should be the first to know where her son was. Captain Fillmore Cavanaugh would be the second.

Minutes passed. Then the cuckoo swung out of the clock and screamed once at me. I looked at my watch. One P.M. The tail end of the parade would be to the park by now. It appeared I had missed it.

I got up, went to the west window of the kitchen, looked outside, and saw only the boards of the privacy fence. What is wrong with this picture, I thought? Then I realized what was wrong with it.

Goldie had told me that earlier that morning she had seen Dorothy Sims leaving to work on the parade. But she couldn't have seen Dorothy leaving because of the fence between them. Not at a casual glance, and not unless she was watching from some vantage point. Which meant that either Hayden Sims had told Goldie where Dorothy had gone, or that Goldie was watching for Dorothy to leave, then guessed at her destination. In either case, Goldie was on her way to meet Hayden when I arrived at the house earlier. And on her way to find him, when I saw her in the alley.

I ran home. When I got there, I couldn't tell which hurt worse, my chest, stomach, or legs. Then I couldn't find Ruth downstairs. Bent over nearly double from the pain, I put one hand on the banister of the stairway and held on until I could breathe again.

"Ruth!" I yelled. "Are you here?"

"I'm here." Her voice came from upstairs.

A surge of relief passed through me. I thought she might have gone to watch the parade after all.

"I need to borrow your Volkswagen."

"Why?"

"I don't have time to explain."

Her keys were flying down the stairs and landed at my feet.

"Thanks," I said, after picking them up.

306

"Where are you going in such a hurry?"

"Hidden Quarry," I said on my way to the back door. But I wasn't sure that she heard me.

The first thing I saw when I reached Hidden Quarry was Goldie Samuel's green Torino parked there not far from the rim of the quarry. I got out of the Volkswagen and cautiously approached the Torino from the rear. Both of the Torino's side windows were rolled all the way down, but I didn't see anyone inside it. What I did see, when I drew abreast of the Torino, were Goldie's purse and a pistol lying on the seat.

I reached through the driver's side window, picked up the pistol, and examined it. The pistol was a well-worn twenty-two caliber revolver. Its white plastic handle grip was cracked and its bluing was almost gone.

I eased the hammer back and slowly spun the cylinder, counting six bullets in all. Then I smelled the bore. The revolver hadn't been fired recently.

I knew I should get back in the Volkswagen and go get help. If I didn't go get help, I might not have the chance later. But I didn't get back in the Volkswagen, and I didn't go for help. I walked to the rim of the quarry and looked down.

Goldie lay on a shelf of rock about ten feet above the water and thirty feet below me. For several seconds I stood staring at her, willing her to move. Then I emptied her revolver, put the shells in my left pants pocket, the pistol in my right pants pocket, and started down the rock toward her.

She lay face down on the limestone shelf with her left arm at her side and her right arm curled out in front of her as if she were in sleep, as if the arm were curled around her pillow. She had landed that way. There were no blood stains on the rock to show that she had crawled anywhere. There was only one small puddle of blood beneath her face. Still red and life-like, it had only now started to dry.

A shadow appeared on the shelf beside me, then left as quickly as it had come. I looked up, but didn't see any clouds or birds overhead.

"I found your son, Goldie," I said, kneeling to touch her hair. "I just wanted you to know that."

The shadow reappeared. This time it brought a rock with it. The rock struck the shelf exactly where I had been kneeling.

"God damn you!" I yelled at Hayden Sims. "Enough is enough!"

He answered by throwing another rock. This one struck Goldie in the spine and made her momentarily jump to life.

"I'm going to splatter you all over that

rock," he yelled from above. "And there's not a damn thing you can do about it."

Up until then Hayden Sims had seemed to be the consummate strategist. He had weighed the consequences of each and every action and reaction and so far had not had a false step. But something must have happened on the way to the quarry to change all that. Like a wounded lion, he didn't seem to care about escape, only about destroying his tormentors.

I dodged another rock, then backed against the wall of the quarry where, because of a slight overhang, it would be harder for Hayden to hit me.

"For God's sake, Hayden," I said. "You're only making things worse."

Screw you, was the gist of his answer.

The next rock, which was big, flat, and heavy, and looked like a house coming down, hit the shelf with such force that it shattered on impact and nearly knocked my legs out from under me. I glanced at Goldie and watched its dust rain down on her. I didn't stand a chance as long as I was there. On one of his throws, Hayden was going to get lucky and squash my head like a pumpkin.

"It's over, Hayden," I said, trying to reason with him. "Go out with some class at least."

"It won't be over," he said, bending down

309

to pick up another rock, "until you're dead."
If he were winded from all the exertion, he
didn't show it.

"Why me?"

He threw the rock. I misjudged its speed
and direction and didn't get out of the way in
time. It struck me a glancing blow, tearing a
hole in my jeans and peeling a large patch of
skin from my hip. But it missed my foot, for
which I was grateful.

"Because," Hayden said, as I scrambled
away from under him. "I wouldn't be here, if
it weren't for you."

And I wouldn't be here if it weren't for you,
I thought about saying, but decided against it.
I might as well save my breath. Hayden Sims
had never been a good listener.

My next move was instinct. I saw him raise
his arms, saw the rock leave his hands, and
dived headfirst into the quarry.

I should have jumped. I hated to dive even
more than I hated to swim. My ears always
filled with water and felt as if they would
explode, before I could surface and shake the
water out.

I surfaced with a gasp, shook my head back
and forth a couple of times, and went under
again. At that same instant a rock hit the water
like a cannonball and nearly burst my ear-
drums, as white hot pain shot down both sides
of my throat and lodged there.

Unable to hear or to swallow, I clawed my way back to the surface, lost my direction and all sense of what I was doing, and began to flail the water with my arms to try to make the pain go away. But all I succeeded in doing was exhausting myself, and giving Hayden Sims another shot at me.

He didn't waste the opportunity. A rock, or more likely a boulder, hit the water inches away from me and drove a slug of water into my eyes and up my nose all the way to my brain. Deaf, blind, dumb, and dead in the water, I waited for the next rock to finish me.

But Hayden had temporarily run out of ammunition and had to retreat in search of some. I used that chance to clear my eyes and ears, and then to start swimming across the quarry, so when the next splash came, it was well behind me. The following splash was even further behind me, as was each succeeding one. But he didn't stop throwing at me until I'd reached the other side.

I couldn't move at first. All I could do was lie there and bake in the hot sun. Then I felt the hard, growing knot in the pit of my stomach. But even though I nearly heaved my guts out, all that came up was a bitter green bile that left a sick and sour taste in my mouth.

From my hands and knees, I rose unsteadily to my feet, glanced once at the sun to curse it, then began the long climb to the rim of the quarry. I was at the south end, at the foot of a talus slope, left behind when whoever had owned the quarry had dumped all of the remaining stone there. Because of the talus slope, the south wall of the quarry was not as sheer as the north wall, but with all of the uneven rocks underfoot, every bit as treacherous.

I slowly made my way up it, using my hands almost as much as my feet. At the top, I rested, and with great effort dug the shells and then the revolver out of my pockets.

My bloody hip had started to attract a swarm of gnats, and my head felt as if it belonged to someone else. Even if I weren't dizzy and disoriented, I was still no match for Hayden Sims one on one. So after letting the sun dry the shells, I put them into the revolver and went into the woods.

Immediately I felt safer, surer, better all the way around. The woods were my natural element, if I had such a thing; and if there were such things as past lives, I had lived at least one of mine in the woods. Probably as an Indian, or a mountain man. Someone who was long on solitude and short on company.

Moving deeper into the woods, I began to circle to the east. It wasn't the easiest way around the quarry. The east side was crisscrossed with sinkholes and ravines, any one of which could break your legs and keep you there. The west side was a highway by comparison. But I wanted to avoid Hayden Sims at all costs. Keeping to the east side seemed the best way to do that.

My plan was to circle the quarry, get in the Volkswagen, and drive out of there. If that made me a coward, then so be it. I'd learn to live with myself later. Right now all I wanted to do was live.

But what I really wished for, almost as much as the sight of the Volkswagen, was a drink of water. Normally there would have been a spring to drink from in nearly every ravine I crossed, but the drought had driven them all underground. Too bad for me. I was so dry I couldn't sweat.

I stopped. Just a few yards ahead of me a bluejay bounced up and down on a limb, screaming "Thief! Thief! Thief!"

I looked to see what he was screaming at. It should have been a red squirrel or another bluejay, or maybe even a hawk or an owl. But none of them were in sight. No other animal was in sight, and that bothered me as much as the bluejay itself.

Retreating a couple steps, I began to circle around the jay. An instant later it flew.

I began to run, as a limb lashed my face and

a brier raked my raw hip, shooting a needle up my spine and bringing tears to my eyes. Then I came to the road that led into Hidden Quarry from the north. Just a few more yards, I thought. Just a few more yards, and I'll be home free.

But when the time arrived, I couldn't do it. I had the key in hand and the Volkswagen in sight when I abruptly veered off the road and stopped.

A moment later Hayden burst into the clearing where the Volkswagen was parked and ran straight for it as if he had been reading my mind. Though it was hot, unmercifully hot there in the woods on that July afternoon, I felt my hands, then the rest of me go cold. Hayden Sims had been a step ahead of me all the way. He still was a step ahead of me. It made me wonder what chance I had against him.

"I'm over here, Hayden," I said. "If you want me, you'll have to come get me."

"I want you," he said, as he started my way.

I waited for him in a stand of white pine. Cool, dark, and close, it was as good a place as any to make my stand.

But the closer he came, the less sure I was of myself. In his kelly green shorts and white collared shirt, with his white shoes and smooth brown legs purposely striding toward me, he didn't look at all worried or fatigued. He looked to me like an angry golfer who had hooked his drive into the woods and now had the inconvenience of having to retrieve it.

When he reached the edge of the pines, I pointed the revolver at him and said, "That's far enough."

"I don't think so," he said without breaking stride.

"I mean it, Hayden. I'll shoot if you don't stop."

"Then fire away."

I'd pulled the trigger three times before I realized that the revolver hadn't fired, wasn't going to fire. It came as a surprise to me.

But I didn't throw the pistol at him in frustration, as I wanted to do. I waited until he got close enough, then tried to hit him in the face with it still in my hand.

He ducked and came in low, locking me in a bear hug before I even had a chance to react. Then he slowly began to squeeze the life out of me.

No wonder Clarkie had passed out almost immediately under his grip. No wonder Scott McBride never had a chance to fight back. Hayden's strength was prodigious. I had never felt anything like it.

Then I heard my spine pop and thought surely it was broken. Frightened to the point of fury, I slammed the revolver again and again and again into his ear until I broke his hold.

But once free, I had no hope of escape. He stood over me like the wrestler he was, waiting for me to make a move so that he could counter it and end the affair once and for all.

So I didn't offer to move. I stalled and prayed and hoped that someone heard me.

"Come on, Garth," he said. "Why not make it easy on both of us. No matter what you do, it's going to turn out the same." His voice had a sugary, almost seductive lilt to it.

I didn't say anything. I didn't want my voice to give me away, to let him know how close to finished I really was.

Instead I stared past him at Sean Ragan, who stood just at the edge of the pines. Sean Ragan, the Vietnam veteran. Sean Ragan, the ex-Marine. Sean Ragan, the carnival worker and man of the world. Sean Ragan, who had done all of the things that I had not done and would never do. Sean Ragan, my hero.

"Damn!" I said, as my face broke into a grin. "I thought you'd never get here." I spoke from the heart, as if Sean Ragan really were there.

It was the oldest trick in the book, and Hayden Sims fell for it. Not hook, line, and sinker, so that he turned all the way around and exposed his back. But far enough for me to roll away and put a pine between us.

316

"You're just postponing the inevitable," he said, advancing toward me.

I struggled to my feet. My legs felt weak and limp, almost as if I had no legs at all. If I had been in his grip a few more seconds, Hayden would have broken my back. Then it really wouldn't have mattered how he finished me off.

Through the force of sheer will, I set one leg in motion, then the other, and began to run. Awkwardly at first, as if on match sticks, as I stumbled over a root, went to the ground, and got up again; then better as I began to put some distance between Hayden and me.

He wouldn't deign to run after me. It seemed to be beneath his dignity. He would wait for me to exhaust myself, or fall and not get up, then calmly walk up and finish his business.

But a funny thing happened on my way through the woods. As I put more air in my lungs and more and more distance between us, I recovered my strength and my fighting spirit, and more importantly, my confidence. Despite his enormous strength, Hayden did have an Achilles' heel. It was his ego.

When I felt it safe to slow down to a walk, I began to search the woods for a weapon. I had discarded the revolver as useless as soon as I had escaped from Hayden. What I wanted

317

was a woods-weapon, one that I could trust with my life.

I found it dangling from an ash head-high off the ground. It was a broken limb about eight feet long. After one hard jerk, I had it in my possession. Then I began to run again.

A hundred or so yards later, I stopped and began to strip the smaller branches off the main limb. They didn't give easily. Ash is one tough wood, which is why they make axe handles and ball bats out of it.

On the move again, I had a long slender pole that looked more suitable for fishing than for fighting. But I wasn't done with it yet.

I had deliberately run in a circle, so when I broke into the clearing above the quarry, I had perhaps a minute to fashion my weapon before Hayden arrived. The first part was supposed to be easy. Since the limb was dry and seasoned, I thought it would break easily over my knee. But it didn't. Instead it almost broke my knee.

Watching Hayden slowly close the gap between us, I ran to the nearest boulder, raised the limb high over my head, and brought it down hard on the edge of the boulder. The limb snapped, but didn't break completely in two. So I twisted it upon itself as I ran from Hayden Sims for the last time.

Finally ready, I had a chunk of ash approximately thirty-two inches long that tapered from a two-inch diameter at its big end to maybe an inch-and-a-half at its small end. I would have preferred for it to have been at least a couple inches longer with a bigger ball and a thinner handle, but it would do for one swing. I crouched down in my old batting stance with my feet spread for balance and most of the weight on my right foot, drew the ash back waist high and parallel to the ground, and waited for him.

He kept right on coming straight at me as if I weren't armed and he were invincible. I knew he would. By then I knew Hayden Sims almost as well as he knew me.

What he expected me to do was to try to take off his head, and he was all ready to counter that move. What he didn't expect was for me to break his knee. As he lay there on the ground, writhing in pain, I could have told him that I was always a better low-ball hitter than a high-ball hitter.

23

Fillmore Cavanaugh arrived in his state patrol car before I even had a chance to figure out how I was going to get Hayden back to Oakalla. Ruth had called him as soon as I'd left, but he hadn't gotten the message until a short while ago.

I showed him Goldie Samuel, told him essentially what had happened, then watched while he cuffed Hayden and read him his rights. Hayden responded with stoic indifference, as if he could have cared less about his rights. I could almost read Hayden's mind. A world champion. With his upper-body strength, he could have been a world champion wrestler—if God had given him the legs to go with it.

"Do you want to make a statement?" Fillmore said to him.

"About what?"

"Anything."

Hayden shrugged. "Just ask me the questions and I'll tell you the answers. I've got nothing to hide."

"You could have a lawyer present," Fillmore said. "It's your right."

Hayden shook his head. "I don't need one. Not at this point."

Then Fillmore left momentarily to go back to his patrol car to get a tape recorder.

"So you won after all," Hayden said to me. "Congratulations."

"Neither of us won anything here today," I said.

"You won the right to go on breathing," he said. "That's something."

I nodded. He had a point.

Fillmore returned with the tape recorder. "I called an ambulance," he said. "They'll be coming soon for Goldie Samuel."

"What about me?" Hayden said. "The last time I looked, my knee was broken."

"All in due time," Fillmore said. "All in due time."

None of us spoke for a couple minutes, as Fillmore played with his tape recorder, making sure it worked. My glance went from Fillmore to Hayden's left knee, which resembled a purple grapefruit, to his torn and bloody left ear, to the sky above us, which had gathered some clouds in the false promise of rain. In a few more minutes the shade from the trees to our west would reach us. I could wait that long.

"I never intended to kill Paul Samuel," Hayden said. "I want everybody to get that straight right off. I liked the kid." Then he qualified himself. "As well as you can like a kid that would rather chase butterflies than chase baseballs."

"Then why did you kill him?" I said.

"It was his own fault," Hayden said. "After he surprised Goldie and me and ran out of the house, she said he'd probably head for Hidden Quarry, to check here first before I did anywhere else. So as soon as I got my pants on, I ran out the front door and jumped into the first thing I came to, which was Butch's old black Chevy truck. I wasn't thinking very clear at the time. All I wanted to do was to catch up to Paul before he told someone about Goldie and me."

"Which could have cost you your job," I said.

Hayden's eyes flamed momentarily. "You're damn right, it could have," he said. "And a lot of other things besides. I had a cozy thing going here. I wasn't about to let some snot-nosed kid ruin it, if I could help it."

Fillmore and I exchanged glances. His said that we would sit there and listen, even if we didn't like what we heard.

"Where did you catch up to Paul?" I said.

"On his way down Hutchinson's Hill. I found his wrecked bicycle there at the corner south of the school and threw it into the back of the truck, thinking that might help convince Paul to get in the truck with me. But when I caught up to him, he didn't want to have anything to do with me. He said to leave him alone, or something to that effect. I said to get his butt in the truck and hear what I had to say. He could be man enough to do that at least."

Hayden looked pensive. I couldn't tell if he were trying to decide what had gone wrong with his life, or what had gone wrong with Paul Samuel that day.

"We drove out here to Hidden Quarry," Hayden said. "And parked about right over there." He pointed to show us. It was right about where Goldie's Torino was now parked. "Then I tried to explain how it was with his mother and me. How two people who aren't married can still need to be with each other every now and then. That when he got a little older, he'd understand. Then I winked at him. You know. Man to man." Hayden looked perplexed, as if the whole chain of events that then followed were beyond his comprehension. "I thought I did a damn good job of it myself."

I didn't say anything.

"He just sat there," Hayden said with a pained note in his voice. "Not saying a word. He just sat there, stiff as a board. Then he said . . . And I'll remember this until the day I die. He said, 'I hate you. I hate your guts.' *Me*," Hayden said in astonishment. "Who had done everything for that kid."

I glanced at the shadows at our feet. The shade had finally reached us.

"The next thing I know, he takes off. I make a grab for him, but he's out of the truck and gone before I can lay a hand on him. Gone," Hayden repeated as if he still couldn't believe it. "Right over the edge of the quarry." He frowned at the injustice of it all. "He might as well have taken me with him."

"You just left him there to die?" Fillmore asked.

Hayden seemed put out by the question. "No. I got on my high horse and climbed down the rock to him. He was laying there on his back, looking up at me. His neck was broken. I could tell that by the way his head bent way to one side at a funny angle, like there wasn't anything to hold it. And there was blood running from his mouth, nose, and ears. But he still wasn't dead. Not until I put my hand over his face and held it there. Then he quivered a little and that was that."

I watched the shade continue to creep across the rim of the quarry. Fillmore watched the clouds gather overhead. Hayden watched his and Paul Samuel's lives end all over again.

"When I was sure he was dead, I carried him back up out of the quarry, put him into the cab of the pickup, and took off out of there. But when I was on my way out, I met a couple of people on foot on their way in to the quarry. The one on my right sort of slid off into the woods, so I didn't get a good look at him. But the one on my left I recognized. It was that long-haired hippie from the carnival that had been screwing my daughter." Hayden's face reddened at the thought of Scott McBride. So did the bald spot in the middle of his head. "I didn't know if he recognized me or not, but I damn sure didn't want to take that chance. The problem was," he said with regret, "I still had Paul Samuel to get rid of. And his bicycle. I figured I could take care of that hippie and his buddy, whoever he was, later."

The next part, when Hayden described how he'd hidden Paul and his bicycle in the interurban culvert under Hutchinson's Hill and what he had done to Paul that night, took more than I could stand. The act of butchering Paul was bad enough. Hayden's calm dispassionate description of it defied whatever humanity I thought we possessed. I had to get up and take a short walk in the woods.

"You used a corn knife?" I heard Fillmore say on my return.

"It was all I had to use," Hayden explained. "It had belonged to my father. For some reason known only to him, he thought I should have it when he died."

I glanced at Fillmore. His look said to keep my mouth shut. But I couldn't do that. Or I would have exploded.

"Maybe he was proud of it," I said. "Proud to have used it. Prouder yet to have survived the use of it."

Hayden's look said he would forgive me. "I put all of that stuff behind me a long time ago, Garth. Once I left the farm, I never looked back."

"Where did the trunk come from?" I said after an awkward pause.

Fillmore looked relieved. He had reason to.

"From some auction that my wife had been to," Hayden said. "She had been wanting me to finish it and put it in our living room. I don't know how long it had been sitting there in the garage."

"Didn't she miss it after that?" I said.

He answered with a shrug. "She said something about it a few days later. But I fed her some line of bull and she went for it." His smile said I'd understand. "You know my wife, Garth. She's no Einstein."

I returned his smile, wondering all the while how well Hayden Sims really knew his wife. Not as well as he thought he did, I bet.

"So then you brought the truck with Paul in it back to your garage and sealed him away in the loft," I said.

Hayden seemed surprised that I knew where the trunk was hidden. But he didn't let it bother him.

"That's about it," he said. "I had some trellises in the loft that I used to hide the chest until I could put that fake wall up."

So while friends and neighbors scoured the countryside for Paul Samuel, he was tucked away in Hayden Sims' garage a few feet from home. Then, when she could no longer stand the sight of Hayden, Goldie built her privacy fence, further walling her away from her son. "Something there is that doesn't love a wall," Frost wrote. He must have had me in mind.

We watched as the ambulance came for Goldie, then as the attendants hauled her body up and over the cliff in a body bag. I had wanted to say goodbye to her, but didn't have the chance.

"And that was the end of it?" Fillmore said. "Until now?"

Hayden looked at me. He, too, had been

watching the body bag make its way up the cliff and into the ambulance. Regret showed on his face. Or what I took for it.

"That was just the beginning of it," he said. "I couldn't sleep, wondering when McBride would show up and put the finger on me. So I found out where the carnival was and went there. But they said McBride had gone home. Then when I came back a couple weeks after that and they said he'd joined the Marines, I thought maybe my troubles were over. That maybe the gooks over in Vietnam would take care of him for me." His smile showed his disappointment. "Little did I know."

Fillmore looked at me for an explanation. I told him about the letters from Vietnam and then the racing poster that McBride had sent to Cheryl.

"The letters were bad enough," Hayden said. "But when I walked into Cheryl's room that day and saw that poster hanging there, it nearly took my head off." Beads of sweat had popped out all over Hayden's face as he relived that moment. "So I went flying down the stairs and told Dorothy that if she didn't get that poster out of my sight, I was going to burn Cheryl's room and everything in it."

Then he went on to tell us what again went through his mind when Scott McBride showed up at his door at noon on Monday, looking for

328

Cheryl. And how he'd followed them out to Hidden Quarry, killed McBride after Cheryl left, and then set up Butch Loveless to take the fall by leaving his wallet in McBride's Firebird.

"Where in the Firebird?" I said. Because neither Cheryl nor I nor the state police had found it when we searched the Firebird.

"In the front seat, wedged down in the seat a ways to make it more believable. You know, like he'd lost it there while he was stripping in the car. But some kid must've come along and taken it. The little bastard."

"And McBride's license and registration?" I said.

"They're in Butch's Bronco, hidden there in the glove compartment under a road map. I had it all set up," he explained, wanting us to know how clever he'd been. "I'd taken Butch's wallet out of his pants when he was in the weight room at school. Then I'd called him there in his office to tell him about Cheryl and McBride, knowing he'd rush right out there, and hoping somebody might see him on the way. Then later on that night I went back out to the quarry, put Butch's wallet in McBride's car, then took McBride's I.D.'s and put them in Butch's Bronco when I got home." He couldn't hide his anger. "It was a perfect plan. Until that little bastard, whoever he was, came along and ruined it."

329

"What if somebody found McBride's body in the meantime?" Fillmore said. "Then your plan wouldn't have been so perfect."

Hayden shrugged. "Then I hadn't lost anything. Vietnam vet, and washed up race driver dies from plunge into quarry. That's the way it would've read. Suicide or accident, who's really going to care?" He looked at me. It wasn't a friendly look. "Except for Ryland here. And that pea-brain we've got for a sheriff."

"McBride was Clarkie's hero," I said. "But he had no idea you were involved. He thought if anybody was involved, Butch was."

For Hayden, the fates had just kept getting crueler and crueler. I could read it on his face. It made me realize how easy it was for some of us to blame fate for our own stupidity. And our own unhappiness.

"Too late I know that now," Hayden said. "I gave him more credit than he deserved. I was out watering my roses when I saw him park in the alley and then sneak up to Butch's house. Good, I thought. Maybe things are going to work out after all. But then I got to thinking what was he really doing there, since after a while it became obvious that he'd come to spy on Butch, not arrest him. That's when I outsmarted myself. Because thinking back twenty years to that day at the quarry, I remembered

330

it was Butch's pickup I was in that day. And maybe it was Clarkie that I saw slip off into the woods. And maybe when he found out it wasn't Butch in that pickup, he'd put two and two together and come up with me."

"So you disabled him and then arranged his accident?" I said.

"Yes."

"But if you were so afraid of Clarkie, then why didn't you kill him while you were at it?"

I'll never forget the look he gave me. It was the soul of conceit. "When I twisted his neck and heard it pop, I thought I had killed him." He looked sadly at his hands that twice had failed him, once with Clarkie and once with me. "I must be getting old," he said.

"I've heard enough," Fillmore said, shutting off his tape recorder. He looked at me. "If you have?"

"A couple more questions," I said. "Off the record."

"If Mr. Sims is agreeable."

"I'm agreeable," Hayden said, showing the fatigue that we all felt. "If you make it short." He glanced down at his knee, which now looked overripe, about to pop open. "It's really starting to hurt me now."

"Twenty years ago," I said. "Are you the one who called Butch back here from wrestling camp?"

331

"I'm the one," he said. "I didn't want Cheryl running off with that hippie McBride. I figured Butch could stop her easier than I could."

"You had reason to think she might run off with him?"

"I had followed her and Clarkie to the carnival one night and saw them spending a lot of time with McBride. I followed her because I was concerned about where she was going in that pickup after she was supposed to be in bed for the night. Seeing her with McBride, I thought I knew. So when she sneaked out of the house later that night, I followed her again, first to the park where she picked up McBride, then to Hidden Quarry where you can guess what went on." At the moment he looked like any caring and loving father. "So you might say, yes, I had some reason for concern."

"And me," I said. "You were the one who ran me off the road Wednesday night, and then tried to run over me the next night?"

"I am. When I saw you there at Goldie's Wednesday morning, I didn't think too much about it." He smiled. "You know, you might have had something going with her, like I used to. And when I followed you from there to the bank, I figured I had nothing to worry about, so I went home. Then that evening I'm

332

just driving around to see what's going on when I see you get out of a Volkswagen up at the Marathon. So I go around the block, then park and wait for you, figuring you're on your way to work or something. But you head out of town, so I follow you, keeping my distance. I start to get a bad feeling when you pull into that motel there at Balboa. The feeling gets a whole lot worse when I find out who's staying there in the room you just went into." The next part Hayden hated to admit, even to himself. "I panicked, which if you know me, is not like me at all. I thought about running you down in the motel parking lot when you came out of Dick's room, but that didn't seem wise, not with all the people sitting around the pool. So I followed you, waited to pick my spot, and came after you. But you saw me coming and got out of the way." Hayden looked relieved. "But afterwards, I was glad you did. I hadn't thought it through, not at all." Hayden's voice had begun to ebb, lose some of its certainty. He looked more than tired. He looked defeated. "I don't know how I missed you that next night. You never saw me coming, I know that."

"Serendipity," I said, not wanting to dwell on it. "But what about when they found the dent I made in your Continental?"

"I wasn't in my Continental," he said. "I was in Butch's Bronco. He's got a bad habit of leaving his keys in his ignition."

That about wrapped it up, except for one last question. "Goldie," I said. "Why, after all of these years, did you decide to kill her?"

The light momentarily returned to Hayden's eyes. "It was her doing, not mine. She's the one who arranged the meeting. She's the one who came after me, then drove me out here, pointed that pistol at me, and without saying a word, started pulling the trigger." Without his realizing it, Hayden's hands had made a circle in the shape of Goldie Samuel's throat. "She kept right on pulling it, too, up until the time I throttled her."

"You didn't have to kill her," I said, knowing how useless and beside the point my protest was.

"You don't understand," Hayden said. "I wanted to kill her. Dan Gable called me a few years back and wanted me to be his assistant. Dan Gable, for God's sake, the biggest name in college wrestling, and I had to turn him down because I couldn't leave there with a body in my garage. How bad is that, I ask you?"

"Not as bad as what happened to Paul Samuel," I said.

He shrugged it off. Then he said to Fillmore, "I'm ready whenever you are."

Hours later I stood in the park, watching lightning streak across the sky, but without

334

thunder, like a storm of the mind. Homecoming was over for another year, the carnival and rides gone, and the now empty park flickered in and out of sight with the lightning, leaving me with an empty feeling deep in my guts.

Before I had gone home for a drink and a shower and to have Ruth patch me up, I had stopped here to find Sean Ragan, greasy and sweaty, working on one of his rides, while a long line of unhappy campers waited for him to finish. I limped over to where he was working.

"What happened to you?" he said, noting my less than perfect appearance, as had several in the crowd behind us.

"I was chasing butterflies. I got mugged by a zebra swallowtail."

He went on working as if he hadn't heard. "Whatever you want, make it short. As you can see, I'm busy."

"In short, I found Paul Samuel. I thought you might want to know."

He glanced up at me, but there was no hope in his eyes. "Dead?"

"Yes, dead. For twenty years now."

Momentarily he stopped working to gaze at something frail and fleeting, and beyond recall. "There was always a chance," he said.

"Yes," I echoed, "there was always a chance."

Having said what I'd come for, I started to leave.

"Thanks, Ryland," he said without looking up.

"You, too," I said, then left.

Picking up a half-eaten candy apple, I threw it into the nearest barrel, then ducked as a cloud of flies swarmed out at me. The kid who dropped it on the ground probably wouldn't remember the apple, but there were moments, happy, carefree, wonderful moments, primary and irreducible, that he would remember about this week. And they would help on a night like this, give him something to smile about, when at age forty-six he ran out of answers before he ran out of questions.

I only wished I was as smart as I thought I was at sixteen, or half as smart as I knew I was at twenty-one. Then perhaps I'd know whether, given the chance, Paul Samuel would have gone on to do great things, or if his death was only one more offering to a world that has eaten so many kids before their time.

I watched a bolt of lightning drop straight down and waited for the thunder that was sure to come. When it didn't come, I went home.

24

A week later I stood at sunset in front of Hayden and Dorothy Sims' house, watching a purple fan of clouds rise in a pale yellow sky. A cold front had come through the night before and brought some rain with it. Not enough to end the drought in either Oakalla or me, but enough to lay the dust and clear the air.

Paul and Goldie Samuel had been buried in Fair Haven Cemetery. Hayden Sims was being held without bond on three counts of murder, one count of attempted murder, and one count of aggravated assault. Clarkie was out of the hospital and back on patrol in a new patrol car. I was out of Ruth's doghouse for scratching up her Volkswagen, but only after promising to either get Jessie fixed for good or to fix her for good, which was Ruth's preference. So all in all things were getting back to normal in Oakalla, if *normal* ever describes Oakalla.

The reason why Goldie Samuel's revolver had failed her, and then me, was that it had a defective firing pin. Ironically, Dick Samuel had bought it for Goldie's protection at a yard sale about a month before. Caveat emptor! As a lifelong salesman, Dick Samuel should have known that.

The reason why the carnival worker had lied about seeing Clarkie's patrol car in the park the night that Clarkie was attacked was that the carny was angry with Sean Ragan for, in the carny's words, "getting on my case so much." His goal was to direct suspicion toward Sean Ragan, and to cast the carnival in an unfavorable light, but all he succeeded in doing was to get himself fired.

With one hand on the wrought iron railing to support my sore hip, I climbed the two steps to the Sims' front door and knocked. Dorothy Sims opened the door almost immediately.

"Do you mind if I come in?" I said.

"Why don't we sit out here," she said, "since it's such a nice evening?"

So I gingerly lowered myself and we sat side by side on her front porch the way Goldie and I had done ten days earlier. But the feeling wasn't nearly the same.

"Here," I said, handing her the clipping that had started me on my search for Paul Samuel. "I thought you might want it back."

She took the clipping from me and laid it on the step beside her. After all of the excitement of the week before, she seemed particularly subdued that evening. Maybe it was the cold front, which had wrung all of the electricity from the air. Maybe it was the fact that she was now on her own again after thirty-five years. Whatever it was, in her white shorts, black blouse, and short hair, she looked like a lost child sitting there. But not an unhappy one.

"How do you know it's mine?" she said.

"The process of elimination. Since Goldie didn't send it, and Hayden wouldn't have sent it, that leaves you."

I could smell Hayden's roses, fresh from the rain, and wondered if Dorothy would continue to care for them as Hayden had, or if eventually they would die from neglect. I wasn't willing to bet either way.

"I just wondered why you sent it?" I said.

"That's not an easy question to answer," she said.

"Try anyway."

She took a deep breath and stared out at the

339

street. "Well, it wasn't for all of the obvious reasons. It wasn't because he drives a new Lincoln and I drive an old Dodge; or because I put him through college and then graduate school, and never even received a thank you in return; or because I cook every meal, when and if he decides to eat at home, wash all the dishes, all the clothes, pick up after him, and hand over my check to him every two weeks; or because I keep the house for him just the way he wants it or because I'm always on call for him whenever he wants sex, which is not very often, but too often at that, if you know what I mean; or because it's my fault we had only one child and she was a girl and it's my fault that he's not coaching at the University of Iowa right now because I didn't want to move; or because he treats Cheryl the same way he does me, always leaving her feeling that she's not quite done enough for him, no matter what she does do." Her look was grim, but somehow soft. "No. It wasn't for any of those things, or even the fact that he's a murderer. It was because he thought I was stupid. Or in his words, 'Too damn dumb to cross the street without asking directions.'" She looked at me with a smile in her eyes. "But I'm not as stupid as he thought."

I nodded my agreement with that. Then I said, "When did you first know about Paul Samuel?"

340

"Just this year. Not more than a month ago. I'd always wondered, especially when Hayden got up in the middle of the night the day Paul disappeared, and then was gone for several hours without any explanation whatsoever. Then there was my missing trunk, which he said he'd sold to Mike Jacoby after Mike made him an offer he couldn't refuse, and then that lumber and paneling he'd bought that I wasn't supposed to know anything about; and a lot of other little things, like all the time he began to spend in the garage that, like I said, just made me wonder."

The sun had gone down. Dusk was coming on, bringing the bugs with it. "Did you know about his affair with Goldie?" I said.

She shrugged. "I guessed something was going on. But, like always, I looked the other way."

We neither one said anything. Somewhere nearby a nightbird had started to sing.

"Anyway," she said, "a couple months ago I was in Sheila Jacoby's house and just for something to say asked her how she had been enjoying my trunk these past twenty years. What trunk? She said Mike had never brought any trunk home that she knew about. When I described it to her, she still didn't know what I was talking about, so I took it upon myself to see if I could find out what really did happen to it."

341

"Then those were your footprints in the dust of the loft?" I said.

"Yes," she said, her eyes sparking with excitement. "My heart was in my mouth the whole time I was up there, afraid that Hayden would come home and find me. But when it was over and I was finally down from there and safe . . ." She smiled at me. "I can't describe how it felt. It was like I was alive, really alive for the first time since I don't know when."

"So then you sent me the clipping?"

"Yes. But not right away. I wanted to wait until the week of Homecoming. You know, when it all happened before. That would make it seem more real somehow."

"Why didn't you just blow the whistle on Hayden?" I said.

I saw the fear in her eyes and already knew the answer. "I thought about it," she said. "But what if something went wrong? What would I have done then?"

"Thanks, Dorothy," I said, rising slowly from the porch. "As I said, I just wanted to know."

"Wait a minute," she said. She rose and went into the house, returning a moment later with Butch Loveless' missing wallet. "When you see Butch again, will you give this to him?"

342

"Where did you get it?" I said. Then I knew where she had gotten it. At the quarry in Scott McBride's Firebird. Hers were the fingerprints that Clarkie had found along with Cheryl's.

"Ask me no questions," she said with a smile.

"You followed Hayden out to Hidden Quarry and then took the wallet he had left there?"

Her eyes seemed to say yes.

"But how did you manage to beat him back home?"

"I didn't. He crawled into an empty bed beside two pillows. And slept that way until morning."

"And if he'd found you out?"

She shrugged. "I'd have lied about where I'd been. Just like he did when I asked him."

"So what do you do now?" I said.

The thought was a sobering one for her. The hunt was over, the quarry bagged. It was now back to real life.

"I don't know, Garth, what I'll do," she said. "Maybe I'll stay here in Oakalla and maybe I won't, and maybe now's not the time to decide. But whatever I do, I'll do it on my own from now on." She glanced at the house, then one by one at Hayden's roses. "It's not that I won't miss him. I already do a little. But not in any way that counts."

I left, crossing the street so I wouldn't have to pass in front of the Samuel house, and

343

hobbled east toward the heart of town. But when I got to School Street, I stopped, not knowing which way to go.

Home was to my left, but Ruth was bowling, so no one was there. The Corner Bar and Grill was also to my left, if all I wanted was company. Ahead about six blocks was my office where I could kill most of the evening, straightening and puttering and avoiding real work. Or I could walk around town until I got tired and then go home.

. I had been like that for a week now—unable to stay in one place for very long, unable to concentrate on the matters at hand, unable to enjoy life's simple joys that had given me so much pleasure in the past. My own company, which had once been a comfort, had become a burden to me. My past, which had once been my solace, had become my tormentor.

Then a breeze shook the tree beside me and down came a couple walnuts, one of them landing at my feet. I picked it up and smelled it, then again and again until I made myself dizzy.

In it was the past, present, and future. In it, too, was a crystal scent of my childhood, distilled through ten-thousand memories, yet as fresh and pure as my first walnut.

Feeling better, I put the walnut in my pocket and started home.